LOOKING BACKWARD
IN DARKNESS

Borgo Press Books by KATHRYN PTACEK

Looking Backward in Darkness: Tales of Fantasy and Horror

LOOKING BACKWARD IN DARKNESS

TALES OF FANTASY AND HORROR

KATHRYN PTACEK

THE BORGO PRESS

MMXIII

LOOKING BACKWARD IN DARKNESS

FIRST EDITION

Published by Wildside Press LLC

www.wildsidebooks.com

DEDICATION

For true friends who helped during dark times:

Mary Jasch and Nanci Schwartz

(who also suggested the title),

and for

Charlie,

Who would have said,
"It's about damned time, Chip!"

CONTENTS

ACKNOWLEDGMENTS

"Three, Four, Shut the Door" was originally published in *More Phobias*, Pocket Books, 1995. Copyright © 1995, 2013 by Kathryn Ptacek.

"Bruja" was originally published in *Deathport*, Pocket Books, 1993. Copyright © 1993, 2013 by Kathryn Ptacek.

"Mi Casa" was originally published in *Gothic Ghosts*, Tor Books, 1997. Copyright © 1997, 2013 by Kathryn Ptacek.

"Little Contrasts" was originally published in *White of the Moon*, Pumpkin Books, 1999. Copyright © 1999, 2013 by Kathryn Ptacek.

"Driven" was originally published in *Dark Love*, Penguin/ROC, 1995. Copyright © 1995, 2013 by Kathryn Ptacek.

"The Grotto" was originally published in *Graven Images*, Ace Books, 2000. Copyright © 2000, 2013 by Kathryn Ptacek.

"Hair" was originally published in *Phobias*, Pocket Books, 1994. Copyright © 1994, 2013 by Kathryn Ptacek.

"The Home" was originally published in *In the Fog*, Tor Books, 1993. Copyright © 1993, 2013 by Kathryn Ptacek.

"Living to the End" was originally published in *Fantasy Tales #7*, Robinson, 1991. Copyright © 1991, 2013 by Kathryn Ptacek.

"Dead Possums" was originally published in *Doom City*, Tor Books, 1987. Copyright © 1987, 2013 by Kathryn Ptacek.

"Rideau" was originally published in *Northern Horror*, Quarry Press, 2000. Copyright © 2000, 2013 by Kathryn Ptacek.

THREE, FOUR,
SHUT THE DOOR

One. Five. Fifteen. One. Five. Fifteen.

Dottie Brewster counted to each number. One. Then to five, and then to fifteen. Then up to fifteen, then to five, then one.

And repeat.

At the back door, she rested her gloved hand on the shiny brass knob, polished from many such sessions. She frowned. Was she counting to five, or fifteen now? She'd lost track.

It didn't matter, she told herself.

Really.

It. Didn't.

But it did.

Her hand fluttered as she gnawed at her lower lip. One, two, three...all the way up to fifteen. Then she started over. One. One, two, three, four, five. And then the next sequence of numbers to fifteen.

She had to get it right.

Then she could open the door and go through it. Close it behind her. Go outside.

Had to get it right because nothing in her life went the way it was supposed to—the *right* way—when she didn't get the sequence correct.

After all, she hadn't been counting the day her mother and sister's car had been broadsided by a semi and they'd died in the flaming wreckage.

She hadn't been counting the day that Farron left her.

She hadn't been counting the day she got fired from the job she'd held ever since college graduation, the job she'd been groomed for during those four years of school and the two years of postgraduate work.

None of this would have happened, she told herself, if she'd been counting.

One...two...three....

Suddenly the lines from the old nursery rhyme drifted through her mind.

One, two, buckle my shoe.

Three, four, shut the door.

Damn.

She'd lost count again.

She leaned forward slightly, her forehead against the chilly glass of the door's pane, and closed her eyes. Tears trembled beneath her eyelids, gumming her thick lashes.

She hated this. Truly she did. With all her heart she wished she could get over it. But it wasn't like some virus where you got sick and went to bed with fever and chills and after the illness had run its course, you got up and got on with your life.

Her problem didn't work that way.

One, two, three....

She knew she had a problem, had known that for some time, and she knew there were people who could help her, or at least try to help. She wasn't so sure they really could be of use. Psychiatrists, Farron had suggested, go see a psychiatrist or a psychologist.

Although she recognized the truth of his words, she'd responded angrily, telling him that she wasn't crazy.

"I never suggested that, honey," he said plaintively.

One, two, three, but she hadn't heard his apology, hadn't seen the look of anguish on his face because she had been counting. Seven, eight, nine. Farron had tried to convince her that it was for her own good, but she wouldn't hear of it, couldn't hear his words. Thirteen, fourteen, fifteen.

A feeling of relief: good.

Time to start over.

Farron hadn't understood, she told herself, as much as he claimed he did. It wasn't the counting that was driving her bananas, not really, although that was annoying. It was the fear that she *wouldn't get the counting, the sequences right.*

Don't get it right, and you screw up your life.

She had ample evidence for that.

Farron, her job, her mother and sister's deaths. There was her father's cancer too. She knew that was related. Somehow. It was her fault. Somehow her father had died, because she hadn't gotten it right.

There were other episodes, other times from her early childhood, her teenage years when she hadn't gotten it right, and things didn't turn out the way they were supposed to. Her mother's closet alcoholism. Her best friend from childhood dying from complications of diabetes. Her boyfriend ditching her right before the senior prom. Her sister's botched abortion.

All these incidents were tied together with a thread that ran from her; she was the loom, and because she was coming unraveled—because she *wasn't getting it right*, the fabric had developed holes. And *it was her fault.*

Three, four, five, sang the litany in her exhausted mind.

Out of the corner of her eye she saw movement. She watched as a huge fly crawled across a food-flecked dish in the kitchen sink. Plates and glasses and saucepans, all dirty, piled high in the stained enamel sink. Something buzzed—a handful of flies at the window over the sink.

She wrinkled her nose, noticing for the first time the odor of sour milk, the sickeningly sweetness of over-ripened) fruit. The stink of something else underlay all the others, and she wondered what it was. She couldn't identify it, not immediately.

She had to do something first.

One, two....

She should wait a bit before she went out. Yes, that was right. She could wash the dishes with really hot soapy water and dry them with some of her linen hand towels bordered with the fancy embroidery she used to have time for, and put them away in the cabinets, and then she would make herself a nice lunch.

Or was it dinnertime?

A sandwich...she could make that for either meal, and so it didn't matter *which* meal it actually was, because the sandwich would be for lunch or dinner.

No, she had to get it right. She looked out the window, saw it was still light, but couldn't see the sun's position. It could be afternoon. It had to be, since she was wearing gloves which meant that it was cooler outside which meant that it had to be autumn or winter or spring, and night came so much earlier then. Afternoon.

Or late morning.

One, two....

Buckle my shoe.

She almost giggled aloud.

In the last few months of her job she had grown increasing late. She had recognized that—she certainly didn't need anyone, much less Farron and her boss telling her—and so had started out of the house earlier and earlier each day. In the beginning she'd left on time, then that had graduated to twenty minutes earlier, then an hour earlier. Finally she was getting up at 4:10, so she could get out of the door and get to the University by nine.

It didn't take her long to get ready in the mornings—she showered, dressed, threw on her makeup, ate a quick breakfast. What took so long was the ritual of going through the door, because she had to do it right—*or else*—and every time she blew it, and she had to start over, and the ritual grew longer and longer.

Three, four, shut the door.

Five, six, pick up sticks.

Seven, eight, nine....

Thirteen, fourteen—

Why hadn't she chosen longer numbers? Something like a hundred would have been better. It would take more time to reach; but she hadn't selected the numbers. They had chosen her. Her mother had always told her to count to ten before responding when she was angry. She remembered as a child counting slowly to ten, and then over again because she liked the feel of control it gave her. She realized she could count and even as she was doing that, she felt her anger or frustration melting away.

She didn't remember having a temper, but her mother always insisted she did, and her mother must be right.

She counted as high as she could go the first time her father put her in the closet and left her alone with the darkness. She had counted because she had nothing else to do. Counted. And eventually he had come back and let her out. He had said then that she was a good girl, not the screw-up she normally was.

She came to realize during the long hours when she was alone that it really was all her fault, and that she had better learn to get things right.

And the numbers had just popped into her head, and without warning, she started counting—to one, to five, to fifteen, then to fifteen, to five, to one. She tried to draw out the ritual sometimes, tried to slow the counting, but it didn't always work, and so she would count over and over and over, and the quickness of it irritated her.

It had become her mantra. When she was angry, she summoned it; when she was tired or stressed out, she did the numbers. Knowing that somehow things would be right again.

Only the reassurance she obtained from it had decreased, and so she had increased the number of times she counted. Doubled the times. Then tripled.

Quadrupled.

Until the numbers bled together in her mind, jumbling—one, six, eleven, five, ten—and she had to start over from the beginning. Sometimes it seemed like every minute, every second of her life was devoted to the numbers...to getting it right.

Eventually, even her boss had noticed, and he'd taken her into his office one morning, and asked gently if there was a problem.

"What do you mean?" she asked, her voice trembling. She had been so upset that she forgot to count.

"You've been late six months in a row now, Dottie," Hal said. "I've looked the other way because you've been here so long and you've always been on time, but you're getting worse. You've got to do better. You've had a perfect record—and now this. And you're making mistakes in your work—you've never done that before. It's like your mind is on something else. Is something going on at home?" He had leaned across the desk and for a moment she had thought he was going to place his hand on her shoulder.

"No, there's nothing wrong," she lied.

"It's got to get better," Hal said.

She nodded.

Only it hadn't, and finally he had said regretfully that he must fire her, and they'd given her a generous severance check because of the years she'd been there, and she had gone home and sat in her living room and looked out the window at the dying flowers and counted.

To one, to five, to fifteen.

Too late now, she told herself, because she hadn't gotten it right.

She should have been counting more, should have slowed it down, made it last.

Only she hadn't.

The fear wrapped itself more tightly around her heart and squeezed.

The tears flowed freely now, and she brushed at her cheek with her other gloved hand, and left a streak there. She stared down at the dirt on her glove and wondered vaguely how it had gotten there. They had been clean when she put them on.

To one, to five, to fifteen.

One, five, fifteen.

She listened to the house, and heard nothing. Didn't hear the sound of the furnace, didn't hear the grandfather clock in the front hall, and wondered why. The clock must have run down, and she wondered when she had wound it last. Hadn't it been yesterday? No. Friday. No...before that. But when she didn't remember.

Five, six....*seven, eight, open the gate.*

She told herself she would get through the door now. She had things to do. She had to get outside and get to—

Get to where? She frowned, wondering if she'd been heading to the store or someplace else. Maybe a job interview? Yes, that was it. After she'd been fired, she'd pored through the classified section of the newspaper for jobs that interested her. A number of positions called for workers who stayed at home, which appealed to her. So she had called for an appointment, and she was headed for it.

Only...she frowned...only that appointment had been yesterday.

Or the day before.

She had blown it again.

One, five, fifteen.

She must have stopped the sequence somewhere, some place, and she'd royally screwed up again.

She hadn't been counting last week when she'd been singing along with the old Bee Gees song on the car radio, and she hadn't seen the van in front of her stop abruptly and so she had thumped into the back-end of it. Her car had been more damaged than the other driver's, and she'd had to have it towed away, and she wasn't sure how she would get it back, because the bill was so huge, and she was running out of money. Farron tried to help her with money from time to time, until she got on her feet and got another job. But she hadn't gotten another job. She wouldn't be getting another job if she couldn't get out the door.

Three, four, five.

One, two, three, four...thirteen, fourteen, fifteen.

She was so tired. So weary of the repetition. Over and over those numbers floated in her head, drifted through every waking thought. She was so tired of them. She should try them in foreign languages, she thought with a sudden giggle.

Unos, dos...cinco.

It wasn't the same.

...three, four, five....

She yawned. She could lay down on the couch, and take a nap for a while, and then when she woke up, she would be rested, and she would get up and wash the dishes and she would go out the door.

For whatever reason she had to go out the door.

But first she had to count. And she had to get it right. Because if she didn't...she shuddered, thinking what might happen.

One. One, two, three....

She didn't count in her sleep. At least she didn't think she did. Usually she woke, and for the first few minutes of her day, didn't think about counting.

Maybe that was a mistake.

It had been morning, after all, when Farron told her he was leaving her. She had cried and screamed at him, and then fallen into a silence and simply stared at him. Why, she wanted to say, why? But every time she opened her mouth, all she could do was cry.

She had counted much too late then. She had counted to one, to five, to fifteen as he picked up the suitcase he had packed before she woke, had counted as he went down the stairs and she trailed after him, had counted as he walked out the door and she had stared out the front window as he got into the car and drove away, counted as the only man she'd ever loved left her.

Counted.

Too late.

She hadn't gotten it right.

Her father was right; she was such a screw-up.

The fear was in her veins, in her lungs, in her tissue; it permeated every bit of her body.

She wept then, loudly, forlornly, and she wanted it all undone. She wanted it to be all *right* again, although she never knew it would be.

Suddenly she felt a warmth in her groin, and then down

her leg, and she looked down and saw the piss running there, making the pool at her feet even larger, and she recognized the foulness she'd been vaguely aware of, and realized then that she hadn't been there for a few minutes, she hadn't been there at the door even for hours.

She had been there all day.

Maybe all night. Maybe longer.

One, two.

Three, four, shut the door.

But how could you shut the door, if you couldn't even open it?

Seven, eight....

How long before you begin to decay? she wondered vaguely, and knew now why there were so many flies.

Nine, ten, do it again.

She *would* get it right. It was just a matter of time.

BRUJA

Chato Del-Klinne looked around at the airport terminal as he stepped out of the jetway. Not precisely Kansas, he could hear Sunny say teasingly as if she stood next to him, and he would have smiled, except he didn't feel like it; he felt...uneasy.

Not precisely Kansas, no.

Southern Texas along the Mexican border, to be more precise. He'd been asleep on the plane, thinking he was heading back to Las Vegas when the captain announced that because of the vigorous storm system to the west, he had been ordered to change his route and land at Dry Plains International instead of Dallas/Ft. Worth.

"Vigorous." Chato shook his head. He just loved these euphemistic terms. Vigorous...meaning the entire western sky was painted a sickly yellow green, twenty twisters had been spotted between Dallas/Fort Worth and Amarillo, and if everyone was lucky, the tornados wouldn't remove the top six inches of soil throughout the state of Texas, not to mention every single trailer park in the Lone Star State.

And so here he was. The airport was bigger than he'd expected. It was, after all, an international airport, but mostly he had discovered with great irony that in the southwest that term meant flights scheduled to and from Mexico. Period.

International.

Yeah, right.

What he hadn't expected was the sheer chaos of the place. Many passengers milled around, while some clumped together to speak angrily about delayed or cancelled flights; somewhere someone was sobbing. Children darted back and forth, and several babies wailed.

He had the sense that something had happened, something horrible, and there was only one sort of thing like that that could make an airport chaotic. Yet the captain of Chato's plane had mentioned no disaster.

Maybe it just happened now. No, he would have heard *something*. So, it—whatever it was—had occurred before his flight put down. It must have been after the one announcement, and it must have been too late for the pilot to go to another airport; jets had only so much reserve fuel, after all.

So, they didn't say a thing because they wanted to keep us from panicking, he thought grimly. Swell.

A youth hardly out of his teens and dressed in old jeans and a white tee-shirt smeared with something dark walked by.

Chato grabbed the young man's arm. "Excuse me. What happened here, can you tell me? I just got off a plane from New York and—"

"A bomb!" the youth cried, his voice thick with fear and a West Texas accent.

"Where?"

The kid nodded with his chin toward the line of tall windows opposite the gate where Chato had disembarked. "Out there. Some terrorist had a bomb. I think it was one of them Eye-ranians. Blew up the whole plane right there on the runway. It was terrible, just terrible. They got firemen and ambulances out there, but I don't know if anyone's gonna make it...." The kid began sobbing and Chato let go and watched as he struggled through the crowd.

Chato was stunned. A terrorist here? He moved forward, and looked out toward the line of windows on the left, and now he could see the wreckage in the distance, maybe a quarter of a mile. He saw emergency vehicles, and saw the flames and billowing black smoke, even in the daylight, and he wondered how his plane's pilot had negotiated the landing so that no one aboard had seen it.

Clever, real clever. Chato didn't much like being manipulated like that. Of course, what good would it have done to panic them while they were still in the air? Yeah, right; wait until we're on the ground, then we can panic.

Now, he watched as people scrambled along the tarmac, some into ambulances, others standing with emergency personnel; he sensed futility. No matter what they did out there...it was too late. Inside the building he watched as men and women and children stumbled along, some pushing others, all of them close to panicking. The bomb had set them off, too, he knew; maybe they were afraid that there were other terrorists, perhaps even in the building who might harm others.

Terrorists. In a border airport in southern Texas. Sure. Dallas-Ft. Worth airport, yeah, maybe. But here? Something wasn't right.

He checked a monitor. Most departing flights were cancelled; his was one. Of course.

Someone next to him started complaining that when he got home he was going to write to the president of the airlines about this incompetence—he had important business in Vegas, by God, and it had to be done on time, by God—and Chato was relieved he wouldn't have to fly all the way to Nevada with him; with his luck, the guy would have sat next to him and bitched the whole time.

Now that he knew he didn't have to rush for a connecting flight, he took time to study his fellow strandees. They were a mixed bag: young and old and in-between, a few in wheelchairs or with canes, a fairly equal combination of Anglo and black and Hispanic, with a handful of Asians. Knots of businessmen in anonymous gray suits and look-alike leather briefcases, and several elderly nuns in old-fashioned habits, a Dallas matron with bouffant hairdo and too much eye makeup, a black kid with gold chains and a gold front tooth to match, two little girls in matching pink and lavender outfits each clutching a stuffed animal, a tall Sikh in all white, and more, dozens more. These people didn't seem to know where they were going, only that they didn't want to stay here, didn't want to stay in one place for too long. And beneath the anxiety and disorientation....

He felt...*it*.

He supposed he'd been vaguely aware of it before this; perhaps it was what had troubled him when he first arrived. But now that he stood there, not moving, he felt it, felt that touch of *something else*, of *somewhere else*.

He had had several close brushes with the supernatural before, and he knew its caress.

An Apache shaman, he'd trained with his teacher long ago before leaving home; for a long time he had turned his back on his discipline. But in the past few years he'd gone through a lot, and his instruction had come in handy.

There was more here than just the explosion out on the runway. God knows, that would have been enough for most places, but not here. There was more...much more.

Blood had been spilled here, he could smell it, and could sense, too, that something had awakened with the spilling of the blood.

He felt as if something shifted under his feet, but when he looked back he saw nothing but the innocuous gray tile.

Sunny, he thought suddenly. He had to get to a phone and let her know that he was okay. He checked his watch. 6:15 here, which meant 4:15 at home, and she'd be expecting him in a few hours. Only he wasn't going to be at McCarron in a few hours.

Mechanically he moved toward the phones, then stopped when he saw the lines there. They snaked back away from the handful of booths, back toward the waiting area.

Determined, he walked into another gate area, but the situation was the same there. At the newsstand no one stood behind the register. Several customers waited patiently to pay, if only someone would appear; one guy was busy reading the *Wall Street Journal*, not even aware of what was going on around him. Behind him a short Hispanic woman stood with a magazine in her hand.

As he studied the area, he realized that since he'd arrived he hadn't seen a single airport employee. No one manned the ticket desks at the gates, nor had there been any announcements about incoming flights or departures. There was nothing but the damned Muzak inanely playing some cheerful mishmash of a Beatles' tune.

He had the feeling someone was watching him, but when he looked around he saw that everyone else seemed occupied in their own little drama. Still, he couldn't shake the feeling. The hair at the back of his neck prickled, and he rubbed the area. He tightened the band holding back his long black hair, then sighed.

Puzzled, he took the escalator to the lower level where the barrage carrousels were located. The carrousels moved, all right, going around and around, but no luggage shot out of the chutes. He checked the rental car desks; no one. No one stood behind the ticket reservation counters, either.

In fact, except for hundreds of panicked passengers the airport was deserted. He looked outside and saw no taxis waiting along the curb. There were no porters, either.

Where were all the airport employees? Off somewhere having a union meeting? On a mass coffee break, perhaps?

Or had they fled?

He thought he smelled burning french fries drifting down from the upper level, and he hoped that someone would go into one of the restaurants and investigate before the whole place caught on fire.

The music system was now playing "Raindrops Keep Falling on My Head." God, how he hated bouncy tunes like that. It was all so...pasteurized.

He went outside and winced as the oppressive heat of the Texas summer afternoon hit him. Then all at once he smelled the acrid fumes from the bombed airplane. He watched now as one of the ambulances he'd seen earlier swung around the building and shot out toward the highway. The vehicle abruptly began swerving back and forth; suddenly it flipped over onto its side and burst into flames. The second ambulance, following some distance away, stopped with a squeal of brakes, and the side and back doors flew open and the emergency crew raced away, just seconds before the vehicle exploded.

For a while Chato had thought about taking one of the rental cars—he couldn't call it stealing in an emergency situation like this—and getting the hell out of this weird place, but seeing what had happened to the two ambulances made him change his mind. Maybe it was just a coincidence, he told himself. And maybe not.

Maybe something didn't want anything or anyone leaving the airport area.

It wasn't a thought he wanted to contemplate for long.

He studied the countryside surrounding Dry Plains International. Well, whoever had named it had certainly gotten that name right. He didn't see anything except a flat brown expanse stretching off to the horizon, and above it a murky faintly blue sky, almost as if there was a haze. No mountains, no rivers or lakes, no buildings, no trees or bushes or strange cacti, no landmarks whatsoever. It was as if a tabletop had been swept clear and this airport plunked down in the middle. He had seen some desolate places, but man, this beat 'em all.

Comforting, he thought, real comforting. Just where the hell was this place?

To further increase his apprehension a dry hot wind howled around the corner of the building, and in the wind he thought he heard voices, strange voices that seemed to whisper his name.

Quickly he went back inside through the automatic doors before the electricity decided to go off and strand him outside. He wasn't sure which was worse: being stuck outside or in. As if something had read his thoughts, the lights overhead flickered momentarily, and somewhere there was a high-pitched scream.

He decided right then and there to go where there were people. Safety in numbers? he could hear Sunny tease him. Damned right, honey. This level was far too deserted for his liking. Again, he felt like something was watching him, but again when he looked around, he saw no one.

The escalator stopped halfway between floors, and he was getting ready to walk up the rest of the distance when it started up again, only this time it went backwards. He managed to turn around before he got to the floor, then stood and stared at the slow-moving steps.

Well, he'd take the stairs now. Damned if he go on an elevator or try the escalator again.

As he walked toward the staircase, he thought he heard a sound like a moan. He stopped. There was no one near the escalator. Still no one at the car rental desks or airline counters. All that was left were two doors, each with its bland symbol symbolizing a man and a woman. He entered the men's restroom first.

"Hello?"

No answer. He checked all the stalls. Nothing.

He went next door to the ladies' restroom.

"Hello?"

He heard a movement in one of the stalls, and pushed open the door which hadn't been locked. A young blonde woman—she couldn't have been much over eighteen, he decided—huddled there. A very pregnant young woman, he thought, when she shifted.

"Do you need help?" he asked gently.

She nodded. When she looked up at him, he could see that tears had left mascara smudges down her cheeks.

"Let me take you back upstairs where there are other people," he said.

"I-I think the baby's about to come. I came in here. I didn't know what else to do," the girl said.

"Maybe there's a doctor or nurse on the second floor," Chato said as he took her by the hand, easing her to her feet. She shuffled forward a few inches, then groaned. He realized she needed to lay down right away, but he would have to get her upstairs for that. Maybe they could break into the airlines' lounge. Surely they had couches in there.

But once he got the girl outside the bathroom and halfway to the escalator he realized they weren't going to get upstairs. She could barely hobble and kept crying the entire time.

While he had been looking around, he'd seen an area back of the stairs that made a protected nook. He took her there and told her to wait, then searched the lower level until he found a chair for her. She sank into it with a grunt.

"I need to go up and see if there's a doctor, okay?"

"No! Don't leave me!" She gripped his hand.

"Look, miss—"

"Gail."

"Gail," he said, trying to keep his tone reasonable. He needed to calm her, reassure her somehow that everything would be all right, when he wasn't at all sure himself that things would be all right. "It'll just be a few minutes. You're okay here. You've got this comfortable chair and—"

She squeezed his hand harder. "No, please, don't leave. I think someone's after me."

"No one can see you back here," he said. "It's out of the way. You can't be seen from the stairway or the doors or—"

"No, no, no! You don't understand. I've been hearing this voice ever since I got off the plane. Gail, it's been saying, give me your baby. I want your baby. I need your baby."

Chato stared down at her tear-streaked face, and knew then that this wasn't something she was imagining. She *had* heard the voice.

"Right. Okay. Look, give me a few minutes to scout around." He held up a hand when she started to protest. "I won't be long. But I want to see what I can find to make you more comfortable. Okay?"

She nodded.

"Just sit here and be quiet, and if anyone approaches...scream like hell, and I'll come running."

She nodded again, pressed a hand to her abdomen. "Thank you. You know, I don't even know your name."

"Chato."

He ducked out of the nook and glanced around the lower

level. Empty as before. Or was it? The hairs along the back of his neck prickled again. Someone watched. He had thought that before. Now he knew he wasn't imagining it.

"Some Enchanted Evening" played on the music system.

That, he decided, could go off any time soon, and he'd be all the happier for it.

One airline counter over he found a door leading into an employees' lounge. Lots to loot here, he thought with a wry smile. He dragged the seat cushions from some couches back to the nook. He would have brought a couch, he explained, but he didn't think he could get it through the doorway.

"I'll be back," he said.

He returned to the lounge and found a closet full of the lap blankets that flight attendants give passengers, along with a dozen or more small pillows. He took everything there he could carry back to Gail. He tucked pillows around her, and covered her with the blankets, and stacked some nearby.

Just in case, he thought. Just in case when the baby comes, and I have to deliver it. He felt a spike of panic. His shaman training didn't include lessons in childbirth. This he'd have to wing.

He'd been aware for some time of more noise from above, and it sounded now like screaming and shouting and assorted bumping and scraping. He wondered what was going on, but he wasn't about to go and investigate. And he hoped whatever was up there wouldn't make its way down here.

Not for the first time he realized they were virtually trapped in the nook. The safe place could become in a moment's notice a prison.

But what choice did they have? He didn't want to settle her in the middle of the deserted level, where anyone—or anything— could see them.

He went scouting again and came back with two fire extinguishers. Not the best choice of weapons, he told himself, but when you have nothing else at hand. Well, that's not precisely true, he realized. He did have his Swiss army knife. Yeah, that would be a lot of use, wouldn't it? Besides, if he had smelled something burning earlier, these canisters might come in handy. If the electricity went off, he could always break the windows with them so they could escape outside.

He saw that Gail had fallen asleep, and so he sneaked back to the employees lounge. When he saw the vending machines again, he realized just how hungry he was. He had slept through dinner on the plane, and hadn't had anything since he'd left New York City that morning. And he knew Gail would be hungry.

He reached into his pocket for change, and thought, what the hell am I doing? He didn't have enough for two candy bars, much less what he knew they'd need.

He studied the first machine, one for sodas, then took out his pocket knife, selected a blade he thought would fit and inserted it and began jiggling it back and forth in the lock on the front panel. Finally he was rewarded with a snick, and the panel opened. He did the same for the other machines.

Something thudded onto the floor above and he half-expected to see someone or something falling through the ceiling. But it held. For now.

He located several empty cartons and put all the cans of soda in there, as well as dozens of packets of cookies and potato chips and cellophane-wrapped sandwiches and candy bars. He threw in what paper napkins and plastic cutlery he found; he opened all the drawers and doors he could find to see what other goodies he could liberate. When he left, he thought the room looked like locusts had swept through.

He winced. Somehow he didn't like the imagery.

When he got back, Gail was awake and had struggled up to a sitting position. He put the boxes down with the others he'd brought back earlier.

"Hungry?"

She nodded.

He pawed through the contents of a box. "I have ham and cheese, or ham and cheese, or ham and cheese." She giggled and suddenly she looked much younger than her eighteen years. "Or the ever popular ham and cheese."

"It's such a hard decision. Umm. Let me have the ham and cheese, please."

"An excellent choice. And what will you have to wash it down with? Here we have more choice. Clear soda, orange soda or brown soda."

"Orange, please."

Somehow he knew she would choose that. He opened the can and handed it to her. He was sitting on the chair now.

"I'll be back."

He went back to the airline counters and hunted around until he came to another fire alarm box. He took the fire axe. A better weapon.

On his way back he grabbed some pads of paper and pens. They might as well keep occupied while waiting for the baby.

He was heading back to the nook when he saw something on the now-stopped escalator. He edged closer. A thin trickle of blood dripped down from the floor above to the first tread of the escalator, crawled along the grooved metal plating, then dribbled down onto the tread below. Tread after tread, the blood dripped slowly down.

He backed away quickly.

"What's the matter?" Gail said, looking up from her sandwich when he came back.

"Nothing," he said with what he hoped was a steady smile.

"You're a bad liar," she said.

"I know. Sunny—my girlfriend—always says that."

He thought Gail seemed steadier now that she was eating and drinking something. Plus, he reminded himself, she wasn't by herself. That had to be a bit more reassuring, even if he didn't know what was going to happen.

"I don't know anything about you," he said after he finished his first sandwich and started on a second. He had never realized how good stale bread and dry cheese could taste. "You married?" She shook her head. "About to be?" She nodded. "And your boyfriend abandoned you, right?"

"Yeah, how did you know?"

"Lucky guess. Well, you're better off without him. He wouldn't have been much help now, I suspect."

"No, Randy said I was getting too fat and ugly."

"You're certainly not ugly. And you're not fat. You're pregnant. There's a big difference."

She flashed him a grateful smile.

"Where you going to?"

"Home to Omaha. I wanted to be with my family. My parents don't know about...my pregnancy. I guess my dad will yell a bit, but he really loves me, and my mom will just glare at him until he shuts up. It's the only place I can go. I was running out of money."

"Sounds like a good place, basically."

"What about you, Chato?" She was gnawing on her lower lip. She hadn't made any noise for some time, but he knew she was hurting.

"I live in Las Vegas; I was coming from New York City going to Dallas-Ft. Worth, but got diverted here. I do odd jobs, I guess you could say, sort of this and that. Sunny is a blackjack dealer at a casino. What else? Well, I grew up in New Mexico."

"And you're Indian," she said softly.

"Yeah. Chiricahua Apache."

"I went to school with some Sioux. There are a lot of Indians in Nebraska, you know."

"Yeah, I know." He paused as he thought he heard someone speak. Hadn't they said *Gail*? No, it couldn't be. "Hey, I brought along some paper and some pens, and thought after we have our dessert of Paydays or Hershey bars, we could have a rollicking game of hangman. How's that sound?"

She winced slightly from pain. "Great. I think I'm ready for my dessert now. What were you doing in New York?" she asked as she peeled back the wrapper.

"Business. Okay. I was at some meetings in northern New York state."

"Are you an Indian activist?" she asked.

He was surprised by her question.

She smiled. "I heard about the protests up there with the Mohawks, and just wondered."

"Yeah, well, I was there at the same time, although for different reasons. I'm not really an activist, though." He didn't want to go into details of the matter that he had handled; he thought it would be too upsetting for her now. There had been some misunderstandings, some deaths; nothing was ever as easy as he thought it would be. He rubbed at a scar on his arm, an red angry-looking scar all too recent. He should know better by now; except that he didn't.

She sensed his reluctance and didn't pursue it. "How about that game now?"

"Fine."

He drew a hanging tree, and twelve spaces below it, then showed her the pad of paper.

"Twelve letters? Oh, no! I was never good with long words!"

She had guessed eight of the letters when the really big pain shot through her, and she groaned so loudly he dropped the paper. He realized she'd been huffing her breath for the past few minutes, and he hadn't even noticed.

"Oh, damn," he muttered when he saw her face, and leaped to his feet. The baby was coming.

Rolling up his sleeves as he dashed into the bathroom, he scrubbed his arms with soap and hot water, dried them, then came back to where Gail lay moaning softly.

He checked his supplies. He was as prepared as he'd ever be—rolls of paper towels, spare blankets, a bucket of water and sponges. Now, if he just knew how to deliver a baby, he'd feel a little happier about the situation.

He helped her lay back down on the couch cushions, settled a pillow beneath her head.

"Okay?"

She nodded, her breath huffing faster. She seemed to be counting silently. Then she said, "I have too many clothes on. You-you're going to have to help me."

He was embarrassed for himself and for her, too. He helped her remove her panties and push back her dress, and then he draped a blanket over her upraised knees.

Oh, God, Sunny, he thought, where are you when I need you? He didn't know that Sunny had ever birthed a baby, but he wouldn't put it past her, and he knew she'd just stride into this little maternity cubbyhole, take in the situation at once, roll up her sleeves, and that would be that. Sunny would take care of everything.

Only Sunny wasn't here; he was.

"Oh, God!"

Gail gripped his hand as he told her to push. That's what they did on TV, he told himself, so he assumed it was close enough to truth.

"Push again. That a girl. Good. Again."

The umbilical cord. What was he going to do about that? Oh, Jesus, what had he gotten himself mixed up in? Then he remembered his pocket knife. He'd clean a blade off the best he could and he'd use that.

What if the baby died? What if Gail died? What if she bled to death right here? He'd have to go get help, he knew it. But upstairs...was there any help upstairs?

No. There was just him and Gail and a baby about to be born.

And almost before he knew it then the baby was coming, and he could see its head, and he told Gail to push harder and harder, and she screamed at him that she was, Goddamnit, and he told her she was doing good, really good, and then all at once there was a baby in his hands. A tiny warm thing covered with blood, and the wrinkled faced contorted itself, and he remembered some dumb medical show he used to watch, and he gently pried open the baby's mouth and removed mucus, and the baby coughed and started to cry.

Gail, her hair plastered dark against her forehead, smiled weakly. "Girl or boy?"

"Girl."

"Good. Boys are nothing but trouble. Does she have all her

toes and fingers?"

"Sure does."

He cut the umbilical cord, and cleaned the baby gently with the paper napkins and towels, then wrapped her in one of the blankets. He had to clean up. And he had to help Gail clean about.

Still holding the baby, he stared down at her and she blinked up at him. He felt himself an inane urge to grin foolishly. Babies did that to people, he knew.

He heard a sound behind him.

A small white-haired woman stood there. It was, he realized, the woman from the newsstand.

"I will take over from here," she said softly, and her eyes were the yellow brown of a wolf's.

And he knew that this woman was the part of the reason for his unease.

He knew in an instant what she was. *Bruja. Witch.*

Beyond her something shimmered, and at first Chato thought it was fog that had somehow crept into the terminal, but then he squinted and the fog coalesced. In the rippling light he could see figures that were there but not there, men from the past, dressed in feather headgear, cotton tunics and shields. Their dark bodies glistened as if oiled, and the men grinned fiercely.

"These are my ancestors," the woman said. "They suffered much under the whites. And they are hungry for their revenge."

Chato didn't have to ask how they would be brought into this time. He saw the bruja eyeing the baby, and he knew without question she would harm the newborn, would...sacrifice...it.

Not if he had anything to say about it.

Suddenly she leaped forward and grabbed the infant, and turned and ran.

"No!" Gail shrieked and tried to stagger to her feet.

"Stay there!" he yelled back at the girl as he raced after the woman. For someone so little, she certainly ran fast, he thought. He risked a glance back over his shoulder, and saw that Gail had obeyed and was back by the nook. Good. He didn't want to have to worry about her as well. God knew what else was wandering around this airport.

This part of the building had grown darker now, as if it were close to nighttime, yet Chato knew it wasn't. He glanced out the windows as he ran, and saw a gloom. But he didn't have time to think any more about it. He saw a door closing ahead, and knew the bruja had gone through it.

He stopped moments before he slammed into the wall, wrenched open the door and stepped through....

...and fell down a steep and rough slope. He tumbled and twisted and bounced, and once slammed his knee against a boulder. Finally, he came to a rest at the bottom. Puffs of dust rose around him, making him cough.

Nothing vital, he thought, was broken, although when he managed to get to his feet he knew he was bleeding in several places; certainly he was bruised, and when he touched his side with his fingertips, he winced. He thought he might have cracked a rib or two.

Swell.

And just where the hell was he?

He seemed to be in a tunnel, rough-hewn from rock and the earth. The ceiling wasn't high, and when he lifted his arm, wincing with pain from his ribs, he found he could touch the surface easily. He was not given to claustrophobia, but he would have liked it if the place were a tad more spacious. The walls were scarcely an arm's length away on each side. The air smelled of must, of rich loamy earth...like a newly dug grave.

The tunnel should have been pitch-black, but it wasn't. It was faintly lit, as though the earthen walls around him was phosphorescent. He scraped some of the dirt away, and his fingers glowed slightly. Quickly he wiped his hand on his jeans.

His eyes had adjusted to the semi-darkness now, and he could see that the walls weren't made of just dirt; objects seemed embedded in them. He stepped closer, and brushed away some grime so he could better see. He backed hastily away when he saw the gleaming white of a human skull. The matrix of the walls were human bones: skulls and femurs, shin bones, and the thin bones of fingers and toes. Here and there stiff hair and parchment-like skin clung. Here and there he could see a bas relief carved, images of skulls and skeletons and pyramids of bones.

He looked back up the slope, but couldn't see the doorway. There was no way out there; that much was obvious.

He would have to go down the tunnel.

He didn't want to go down the tunnel.

No choice, old pal, he told himself, and it almost sounded like he had spoken aloud, although he knew he hadn't.

Something brushed by his ear, and he shook his head.

The floor, he realized then, was made up of crushed bones. Inside his boots his toes curled, but he had no choice. He had to walk upon the dead.

Carefully he moved forward, suspicious there might be some trapdoor waiting for him; but the ground seemed solid enough. For now.

He noticed masks suspended from some of the walls. Intricately carved images that leered or glared down at him with the countenances of stern-faced warriors and eagles and reptiles and pumas and other feral beasts. Masks with elongated earlobes, exaggerated noses and lips, eyes that were narrow slits, tear-shaped or round as if with surprise. Masks hewn of coconut husk, of wood, of copper and silver and tin. Some had elaborate headdresses in turn, those the visages of jaguars and parrots. Bright feathers and plaits of human hair and strands of beads and teeth and shell dangled from the masks, and he saw the glint of gold and precious stones in the rings in the ears.

More light came from ahead, and he reached an opening on the right. There was a smallish room that seemed empty, and when he stepped into it, he saw himself as a boy of fourteen when his father had taken him to Ryan Josanie. His old teacher, the man who had taught him to be a shaman.

Josanie was showing the then-Chato how to control his dreams, and the youth was complaining that it was hard, and

Josanie, not smiling, was saying that everything worth having is hard, and the then—Josanie glanced up and saw the now—Chato.

"Josanie." Seeing the old man brought him such sadness and regret. His teacher had been dead for years. Chato took a step forward, and with a shimmer, as it if were simply an image in water, the scene disappeared, and he was standing in an empty room.

He went out into the tunnel, which now turned to the left. Sometimes, he thought, the eyes of the skulls in the walls seemed to watch him, but he dismissed that thought. He was just getting spooked; that was all. Nothing was watching him.

Or was it.

He encountered another room. There he saw himself and Ross, his brother younger by three years, and they were at a state championship football game, and the then-Chato was in uniform, and Ross was saying how much he admired his brother, and Chato was laughing and telling him he'd know better when he got older, and Ross saying he'd always respect his brother. Ross...whom he'd not seen in years, hadn't talked to for more than a year. Ross...they'd been close once. Now they had drifted so far apart.

Once again Chato took a step forward, and once again, the image, as if mirrored on the surface of water, disappeared.

Out in the tunnel he grew aware again of a sound that had been with him since he'd entered this stygian world. Its rhythm was regular, he realized, and he thought it might be water dripping somewhere. No, more than that. And he recognized it then as the sound of a heart beating, and whether it was his or something else's he didn't know.

Some yards away he found another room, and this time he saw his mother and father working, working hard as they had always done to make a better life for his brother and him. They never complained, even though they often held down as many as two or three jobs at once, all so that their boys could go to school, would not live in the desperate poverty which they had known all too well.

In still another room he saw himself at the university, saw him getting his degree, saw his parents in the audience, and he knew their pride. He was the first in the family to go beyond high school. He was proud, and yet he felt as if he had lost something that night, something of his people, and he didn't know what.

In yet another room he saw a woman he had loved long ago; they had parted amicably enough; and then he saw his old house in Albuquerque where he had lived when a professor of geology there, and he remembered all the good times he'd had then, all the good friends he'd left behind long ago, all the memories that he had stepped away from.

Another chamber contained niches carved deep into the earth, and in the niches lay mummified bodies. Bodies that had been dead for decades, for a century or two or even longer. The dust was thick in this room, and he did not step inside. He feared to. Here and there he could see a scrap of cloth still sticking to the leathery skin of the mummies, and the air smelled faintly of herbs. Something moved opposite him, and he watched a centipede crawl out of one of the body's eyes.

His stomach rebelled, and he hurried away.

The path twisted to the right, and he stepped into the room and saw a man on a bed. The man was naked, and a blonde woman, equally exposed, sat astride him and ground her hips and moaned. Her hair was plastered in long sweaty strings down her back. The man on the bed reached up and brutally squeezed her breasts, and she cried out as she arched her back, and then she swiveled her head around and leered at him, and Chato saw with horror that the woman was Sunny.

"No!" he screamed. He stumbled from the room, and when he glanced back it was dark. No, no, no. Sunny wasn't with a man, wouldn't be; she loved *him*. Or did she? one part of him slyly whispered. She did, she did, she did. He repeated it to himself as if it were a mantra.

He rubbed his hand across his face, felt the sweat and grime there, and knew then that what he had seen was false. He had been misled, deliberately. Whoever—whatever—was doing this wanted him to lose heart, wanted him to give up.

But he wouldn't.

He took a deep breath, and followed the curve of the tunnel which was now heading downward slightly, and he wondered how far below the airport he was now. If that was really where he was.

Abruptly the tunnel ended, and there before him stretched a pool of water. He edged closer and saw reflected only himself.

Now what? he asked himself.

He inspected the wall beyond the water, the walls alongside him. Were there hidden doors somewhere? No. He knew that this was the way.

But if he jumped in, he would drown. Who knew how deep this was? He might just sink like a stone, and that would be the end of him. Or perhaps there were...things...slimy things waiting for him beneath the water, things that would suck the very breath from his body, and crush him with their rot-encrusted tentacles.

No, no, he couldn't do it. He had to go back, had to find another way to rescue the baby.

No, said a voice in his mind, and he knew it was old Josanie. *Think.*

He studied the water's tranquil surface. Nothing seemed to move below it. Nothing disturbed it.

Taking a deep breath, Chato took one step into the water and sank and sank and sank until he thought his lungs would burst from lack of oxygen, and then suddenly he was in another room, this one much larger than those lining the tunnel.

Firelight flickered, casting elongated shadows, shadows that seemed almost to move as if they were alive.

And there beyond the blaze stood the bruja, and she held the baby by its tiny heels, and dangled the child over the flames. The baby wailed miserably, and flailed its arms uselessly.

"You will pay," the woman whispered, and in that moment he saw she was not an old woman as he had first thought, but that her skin was dark and mottled, like that of a lizard, and her teeth were long and yellowed, something red staining them. From her back arched wings of jade and ebony feathers, feathers that *moved*, from the lice and maggots that crawled across them. She looked like a feathered serpent.

He blinked, but the image stayed the same, and in that moment, he saw she wore his mother's face, then that of Sunny, then that of a girl whom he had known long ago at the university, and then it was the face of the old woman, but only as she must have been long, long ago. She was at once beautiful and terrible to see, and he saw now that she was completely naked except for the necklace of bones draped across her full breasts, and her bronzed skin gleamed.

She smiled at him, and beckoned to him with one hand, and in that hand he saw an obsidian knife.

He remained rooted where he was.

Her skin was tattooed. At least he thought they were tattoos. Tattoos of eyes, like the masks in the tunnel: mere slits, round, tear-shaped, and then with growing horror, he realized the eyes were watching him and that some had winked.

The woman's smile broadened. She raised her arm, the knife rising, and now he watched as the dagger came hurtling down and—

Without thinking, he threw himself across the fire. He was only dimly conscious of the sparks singeing his hair, burning his face and hands, and he grabbed the baby just as the knife slashed downward and pain shot through him as the obsidian cut through his sleeve into his flesh, and he yelled, and kicked out, and his boots connected with the woman, and she screamed as she lost her balance, and fell into the fire.

He scrabbled to his feet, the child cradled tightly in his arms, and watched as the woman writhed and howled as the flames licked up and down her body, melting the flesh away as if it were nothing more than thin tissue paper, and he watched as her bones burned, watched until there was nothing more than charred matter. Abruptly the fire died down, and there was only embers and what had been left of the bruja.

Tentatively he touched one of lumps with the toe of his boot, and he thought he could hear a faint cry.

He hurried away from the fire, then examined the room. It was elongated, the now-dead fire at one end, a pool of water at the other. He had come *down* before. Would he have to go down again? It didn't make sense. After all, he wanted to go *up*, but then maybe none of this made sense, at least as far as the rules of science went. This was a matter of something much darker, much older than science, after all.

The baby was whimpering, and he tried to shush her, but he knew she must be scared and hungry, and with a prayer that this was the right thing, he jumped into the water, and suddenly he was bobbing up and up and up through clear water, and his head broke the surface and he scrabbled out of it before the baby could drown.

Once more he was standing in the tunnel, and as far as he could see there was still no exit. It looked liked he'd have to head up that slope. There was no way around it.

He clasped the infant closer to him and started toward the slope. He ignored the rooms on either side of him; he wanted to see nothing that they held. The walls seemed to grow closer upon him, and things with long plucking fingers reached out and grabbed at his tattered shirt, his burned skin, and he gritted his teeth against the pain.

Finally he came to the slope. He started climbing up, holding the baby with one hand, helping himself find a purchase with the other hand.

What if, he wondered halfway up, what if he got to the top, and he didn't see a doorway, just like when he fell down the slope.

Believe, one part of his mind said, and it was his voice, though, not Josanie's.

He reached the top, and rested, but there before him was the door. He pushed it open and stepped through, and he once more was in the airport terminal, and when he glanced around, there was only a smooth wall.

He hurried toward the nook, afraid now that he would find Gail gone, but she was there, sitting on her bedding. She leaped to her feet when she saw him and rushed over, and he handed the baby to her.

"What happened to you?" she asked.

He knew how he must look. His hair was partly singed, some of it laying in wet strands across his cheek and forehead. His face and arms were bruised, he had blood and cuts and dirt all over him, not to mention the burns and scorch marks.

He grinned.

"It's a long story." He took a deep breath and felt the sharp pain in his ribs; he had forgotten about them during all this; now he was very much reminded. "I think I'm going to wash up as best I can in the bathroom, and then I think we ought to get the hell out of here. You agree?"

She nodded. "I agree."

When he came out of the bathroom a few minutes later, he found she'd make a makeshift bed for the baby from a small carton, and that she'd packed some of their things—mostly the food and drink and blankets—into a few other boxes.

"I didn't know how far we'd have to walk," she said.

"Walk? Hell, we're going to drive," he said, and he strode over to one of the rental car stations, and grabbed a handful of keys. "We're going to go to the rental lot, and find what fits where, and when we do, we're getting in and not looking back." He didn't mention the vehicles that he'd seen earlier, the ones that couldn't get out of the airport. Not now.

He wasn't about to stop for anyone or anything now, not after what he'd just gone through.

It took them half an hour but they found a blue T-bird, and got their boxes settled in. Gail strapped herself in, then held the baby tightly.

Chato got behind the wheel, put on his seatbelt, adjusted mirrors and seat, and turned on the car, and without thinking, flipped on the turn signal. He grinned when he realized it wasn't necessary. Old habits.

Then they drove out of the deserted rental car lot, and into the outbound lane, and when they reached the shells of the ambulances, he saw that Gail started to shake as she realized what had happened earlier, and he said, looking into the rearview mirror and seeing the dark eyes of old Josanie, "I believe."

Chato drove away from the airport, away from the fire and the death, and it was only when they had driven over twenty miles further that he remembered he never had picked up his luggage. He began laughing.

That was okay. He'd pick up some more bags. After all, he told himself as he look over at the sleeping mother and child, luggage was cheap; life wasn't.

MI CASA

Anita Rodríguez stared out the window, but could see nothing but her reflection, almost watery in the glass. Dark hair pulled back severely, dark skin, dark eyes...dark, dark, dark... everything was so dark.

And darkness had come prematurely to the northern New Mexico mountains, blanketing everything with a wintry breath that even now puffed against the house, trying to get in.

She saw no other lights outside. How could she? The house was so far away from others that it might well have been the only one in the county.

Shivering, she turned away, the old lace curtain fluttering back into place. Anita hitched her shawl up around her shoulders, then settled on a low bench and picked up the book she had been trying to read for the past hour. She was still on page one.

Tears blurred her eyes, and swallowing rapidly, noisily, she studied the large room, almost Spartan in its simplicity. Whitewash covering the adobe brick walls, the room contained only a few pieces of furniture: the plain bench, a chair with a high leather back, an immense double-doored wooden cabinet dating from the colonial Spanish days, and a weathered table with a carved *santo* atop it. The floor displayed a Southwestern pattern of inlaid Mexican tiles in vivid turquoise and salmon and canary and beige. Two doors: one to the outside, one to the rest of the house. Light came from the pierced tin wall sconces, once holding candles but now electrified, and the *horno*, the rounded fireplace in the corner, where pinõn logs crackled as they burned. From the hallway she heard the steady ticking of a clock. The doorframes and windowsills, inside and out, were painted blue.

To guard against evil spirits, or so the tradition claimed.

But tonight nothing would keep the spirits—the remembrances—out of the house. The pungent fragrance of the burning *piñón* alone was enough to make her cry, without all the memories crowding her tonight.

Softly the clock chimed, and she recalled the day her father had presented it to her mother. He had saved all year for it, this tenth anniversary gift, and he was so proud of the beautiful walnut veneer grandfather clock with its silver embossing. And her mother's eyes had welled with tears and—no.

Why had she come back?

To escape?

Hardly.

Yet that was the precise reason Jerry had urged her to return home—to get away. Her mother had finally entered a nursing home, and Anita had wept long hours since, even though she knew there had been no choice.

"It's not really your decision any longer, hon," Jerry had said as he comforted her in his arms. He kissed the top of her head.

Anita had nodded against his chest, knowing he was correct; that she had done the right thing. And still the guilt and unhappiness flowed through her.

She could no longer do anything for her mother who had laid so still in the bed with eyes closed, rarely responding to anyone's voice, nearly comatose, but not quite. Monitors and machines beeped, hissed and hummed, while tubes snaked and coiled out of the woman, and after a while Anita couldn't separate in her mind what was really part of her mother, what wasn't. Sometimes she thought she remembered her mother having the tubes coming out of her skin years ago, back when Anita was a child, but she told herself that was nonsense. It was, wasn't it? But the memories from before were fading, were changing, and she didn't like it.

Anita had done what she could to make her mother's life easier, and her brother and sister were not willing to help. In fact, they had proved quite vocal, informing her that they didn't want the old woman living with them. Their conversations had stayed with her all too well.

"Old woman?" Anita had said, not believing she'd heard the scorn in her siblings' voices. "That's our mother there."

"That's a shell," Raymond had said, his voice devoid of emotion. His eyes would not meet hers. "Nothing more, Nita."

"No," she'd whispered.

"Face it," Anna had said, "that hasn't been our mother since the accident. You know that—God knows, we've been telling you that for a year now. But you never listen to us; you never have, even when we were kids. It's for the best, you know."

"But—"

"No," Raymond had said, holding up a hand. "We've heard all the arguments. There's nothing new you can tell us. And face it, Nita, you'll be better off with her in the nursing home. We all will. We can get on with our lives now."

After that, Anita knew they were right, that it was time for the professionals to take over, time for her mother to go where she would get around-the-clock treatment. It was time. Long past time.

Time...the clock ticked away. One, two, three, four, and she found she was breathing in rhythm with the clock. She held her breath for a moment, tried to break the rhythm, then almost laughed at the absurdity.

Time...one part of her wondered if she should have kept their mother just a little longer. What if she had abandoned her parent too soon? What if it had only taken a few weeks more, a month, two or three even...Time....

No. It was the right time; and she hadn't abandoned her mother. She hadn't. Really.

Even though she felt as if she had.

And so, here she was, getting away to rest in her mother's house, getting away from the situation. The irony, of course, was that it was all she could think of.

It was all her life had turned into. Waiting for her mother to live, to die, to do something other than lay there so still.

No.

She wouldn't worry about her mother and the nursing home any longer. It had been done; the act was completed. There was no turning back.

The door and pane rattled with the force of the cold wind. The curtain trembled ever so slightly, as if something had breathed against it.

The clock ticked and ticked and ticked...ticking away her life, she thought.

She concentrated on the book, forcing herself to finish the paragraph and go on to page two. But again her mind wandered; her eyes lifted, glanced at the dark oblong window.

Something white pattered against it. She rose and glanced out, and saw snowflakes.

That was the problem with coming to this old place set in the foothills of the Sangre de Cristos, east of Santa Fe. Winter came so early here, painting the slopes white long before it ever reached the capital city. It was only mid-September, and yet it might as well have been the depths of winter.

She had not thought she could take the time off—after all, she was a legislative assistant and the legislature was in session right now—but somehow Jerry had arranged it. He insisted she needed the time away, and her boss had agreed, and so she had come home.

To this house.

She remembered when there had been much more here, in this room—when it had been filled with the playful shouts and gleeful laughter of three energetic children, and the cheerful calls of their mother from the kitchen for them to wash up and come to dinner right away.

She remembered when Raymond, not more than nine or ten years old, had drawn in bright red Crayola a picture of Father Martinez from the parish church on the wall; it had not been a flattering representation, but all their mother had done was chuckle and suggest that perhaps he might wish to use paper next time.

She remembered her mother sitting by the window the night they had learned that their father had walked out on them and would never be back. She, not even eleven, had gone to her mother and put her arms around her, her head resting on the dark one below hers, and the others had come to them and held their mother as well. So long ago.

Years before she had gone to the legislature, years before Raymond had bought his art gallery on Canyon Road, years before Anna had moved down to Albuquerque with her second husband.

Years before they had grown apart.

Tick, tick, ticking away....

She shook her head, sighed, then started when she heard a sharp bang in another room. She hurried down the darkened hallway and into the end bedroom—one of the casement windows had blown open, and the lace curtains stood straight back from the wind gusting snow across the sill. She rushed over and locked the window, batted away the damp curtain as it slapped against her cheek, then fetched a towel from the bathroom to wipe the snow up before it melted.

When she finished, she looked around the room, with its blue and white quilt on the wide bed, at the intricately carved pine chest set against one wall, at the painting of a Santa Fe church she had done when she was a teenager and had thought she wanted to be an artist. The room was so...bare...bare of furniture, of belongings, but not of memories.

Again she could close her eyes and recall so easily those days when her mother had let them climb into bed with her, and the three children had piled up onto its softness, then burrowed under the quilt while their mother told them tales of talking rabbits and squirrels. How warm and cozy—how safe—it had all been.

She forced herself to return to the front room, where she

stood before the fireplace and held her hands out to the flames. She was so cold; maybe this would help.

The ticking sounded louder now.

Wind pounded against the door, and she stepped closer to the fire, as if seeking protection. Of course, that was nonsense, she thought when she realized what she'd done.

She shouldn't have come out here this time of the year, she told herself, not for the first time since her arrival. She should have waited for spring; but she couldn't. She'd had to get away now, before the weeks grew into months, the months into years, into decades.

Something white drifted across the floor, and she whirled around.

A snowflake.

It had sifted in through the crack under the door.

Ice crystals had formed on the window, too, and she wondered how long the storm would last. Hours, perhaps; maybe even a day or two. She didn't worry about being stuck here, though, because Jerry knew where she was. He would come for her, if she needed him, if she couldn't get out in the morning.

Jerry. She smiled at the thought of her husband, then sat on the bench again to read. Another page gone by slowly, then she looked up as more snow drifted into the room.

The windows were not as tightly closed as they could be, she knew. Or rather, the old wood frames were warped from cold and heat and age; there was nothing to do but replace them, and perhaps she and Jerry could do that in the spring, when it was warm again.

It hadn't always been this cold, the house; once it had been warm and open. *Mi casa, su casa,* her mother had always proclaimed to friends and strangers alike. *My house is your house.* And their mother had never turned anyone away in all the years she had lived here.

Not like Anita. Anita had turned her mother away.

No, she told herself sharply as she bit back tears; she had not turned her mother away. Her brother and sister had done that;

she at least had nursed her mother as best she could. And when it had grown too much, she had sought help. There was nothing wrong with that.

Was there?

Mi casa, su casa.

Yes; she had told her mother that very thing when the old woman had come to live with them after the accident, the accident that had left her paralyzed along one side, and nearly speechless and her mind rambling, a wreck of the once smiling and pleasant woman who had raised three children by herself. But it was Jerry's and her house, not her mother's.

And then, when the situation grew too inconvenient, she had turned the old woman away.

No!

She shook her head, denying.

Mi casa—

There was a deep roaring, like a dark train barreling a hundred miles an hour or more along a steel track—the wind had become a gale. The walls of the house seemed to reverberate from its power, and she wondered if they and the roof could withstand the escalating wind, this blizzard. Surely, yes, because they had withstood so much else before.

Snow formed a powdery semi-circle inside the door, and the windowsill was white. A trickle of water from melted snow inched down the wall.

The temperature in the room had dropped in the past few minutes, and she shivered, then rubbed her arms briskly with her hands, but nothing would warm her. Not now.

The ticking of the clock dropped to a whisper, as if the clock were winding down. Slowing, slowing, slowing...as if it were more the beat of a heart than a clock now.

Anita admitted it at last. She had turned her mother away. Had abandoned the woman when she needed her family most. She had.

But coming here had been the right thing. This would make it all right. This waiting at the house. She knew it would.

Slower...slowly...the ticking....

She smiled. Nothing ever changed. The snow would come in, as it always did, and in a minute she would get another towel from the kitchen, and she would wipe up the snow, knowing even then that this small action was futile. And she would look once more out into the darkness, and behind her the fire would burn, and the wind would scream.

The snow would continue falling, collecting slowly around the house in gigantic drifts.

And she would sit down and read again.

And she would listen as the wind screamed and the roof shook.

She would.

Just as she had every night for the past five years.

She would wait. Wait until her mother joined her, and once more there would be warmth and laughter, the two of them together.

My house.

LITTLE CONTRASTS

You really have never understood me, Randy. Not from the beginning of our relationship, not through twelve years of marriage, not even now.

I think it's more—much more—than the usual male-female misunderstandings, too, although that's involved to some degree, of course. Everything we do or think or experience is tainted—if you want to call it that—with the nature of our sexuality. No matter how much "they" try to change it, it'll still be the same. Men will be men, and women will be women. Maybe we can change a bit, but you can't buck a million years of genetics.

Excuse me while I reach across you and get into the glove box. I always keep the spare napkins there. Remember how we always used to go to the old drive-in on the other side of town when the kids were really little? They'd be in their jammies in the back—kind of like they are now—and we'd have all these little packets of mustard and ketchup in the glove compartment, along with straws and napkins and plastic forks. We were better stocked than the concession stand!

I hope you don't think I'm being real rude. I'd offer you a sip of my soda, but...well, you understand. My, that tastes so good. I just wish they wouldn't put so much ice in these cups.

It's hot in here. It's supposed to hit over a 100 today, maybe get as high as 105. I know I'm sweatin' like a pig. My mother always said ladies never sweat, they *perspire*; shows you how much she knew.

Maybe I should run the air conditioning for a while. All this heat makes everything kind of ripe, and it *does* smell in here. There's nothing you can do about it, hon. Rotten shame.

I'm sorry, Randy. I shouldn't laugh. Not really. It's not nice. I shouldn't say, "rotten", either. I mean...well—

Now what was I saying before I got sidetracked?

Oh, yeah, the male/female thing.

Everything is just so...polar, isn't it? Black...white...leftist...rightist...innie or outie...navels, that is.

We're all divided into two groups, no matter what. Rich or poor. Black or white. Left or right. Liberal or conservative. Strong or weak. Girl or boy.

Is that what everything in life comes down to? A girl thing? A boy thing?

East is east, and west is west, and never the twain shall meet?

The strong and the weak...I know that's how you thought about us. You were strong. I was weak.

And thinking that, why did you marry me?

Everything I did or said or thought—everything that was the essence of *me*—you seemed to despise or at the very least disapprove of and want to change.

And they say women are always trying to remake their men. Ha! I think you saw in me what I could be, or at least what I could be *in your eyes*. You know, sweetie, you really should have waited longer for what you really wanted and not settled on me.

What the hell did I know about these things? I was practically a kid when I met you. I just thought some great guy had fallen for me.

But I see that we were never very compatible, not even from the beginning.

I liked country, you liked jazz, and neither one of us was willing to listen to the other's musical choices. God knows I tried, but whenever I asked questions about some jazz piece, you always made fun of me in that condescending way you have. Had.

Oh, you didn't know you were condescending? Please. It's

your number one personality feature. Or maybe your bossiness is. Oh, wait. In a man "bossiness" becomes "assertiveness." That's right. It's *only* bossiness when it comes to a woman. That's another one of the weird boy/girl things.

Oops. Sorry. I shouldn't have burped. That's another thing women don't do, my mother always said. But the word she used was "belched." "Burp" to her was so vulgar. Vulgar. Honestly, I can't even begin to think of things in terms like that. Vulgar. Ladylike.

I shouldn't try to laugh and swallow my drink at the same time. Now I've dribbled soda down my front. That's certainly "unladylike." It's so dark on the material...looks almost like blood, doesn't it?

Guess I shouldn't bring that up, huh?

You didn't like my friends much, either. But you got rid of them fast enough—you were rude to them, or came on to them and embarrassed us all, and after a while my girlfriends stopped coming by, quit calling, and effectively you had me all to yourself. You always thought I was a hick. Maybe I was, but I didn't see anything wrong with it. I don't see that all your so-called worldly ways and expensive education got you very far. Some ambition in there would have helped, I reckon.

You laughed at me when I said I wanted to go to college. What did I need a degree for, you wanted to know, when all I'd ever be was a housewife? When I took community college classes, you made fun of me, and asked me if I was taking underwater basket weaving. You even visited a few of the classes in an attempt to ridicule me. The professor asked if I would drop out, because you were disturbing the other students.

Every time I tried to better myself, you knocked me down—figuratively-speaking, of course. I'll say this, Randy, you never laid a hand on me. I would have left you the minute you had. Or at least that's what I hope I would have. Plenty of women leave their men when the hitting begins. Too many don't, though.

But you didn't have to hit me with your hand. You hit me in other ways. Mentally, psychically, emotionally. The bruises were inside.

So, you despised me and my likes, and when I tried to change, you despised me all the more. You wanted to mold me, mold me into what, I don't know.

I may have been young when we married, but I wasn't mindless. That's what you needed. Some mindless little bimbo or groupie type who would have hung on every word you spoke, who would willingly have done anything and everything for you.

You knew from the beginning I wouldn't.

And maybe that's what intrigued you, maybe that's what made you want me all the more. Kind of like a rider who sees a wild horse he's got to tame.

You tried to tame me, you really did. Or rather—break my spirit. It almost worked. Almost.

You despised me because you despised yourself. You were a no-talent, barely-get-by type of guy with zilch ambition. Only you had everyone fooled with your good looks and your charm. Those qualities can go a long way, but not everyone is fooled by them.

And the older you got, the more you realized that—just how empty you were, and how full I was. Empty...full...there's another one of those little contrasts.

And so it wasn't bad enough that you were a total bastard toward me. You decided to turn the kids against me. Every chance you could you ridiculed me in front of them, you told them how dumb I was, how stupid, how this or that, and all the time you were talking about yourself.

Of course, kids listen to their dads, and after a while, they began to see me the same way. No matter what I did, they thought I was dumb.

I almost walked out then. But I wanted to give our marriage a chance, I wanted to give the kids—and you—a chance.

I should have left, Randy, should have cut my losses then.

Then the kids could have seen just what sort of a "hero" you were. I'd like to have seen you try to fix their lunches, and do their laundry and make dinner for them after you'd been at work all day. But I forget...you wouldn't have done that...you would have found some housekeeper right away, or you would have gone around, looking like such a sad sack, "betrayed" by his wife—and before long you'd had some other little girl-woman taking care of you. Your kind never does without for very long.

God, I'm tired. I've been cleaning the house from top to bottom. I've been going room by room, and it's amazing how much you can get done if you really put your mind to it. Of course, there's just me now in it, no one else to track mud through the just waxed kitchen floor, no one to spill soda or fruit juice on the carpet, no one to leave toothpaste gobs in the bathroom sink. I mean, I know I'm a little messy now and then, but I swear, hon, that I think you used to do it on purpose. I would just get something clean, and you'd go and drip something gooey on it, and I'd have to scrub it again. I know you got a big kick out of it—sometimes, even with my head down as I scrubbed, I could see you out of the corner of my eye, and you'd be grinning this big old grin. Yeah, that was a big kick for you. Really got your rocks off on it, didn't you? Just another way to keep me under your thumb. Of course, the times I decided not to clean, not to sweep up after you and the kids, the place became a real pigsty, and I got worried for their health. Not yours, mind you, but theirs.

Not that it matters any more. Nothing much matters any more, I guess.

Except that I have a very clean house.

And I can sleep in as late as I want in the morning. No one demanding to know where their lunch is or their schoolbooks, didn't I iron a shirt, why didn't I do that, just as if the three of you couldn't do a lick of work yourselves. I guess it was just easier to sit in front of the tube and have good ol' Mom run your errands and wait on you like I was your maid.

That's pretty much a pattern in my family, so I shouldn't have been surprised. My mother waited on my father hand and foot, and even though he'd be sitting closer to something, he'd ask her to get it for him. And she'd do it. Her mother did it for my grandfather, too. I hated that when I was going up; I hated my father for using my mom like some work animal, and I hated her for going along with it. Never once did he thank her, or say, sit down, Bess, you're tired, I'll get my beer, I'll make myself a sandwich, hey, do you want something too? Never. Not in over thirty years of marriage. She resented him, of course, and it would come out in little ways, tiny pettinesses, as if she were getting back at him for everything she'd ever suffered. I don't think he ever noticed, though. My mother was too much of a "lady," though, to ever publicly complain. She never said a word to me, either, just pressed her lips together whenever she heard him calling her from the front room.

I vowed that when I got married and had children I'd make them do things for themselves. There's nothing wrong with fetching something for someone—if you're up already or what-ever, but to expect someone to do everything for you...well, they abolished slavery over a century ago, you know.

Somehow all my good plans went awry. All of a sudden, it seems, I found myself getting your cup of coffee, then leaping up during a commercial to get another cup for you so you wouldn't miss your show, and then the kids came along, and I was doing this and that for them when they were too little, and suddenly they were bigger kids and still demanding too much from me.

But when I got sick last week and was too tired to do anything for anyone, you all got so belligerent with me. What the hell did I think I was doing? Who did I think I was? And the unkindest cut of all: didn't I love you all anymore? For God's sakes, I was sick! I was puking up my guts half the night, running a fever, and all you did was peevishly demand to know why I hadn't done the laundry. I could have shit the sheets, and you would have just stood there and complained about the smell and not lifted your hands to change them.

I was getting real worried and wanted to go to the doctor for some medicine, but you kept saying there wasn't anything really wrong with me, that I was just being lazy. Lazy. Right.

I think I almost died I was so sick. I was out of my head with fever most of the time.

I guess that's when I began to see things a lot more clearly. Maybe the fever helped. I don't know. I just know that I started to feel a lot different after I was back on my feet.

And you were still pouting, still whining that I didn't love you or the kids.

Of course, I did, but you can love someone almost too much. You can't smother them, can't do everything for them; kids—and adults—have to do things on their own. It's how they become real people.

I'm still tired, you know. This illness really took it out of me. Let me close my eyes for a while. I just want to rest them. That's what my grandmother always said. We used to tease her about it.

There now. I'm closing them. I'm resting. I'm....

Oh, God, did I doze? Jeez, I guess so. It's nearly two. Excuse me, while I yawn.

You know for a moment there it was almost like old times. You and me and a drowsy do-nothing type of afternoon. You remember how we use to lay on the bed upstairs, with just the whisper of a breeze coming in the window, stirring those gauzy curtains I'd picked up at the flea market? We would talk for a bit, then drift off to sleep, then wake up again, to finish our conversation, just like minutes hadn't passed. That was fun.

There *were* fun times, you know. Don't think I've forgotten them. I haven't. And there are many more memories I cherish as well.

It's just that there were so many more bad times, and in the past few years that's all I've had—bad times with you and the kids.

Sorry, Randy. Yawned again. I think I'm going to go to bed early tonight. I've got a lot of errands to run tomorrow, and I want to get them done before it gets too hot.

Boy, I wish we had a swimming pool. It sure would be nice to strip and take a swim. The best time would be at night, though, feeling that cool water against my warm skin. Lying in the moonlight, then taking another dip…. We were always going to put in a pool, remember, but somehow we never got around to it. There was always something else for us to spend our money on. The truck, the boat, the cabin at the lake. All the things that you enjoyed. Few of the things that I like.

Well, I guess that's water under the bridge, or something like that now, right?

Just where did all our hopes go to, hon? What happened to that eager young woman, that attentive man? When did we become the people we are today?

I don't know. I really don't.

Maybe it all began to change when the kids came.

Everything changes in a marriage, they say, when you have kids. I didn't think it would. Not really. I certainly didn't think our situation would get worse. But it did. The kids might as well have had just one parent for all the help you gave me. If they saw you at all in the first year I'd be real surprised. But boy, when we were out, you sure took all the credit, just like you'd carried them yourself for nine months.

You know, I just never realized how much you envied me. It wasn't just for having the kids, but for a lot of other things. Things I couldn't see before. And here you always told me I was the empty vessel, waiting to have something poured in it.

You were wrong. Dead wrong. You were empty.

And that's all I've got to say on the matter. Maybe I'll be in a better mood tomorrow. Maybe not.

I gotta go.

There. Locked the car doors. I'd crack the windows, Randy, but you understand…the smell and all. I don't want someone just happening by and getting a whiff of that.

Oh, the air out here is so nice and fresh. It *is* going to be a scorcher. That sun is so blistering—I knew I should have worn a hat. Oh, well, it's not that long a walk back to the house.

You know, when we first moved here, I wasn't sure about living in the country, but you told me that it'd be a good thing.

You said it was better that we didn't have neighbors for miles and miles. Who wanted noisy Parkers coming over any old time?

Well, hon, I think you're right. Yes, I'm willing to concede on that point. I like being out in the middle of nowhere, with not another soul around for miles and miles and miles.

And this old shed proved to be perfect. It's nice and remote, and I can keep your car here. And here I wanted to tear down this crummy thing—I mean, it's so ugly, being metal and all, but no, you said we could store things out here.

You were right.

Damn, that's twice, Randy. I've gotta watch that.

You understand why I didn't want to use my car—it's up at the house, by the way. C'mon, you know why...stains. And I just had it thoroughly cleaned inside and out, you know. You were always so picky about your car—there couldn't be a blade of grass or scrap of paper in it, or you'd pitch a fit. That's why we always had to take the kids in my car; little children leave gummy fingerprints on everything, and barf, and just generally make messes, and you couldn't have that in your precious automobile. And you were forever washing it; I'm surprised the paint didn't come off from all the waxing and polishing you did.

You know, I think you paid more attention to your car than to your kids or me.

This must just drive you nuts.

Oh, now, c'mon, you can sob all you want and try to scream, but you know you aren't going to be heard with that gag. It's real secure, and so are those handcuffs and the rope. If you don't struggle, you won't get choked by the noose. See, it's a slip knot. My brother was a Boy Scout, and he taught me all the knots when I was a kid; he said he never saw anyone learn so quickly. I just hope you don't chafe yourself too raw. You might bleed all over that precious leather upholstery. Besides, as you always pointed out, there's no one for miles and miles to hear you or the kids.

I'll just give the old trunk a thump—ah, yes, they're still

conscious. Hush, you two, be a good boy and girl. Daddy doesn't like noise, you know, and you really ought to try to be nicer to him now that you're all having this quality time together.

I'll be back tomorrow, Randy, regular as clockwork. I haven't missed a day in the past week, have I, although I reckon it won't be much longer. I hear it's supposed to get up over a 100 again tomorrow, with no let up in the temperature at all through the weekend. All this heat...and not a lick of wind. This old tin shed is a real oven.

I know I shouldn't laugh, but here I was talking about all this two groups stuff, and it all comes down to this, Randy: alive.

Or dead.

See you tomorrow.

Maybe.

DRIVEN

My life is slowly being sucked out of me...bled away by my miserable existence, as if a vampire has attached itself to me. No, make that a spider. A spider's just as bad—she sits in her web, waiting for her prey, and when she captures it, she sucks the poor thing dry until there's only a husk left.

That's me...fast becoming the husk.

I study myself in the hall mirror, and discover minute lines around my eyes that I know weren't there months ago. My skin looks dry...wasted. I could be ten years—fifteen years—older than I really am.

Dry...drying...dried...dust....

I take a ragged breath as I examine the handful of mail and my hands shake. I know what the official-looking envelopes contain even without tearing them open.

Past due.

Past due.

Past due.

You are X months late with payment.

We are turning your account over to collection.

We regret that you haven't contacted us....

We will be forced to....

And me with all of $38 in my checking account.

I crumple the envelopes suddenly, then carefully smooth the papers.

I don't know whether to cry or curse. I've done both in the months since Jack left.

It hasn't helped.

I've written letter after letter to my creditors explaining that I'm not trying to screw them out of payment and that I really intend to pay but that it will just have to be real slow, and the next week the dunning phone calls continue, the intimidating letters fill the mail box. The calls are so bad now that mostly I leave the phone unplugged. *That* was disconnected twice in the past few months, and the electric company is threatening to shut me off.

Gritting my teeth, I toss the mail onto the hall table along with all the other unopened envelopes, including those from Jack.

I push back an errant strand curl and pick up the painting, my keys and purse and slam out of the house. The glass panes in the door rattle.

I have plenty of time before I go to work so first I'll drop the picture off to be framed. It's an oil that I was commissioned for months ago, and I finished it last week. It's not completely dry— the weather is too humid for that—but I can't wait any longer; I need the money. Time after time I'd started the painting, but it hadn't come together for the longest time. I'm not completely happy with it, but...I wish I had more time and energy for my art, but I don't; I'm lucky to get a bit done each weekend. And it's not easy being creative when you're depressed all the time.

My friends tell me to hang on, and I'm trying; I'm trying to have a positive attitude, trying to hope that things will change for the better...but it's hard...damned hard.

At the corner, I bear left. Ahead, a line of cars sits at a stop sign. There's no reason for this backup—there's not much traffic, and no pedestrians are crossing the street. I drum my finger-nails on the steering wheel. I play with the electric windows, sliding first one, then the other up, then down. I adjust my seat, my rearview mirror and side mirrors, and just as I'm about to honk the horn, the convertible in front of me slides forward a few feet. I inch up, leaving my foot on the brake. A bead of sweat trickles down my back and I lean forward to cool off. I'd turn on the air conditioning but that overheats the engine. It's so hot these days; no rain in sight, with temperatures predicted to hover in the nineties for at least another week or so.

Suddenly something thumps me from behind, and I blink, for a moment not understanding.

Then I know: some idiot has smacked me. I leap out to inspect the damage.

The other driver, an older woman with wispy white hair, slowly emerges from her Jaguar. Her lower lip wobbles as she approaches me and she starts to cry.

"I'm so sorry. I didn't mean to hit you. I just thought you were going to move more. I'm really sorry. I'm so sorry. Really." She wrings her hands, hands dotted with age-spots, hands where the veins stick out in vivid relief.

I remember the last time I saw my mother—her fingers were all gnarled, and the veins stood out so prominently; when I had taken her hand, though, it had been cold, icy cold. I feel the anger build inside, and I lash out, almost screaming. "You dumb bitch, why don't you watch what you're doing? Why don't you pay attention instead of fiddling with your radio or messing with you stupid hair? Lucky for you I don't have my baby in the car."

I march off, and now that the cars in front of me are gone, drive off. Trembling, I glance back in the mirror and see the old woman sagging against the Jag. I bite my lip. I don't know why I blew up. There really isn't any damage to my bumper, and her car had the scrapes. I felt bad seeing her cry, but somehow that had made me angrier, made me really want to lash out.

And why did I say that thing about the baby? I didn't have one.

I shudder. Maybe it's the heat. The heat and humidity. I can't park by the frame shop, so I settle for a space in front of a building down the way. The walk back is hot, the asphalt underfoot sticky; rotting fruit from a nearby tree stains the sidewalk.

The guy behind the counter barely glances at me when I enter. He's on the phone and from the way his voice is lowered, it isn't with a customer. I wait for a minute, then two, then three.

Finally, when I've been there over five minutes, I clear my throat.

"I gotta go. Call me back in a minute."

I think our transaction will take longer than that, but I say nothing.

"Yeah?" the clerk asks as he approaches. His tone is surly, and it's obvious he thinks a customer is interrupting his life.

"I called earlier in the week—I had a hell of a time getting through, too; the phone's always busy." I glare at him, knowing now why I can't kept getting a busy signal. "I have this painting to frame, and the man I talked to said it would take only a few days."

"Yeah, well, Dave isn't here."

"Who's Dave?" I ask, baffled.

"He's the guy who frames. I don't know when he'll be back."

"Can you give me an estimate?"

"I don't do frames."

You don't do much, I want to point out. "Well, don't you have a chart or something?"

"Yeah."

It's such an imposition, I know for me to expect the guy to do *something*.

The clerk takes the painting from me, and I slap at his hand. "Don't touch the canvas. You'll wreck it."

"My hands are clean."

"It doesn't matter. You can leave marks even if you just washed your hands."

He starts to pick it up again, his fingers against the canvas, and I snatch the painting back. He grabs at it, and one of his nails scrapes against pigment, leaving an inch long scar.

All my hard work.... "You idiot. Look what you've done." Tears brim my eyes as I cradle the painting. "Forget it. Just tell Dave or whoever that I'll be back in a few days. And it won't be to have my picture framed, but rather to complain about you."

"Fuck off, lady." As he starts to turn away, he's already reaching for the phone.

I slam out of the shop and return to my car. Something official-looking flaps under the windshield wiper and I stare at it in disbelief. A ticket.

But why?

I glance around and for the first time see the hydrant. I groan. I hadn't even noticed it when I parked. I grab the ticket, nearly ripping it in half in the process, and thrust it inside my purse, then sit in the car and stare at the painting.

I can repair the damage; it isn't that bad, but...but it angers me. Why was he such a moron? Why wouldn't he listen to me? Why hadn't *Jack* listened to me? I take out my Swiss army knife and run the flat of a blade across the raised pigment to see if I can smooth it a bit. It looks worse than before. Suddenly I hate the clerk, hate what he did, hate the painting. I thrust the knife into the canvas, and smile as the canvas rips. I slash over and over, until it's practically in shreds, then I toss it into the back-seat.

My hair straggles into my face, and I slap it back with both hands, unmindful of the open knife. When the point of the blade grazes my temple, I drop it, and it falls onto the floor. I lick my dry lips.

Everything these days frustrates me; little things just pile up and up and up, and bother me. Someone can say "boo" and I'll either cry or get angry. I have to get control, have to get back on even keel, except that I don't know how to do that any more, don't know what I can do to calm things down. Once my life was so orderly; now it seems utter chaos; I'm on a constant roller coaster, that mostly heads down and down and down.

It's okay.... I can do the painting again. Do it better this time. I can still get paid; that's the important part.

I start the car and wince as it threatens to die—and ease out onto the clear roadway, just in time to have someone in a red import race up close to my bumper and lay on the horn. As she swings around me, a teenaged girl flips me the bird.

Give me a fucking break, I think. The girl hadn't been in sight when I pulled out.

My hands are trembling, I realize, as I park in the lot at work.

I retrieve the knife and close it, slip it back into my purse. As I walk into the building, a blast of air conditioning hits me. Maybe this will cool me down, I think—in more ways than one. I greet the usual people in the outer offices. Most merely nod or keep their heads down, and my skin prickles. What's wrong?

I'm barely settled at my desk when the phone rings. It's my boss wanting to see me. I glance at my watch; I'm only a minute late. That isn't so bad; we've talked about it before, and he says he doesn't mind if I'm a few minutes late here and there because he knows I will make it up at the end of the day.

I smooth down my hair, powder my nose, and then slowly walk down the hall to his office and wait outside the closed door. I try chatting with Vickie, his white-haired secretary, but the woman abruptly excuses herself for the ladies' room.

"Come on, Carol," Dick says, sticking his head out the door. His tone isn't jovial—it's polite, nothing more. I enter. The personnel manager is there as well, and several department heads.

There is no chair for me to sit in. None of the others look at me.

I remain standing, while Dick closes the door.

He walks around to his desk and sits down behind it. He picks up a letter opener in the shape of a small jeweled dagger. His expression is grim. "I'm sorry, Carol, but we aren't happy with the work you've been doing for us."

I blink at him. "Aren't happy? But you gave me a raise last month at my yearly review."

"I know, but there were problems then."

"Why didn't you say something? I could have tried to improve or change or something. I can still do something." I try to keep the eagerness out of my voice; I don't want to look like I'm groveling, even though I am.

He strokes the letter opener now, and I hope he cuts himself, hope he drips blood all over his precious month-end reports. "I'm sorry, Carol, but we're just not satisfied with your performance. Over the past year you haven't shown the growth we expected;

you're not as aggressive as we anticipated. And there's the little matter of the personal problems, too. That's taken away from your job, and impacted your performance here."

Impacted? My problems—the "little matter" of Jack has torn my life apart. Not "impacted." Why can't he even speak proper English? When it all began, Dick brought me into his office and told me how sorry he was, and how they all understood, and they would understand if I needed a day or two off here and there, etc. He had been so warm, so friendly...so two-faced.

"...and so we're going to have to let you go."

"Let me go?" Somehow the words don't make sense to me. I realize I've missed other things he said, but it doesn't matter. Just the last words did.

I lick my lips, feel how dry they were, how dry my throat is. Dry...drying....

Dick clears his throat. "Al will take you back to your office where you can clean out your desk, and he'll escort you from the building."

"That's it? I don't get a warning? I don't get put on probation? You're firing me just like that? Without any warning whatsoever? You said before that you all understood about what was going on, you said that you'd cut me some slack, you said—"

"Carol, I said that for some time we haven't been—"

"I know what you *said*, Dick, but why didn't you let me know this before so I could have tried to work harder? Why did you just wait to spring this on me? Why?"

He starts to speak again, and I know what he'll say. We haven't been happy for some time, we haven't this, we haven't that—everything he spewed out just moments before he'll parrot over and over, as if he'd nothing more than a tape loop.

"You'll have to surrender your key."

I want to grab the little dagger letter opener and plunge it into his heart. If he has one. I would love that, seeing the surprise in his eyes as he tries to wiggle away from me...only I wouldn't let him. I'd twist the dagger in his chest and twist and twist and twist, and the blood would spurt all over me, and I wouldn't be so dry any more.

He sits there watching me.

They are all waiting for my reaction, waiting for me to cry, to beg for my job back. The hell with that. I won't give them the satisfaction of me crying. Not that I feel like it; I don't think I have any tears left.

Numbly I yank my keychain out, and unhook my office key and fling it at him; it hits him squarely in the chest. My lips curl into a faint smile. My fingers shake so badly I can't get the other keys back on the chain, so I just thrust them into my purse.

I whirl and leave his office, brush past Vickie who has returned and half-walk, half-stumble to my office.

I know my face is red, can feel the heat of it, and I glance wildly around for a carton to put my things in. Vaguely I'm aware of Al lurking in the doorway. Probably wants to make sure I don't steal my desk or chair. Absurd! I've been a trusted employee, and now this...humiliation...this indignity.

Moments later Nora from accounting comes in, all apologetic and more than a little embarrassed, with a computer paper cartoon. She murmurs that she's sorry, slaps the container on my desk, then ducks out.

I jerk open my desk drawers, sweep the contents into the box. Silently I dare Al to challenge me on any of the contents. I pick up my coffee mug and toss it with the other stuff, then set my purse on top of everything. I pick up the carton and brush past him.

"I'm sorry—" Al begins.

"Yeah, I just bet you are."

I walk through the building, aware that everyone watches me now, aware that Al trails after me. What are they afraid I'll do? Destroy something along the way? Duck into someone's office and hide?

This is ridiculous.

But it is a ridiculous place, always has been.

He opens the door for me and I go out without thanking him, and walk stiffly to the car. I open the trunk and drop the box back there. Slam the trunk lid down. Open it again to retrieve my purse, then slam it. I get in my car and sit there, and stare at the building.

I can see some faces at windows here and there, and I wonder if Dick is watching. Good ol' Dick. Dick the Prick we all used to call him behind his back. How much of that, I wonder now, got back to him. If I don't leave after a while, will he call the police and accuse me of trespassing? The thought is almost funny. One part of me wants to stay there and find out just what he'll do.

Another part of me wants to start up the car, press the gas pedal down *hard*, and just gun that sucker into the front of the building. I smile, envisioning the building's glass front shattering into millions of shards as the car smashes through it, imagine the satisfying crunch I'd make as I hit the receptionist's desk, imagine all the whirling papers and alarmed voices and fragments of glass and wood everywhere.

Fragments. Like my life. Everything is in pieces.

I can feel the tears now, feel their warmth creeping down my cheeks, and I pound the steering wheel with a clenched fist over and over until I know my hand is bruised.

I brush at the tears, and through their haze I see someone coming out into the parking lot. Sending the Gestapo, I tell myself, and back jerkily out of the parking space. I won't give them the satisfaction of seeing me cry. I blot at my tears with a tissue, wipe the sweat off my face and grimace.

Whoever it was goes back inside. No one watches now.

They're spiders all of them. They've sucked me dry and thrown me out, just as they will with everyone else inside that building.

I slam on the brakes, take out the army knife and run back to Dick's parking spot. I unfold the biggest blade and stab at one of the tires. Nothing happens. I try again, and glance nervously at the door. I don't have much time before someone comes out. The tire will take forever. I stand up, and glance inside the Continental, then smile. I open the door and run my hand across the fine leather seat. Then I bring the knife down and slit the seat open in one long very satisfying tear.

I walk back to my car.

I pause at the driveway, wondering where to go. Home? To do what? Just sit and stare out the window and think about how miserable my life is and how I hate everything and everyone at the moment?

No.

Or I can just drive around. And maybe that will calm me a bit.

I switch on the radio, and frown at the music under the crackling. Yeah, that needs fixing too.

I wheel onto the roadway, nearly sideswiping an A&P semi. I don't care. Let 'em wipe me out. It'll be less expensive that way, I think bitterly.

No husband.

No job.

No money.

And just how the hell am I supposed to pay my mortgage? How am I supposed to pay for groceries? At least the old sedan is paid for; that's something they can't repossess for nonpayment. At least I don't think so.

I drive blindly, not knowing where I'm going, not caring. I head out to the A&P shopping center and circle the parking lot, wondering if I should go into one of the stores just to be *doing* something, but all those things to be bought there will just remind me of how little money I have.

I head downtown then, and creep past the video store and the pizzeria and the new Chinese restaurant. I haven't been out to eat in months; too expensive. And I'd always loved eating at the Chinese place.

Then I am past the frame place once more. I pull into a parking lot and stare across at the liquor store. I could buy something. Some wine. A wine cooler. A six-pack of beer. Something. I don't care to drink, though, and that angers me. I would like to get lost in an alcoholic haze right about now.

Maybe getting fired isn't such a bad thing, though. Maybe

that will give me a chance to concentrate on my art. I'll have more time for painting; I can put up some of my business cards on bulletin boards around town. I'll call some of my old contacts, see if they need some artwork done for ads or whatever. There are ways...things to do. It isn't hopeless yet. I can't give up. Not yet. The husk still has some life in it.

I decide to leave, and wait while the vehicle in front of me sits at the stop sign. Another one, I think, and bite down on my lip.

The woman has a fancy new silver van filled with high-school-aged kids. The woman, who keeps twisting around to make some point in her conversation, seems to have forgotten that she's blocking a driveway. Or perhaps she just doesn't care. I wait, and just as I'm about to honk my horn, the woman hops out of the van, and looking around to make sure no one sees, slips a flattened aluminum can under one of the landscaped shrubs. Then she climbs back into her van and turns right.

What the hell is that? I wonder. She can't keep a squished can in her precious van? Her brand new van that cost nearly thirty grand, and which probably has a working radio and doesn't overheat when the air conditioning is on.

I bite harder on my lip, and the wound bleeds more.

I swing into the road, following the van, which swings left onto Ryerson. I turn left.

The van stops at the traffic light. I stop.

The van drives down Ryerson for a mile or so, and I trail behind, sometimes discreetly, sometimes not. I don't care if the woman sees me, if the woman knows I'm following her. I don't care. That fucking woman has tons of money and has nothing better to do with her life than to ferry kids back and forth, and I'm very sure *she* doesn't have to worry about broken windows and or phones being disconnected, and not having a job or money to pay her mortgage or buy groceries or do anything decent in her life, and I am fucking well sure that this woman never felt a creative urge in her body in all her vapid suburban life and that she can't tell an oil from a watercolor, and what the hell is she doing with such a nice fine life when she doesn't deserve it?

The van is out on Main St. now, and I follow. The woman stops at Maple, and one of the kids jumps out and waves. The other driver honks. I honk. The van starts up again, and then stops half a block down. Another kid leaps out.

What? The kid can't even walk a few houses down? I ask myself incredulously, oblivious to the blood that runs down my chin from my lip.

The woman stops next at the Quick Chek and runs inside, leaving the van idling. I park a row behind and watch. Moments later the driver returns, a small bag in her hands. She glances at my car, then away.

The bitch knows, I think, and smile.

The van starts out again, and I follow. The other woman drives out to the streets by the Country Club, and I cruise behind her. She's been driving all over town, I realize, up one street and down another. Like an insect trying to find its way off a web.

I smile.

I'm not the husk, not the hapless prey in the web, I realize. *I* am the spider. I'm not waiting to get zapped by some human arachnid—I'm the eight-legged terror that glides along the silken strands of the web to rid it of these flies, these worthless things that clutter the world. Yeah, that's it.

What a predator I am. I am hunting prey...weak suburban prey. I grin into the rearview mirror at myself and am surprised to see the trickle of blood. I lick it away, and concentrate on driving. I am very meticulous about putting my turn signal on far enough in advance, and not tailgating. I don't want to be stopped by a cop. But I wonder what it would be like to nudge the van a little, just a little, just knock it a few inches forward, or maybe a foot, or maybe just slam full speed into the back and—

I want to see the terror in my prey's eyes.

The woman stops at another house, this one a really fancy one, and I wonder if it's hers. No. She pulls away again. The "fly" seems to be going a little faster than earlier. Is she a little anxious? Good. Let her wonder what's going on. Let her worry like I always have to worry.

I glance at my watch and see I've been following the woman for over an hour now. My grin broadens.

I am hunting this woman, hunting down this moronic creature who has all the time in the world and doesn't know what it is like to paint an exquisite landscape, who doesn't know what it is to have her beloved husband leave her for some two-bit woman in his office, who isn't drying up before her time, who doesn't know anything about living.

Living. Yeah, this is real living.

I am smiling so widely now that it feels like my face is about to crack open. I lick my dry lips, wipe the sweat off my forehead.

I wish I had a gun. A nice handgun that I could take out of the glove box. I can smell the oil on it, feel its cold metallic hardness. I would stroke the barrel, check the chamber, and then I'd raise it up to the windshield, and I'd imagine what would happen when I pull the trigger—

...the shattering of the glass...the sound of the bullet as it rips through the metal...the impact of the slug as it tears into the woman...the woman's scream...the blood and....

...the blood....

...all that blood from hapless victims to be sucked out of them....

...blood....

I taste something coppery on my lips—blood, I realize—and I blink. I glance at the van, then at the clock on the dashboard. Another hour has elapsed, and I have no idea where I've been or even how I've been driving. I don't remember a single thing. Nothing since I thought about the gun.

I wipe at the sweat on my chin and my hand comes away red.

We are back on Maple, I see. I frown. Is it even the same van? Isn't that woman's van silver? This is blue gray. Not the same. Or is it? Maybe it's a trick of the light. Maybe the van really is more blue than I thought earlier?

Maybe.

Or maybe this is a different van altogether.

And how long have I been following this one? How long have I thought it was the same van?

Hours.

Hours gone, hours out of my life.

I have wasted hours of my day.

Tears burn in my eyes, and I swallow heavily.

What's wrong with me? I thought I was coping well enough, and here I've gone and done this...stupid thing. I brush the tears away and back the car away from the van. I have to go home. I am falling apart, and I am scared.

At the stop sign I wait for the street to clear. I glance briefly in my rearview mirror as a red import pulls up behind me. Finally, it is clear, and I turn into the lane.

I don't want to think any more about spiders and webs and prey.

I'll go home and take a bath—no, a shower; that's more invigorating—and I'll even wash my hair, and I'll dress in fresh clothes, and then I'll sit down at the dining room table with a pencil and pad of paper and list my options. I can apply for unemployment, get food stamps, ask my mom for money, sign up for one of those classes they always have for women left in the lurch—well, there are a lot of things I can do rather than wallow in self-pity.

I turn off Maple onto Main, the red car still behind me. It drives neither too fast nor too slow, and the driver seems to be watching me intently.

I swing onto Ryerson; the import follows. I go out to the A&P parking lot. The red car remains behind.

I force myself not to look in the mirror, not to think about the other car, and head back home.

But as I roll into my driveway, I glance back in the mirror. The red car still shadows me, and is now slowing down.

I get out of my car and just as I step into the house, I hear the *click* of a car door.

Jack had a gun, but he took it with him. It doesn't matter.

There are other things around the house...my lair...a knife, a hammer, what's the difference—I know how to use them all.

The doorbell rings.

I stand in the hallway, not moving.

It rings again, and someone knocks.

Patience.

The door is unlocked. Sooner or later she'll try it.

Come into my parlor....

THE GROTTO

Ceil Uccello Wallace had always wanted to visit Tuscany. It was a shame that she had returned to her ancestral home only now, when she was dying.

Ceil slowed her pace, then detached herself from the tour group that she'd been following all morning, and wandered down a narrow cobblestone street, so angled and steep that she thought if she fell she'd just bounce, much like a pinball, off the thick stucco walls all the way down to the vineyard below the walled town. She chuckled.

The tour group was out of sight now, heading toward the town's unassuming church; otherwise she was the only one out and about this close to one. Overhead the sky was a stark cerulean, and a faint spicy smell wafted from the profusion of bright flowers blooming in window boxes. A black and white cat sitting in a doorway yawned as she passed by.

San Damonio, northwest above Florence, had been her family's home for more generations than anyone could count. Local tradition held that her family, the Uccellos, and a handful of others were Etruscan farmers who had migrated to this valley some three thousand years ago.

Ceil thought that was a fanciful story, fabricated to satisfy history-hungry tourists.

Tourists, like herself, she thought ruefully. In a single day she'd played the role: checking the handful of shops—none with the usual tourist knickknacks, which she found refreshing—as well as visiting the church, a most unpretentious structure with nothing of value to offer: not a single marble statue, lofty bell tower, stunning mosaic or fresco, or even a worthy *cappella* or chapel. In fact, she had never seen such a boring church. It was almost as if the place were unused, and yet she had seen some townspeople going inside. Hadn't she spotted a priest earlier...?

Actually, as she thought about it, there was very little in San Damonio of interest to visitors. On her map the town appeared as just a tiny dot, and when she'd tried to find out more about it, she'd met with a dead end.

San Damonio wasn't famous for its nondescript church, nor was it known for the wine from its vineyards—in fact, what she had glimpsed of those on her way into town seemed sadly insignificant to the vast and renowned vineyards she had seen in Chianti, south of Florence. Surely, though, the town must have *something* of note.

As she reached *La Rondine*, the town's one and only inn, a flock of birds wheeled overhead. She shielded her eyes with one hand and peered upward into the bright sky. The flock dipped, barreling straight toward the street, then abruptly changed direction and flew out of sight.

Were they swallows? she wondered, or just common sparrows? She didn't know if there had actually ever been swallows in the area to give the inn its name.

Still, for all that, it was a pleasant place, and the staff seemed quite friendly.

She headed straight for the dining room. It was close enough to lunchtime, if the slight rumbling in her stomach was to be believed. Besides, she'd had only a cup of tea before leaving that morning.

"*Buon giorno*, and how did the *signorina* sleep last night?" Arturo Ventaglio, the owner of *La Rondine*, asked in English. He was an older man, with hair dusted with gray. Marco, the teenaged morning desk clerk who also served as the dining room waiter, smiled widely, revealing a few gaps in that handsome expression.

"Quite well, thank you. It's so restful here." Ceil thought

Signore Ventaglio was being quite diplomatic, referring to her as a young woman. She wasn't old at forty-one, but then she guessed she didn't fall in the young woman category, either...not any more. Still, it was flattering.

Ventaglio bobbed his head. "Very soothing, *si?*"

Marco nodded, too. "Very, very, healthy, too!"

"Yes, so I understand," she said with some irony. "The climate is certainly ideal."

She was grateful both men spoke English, because her Italian was rusty. Her parents had fled the village during the ravages of World War Two and settled in New York City and then later, as the family grew, across the Hudson to Kearny, New Jersey. But always when they spoke of "home" it was the Tuscan village. Once Ceil started school, her parents insisted that they speak only English. Sometimes, though, her father and mother reverted, and Ceil and her brother and sister picked up the language that way.

Her parents had died before they could return, and so Ceil had taken it upon herself to go to San Damonio. Year after year, though, she cancelled her plans, with one decade dissolving into another. Her sister and brother were to accompany her, but early in the year Michael had died in an army training mission, while Lucy had been killed by a drunk driver at two o'clock in the afternoon. Shortly after that, Ceil and her husband of two years separated, and it was the following month that she had had the wake up call of cancer. In that moment she knew she had to go "home."

She'd told no one of her coming; she wasn't even sure any family remained. If that were so, then that made her journey even more poignant—she was the last of the Uccellos.

"More sightseeing today?" Signore Ventaglio asked, escorting her into the dining room. He drew out the high-backed chair with a flourish, and she smiled.

"Yes." He did tend to fuss a bit over her, but as she scanned the dining room she didn't see many other guests—a retired couple by their appearance, and a man about her age. Perhaps

Signore Ventaglio just felt the need to hone his hospitality skills.

"Ah, good. There are many ruins north of town. Very old. Who knows how old, *si*? And you must visit the vineyard—tell them that Arturo Ventaglio sent you, and they will give you a bottle of their best *vino*."

"And the *grotta*," Marco called as he headed toward the kitchen to get her tea. She noticed that he walked with a marked limp.

Signore Ventaglio scowled at Marco. "*Si*, the *grotta*, although that is a difficult climb for most. Straight up." He gestured with both hands. "Much better for a *capra*." He saw her confusion. "A goat."

Interesting, but her guidebook hadn't mentioned a grotto, not here in this out-of-the-the way village. "Tell me more, *signore*."

The man shrugged. "The *grotta*. It isn't very spectacular. Damp. Dirty. Not a place for a lady such as yourself."

"No, no, no," Marco said, shaking his head. He was back with her pot of tea. "Not a place for a lady."

She smiled. "I'm hardly a lady—I'm a historian who's been on many archaeological digs. I've gotten dirty with the best of them."

The innkeeper's frown deepened. "It is not a place for a lady such as yourself," he repeated, then took Marco by the shoulder and shoved him back into the kitchen. The door swung shut behind them as Ventaglio's voice rose, loud and angry. She heard the word *imbecille*. She felt sorry that Marco was in trouble because of her.

But, she told herself, she'd done nothing. The boy had volunteered the information. She read the menu, forcing herself to ignore the shouting. A few minutes later Marco returned, a chastised expression on his face. He stood by her chair, waiting for her to make up her mind.

"Just an *antipasti*," she said. He nodded and shuffled back to the kitchen. Her appetite had decreased over the past few weeks; she knew she should eat more; it was just that nothing tasted or smelled good. When her doctor told her of the cancer, she panicked—she wanted to run from the exam room, as if she could escape her fate. She stayed, though, and listened to him, noted his recommendation for an oncologist. The next few days remained a blur—the cancer specialist saw her; then he gave her the prognosis. Yes, he could fill her body with chemicals and radiation, but it wouldn't matter; nothing would help at this late stage. She was dying. It was just a matter of time.

Curiously Ceil remained somewhat aloof from all this; it was as if it was happening to someone else. The specialist said he would sign her into the hospital that afternoon to start the therapy, but she said no; she thanked him, then dressed and returned to the university where she taught for the past decade. She typed out her resignation, handed it to her bewildered department chairman—summer classes were in session—waved to her fellow history lecturers, packed up the few personal items in her office, and went home.

There, she unplugged the phone and crawled into bed fully dressed, burrowing under the covers. She laid there for nearly twenty hours before finally emerging. She hadn't slept much, just dozing here and there. All the time she did little but think. Mentally she felt like a mouse in a maze...her mind running down first one corridor, then another, and all of them dead ends; there had to be some way out, some corridor that didn't dead end. She did know, however, she didn't have enough time left to lay around the house and feel sorry for herself. She showered, dressed in her favorite pair of jeans and shirt, and called a travel agent. Then she called a real estate agent who was a friend and had the house put up for sale; funds from that sale—she would take the first offer, she said—were to be wired to her. Of her belongings she took only what she would need for a prolonged visit. Everything else she donated to charities.

Four days later she was on her way to Italy.

Any time, the specialist had said; she could die any time. It could be a week from now, a month...a year; it could even be longer...or not. She had medicine for the pain that the doctor said would come later. Mostly, though, she just felt tired.

As she poked at a pepper on the *antipasti* plate, she realized that she still hadn't cried about it. Of course, what good would that do? Crying wouldn't cure her. Besides, she had too much to do yet, so much to see. Better for her to focus on that.

For the past month she had toured Venice, Rome, Naples, and Milan, leaving Florence and the surrounding Tuscany countryside to the last.

And now that she was here...she didn't know. She didn't feel like she'd come home; she didn't feel much of anything, besides a certain curiosity.

She speared an olive as she gazed out the window. The same black and white cat she had seen earlier lounged on a bench opposite the inn. He yawned and rolled over, exposing a white belly to the summer sunshine. A shadow spread across the dozing cat, and the animal leaped up and darted into a shop. She peered up, saw nothing. An eagle or a hawk, perhaps. Did they have eagles here? she wondered and reminded herself to search for a book on the local flora and fauna; the guidebook was certainly useless in that respect.

"Excuse me," said a smooth baritone voice.

Startled, Ceil dropped her fork onto the plate.

"I'm sorry to have frightened you." It was the man from the other side of the dining room.

"You didn't," she replied somewhat crossly. She picked up her fork, then set it down. "I'm sorry. That was bad manners. Please, sit down and join me."

"I could not help but overhear your conversation. You expressed interest in the *grotta*."

"Yes."

"I could take you there, Signorina...."

"Uccello. Ceil Uccello." Until this moment she had been going by her husband's last name. It was time to change, she thought; time...and how much longer of that did she have? Would she stand up after this meal and simply drop dead? Would she simply not wake up one morning? She forced herself to concentrate on what the man was saying.

"Ah. Did you know that your last name means 'bird'?"

She nodded. "My parents told me when I was small."

"Ah. But yes, about the grotto...it's close to the villa up the hill."

"I see." Ceil wasn't sure about this. The man spoke with a slight accent, almost English.

"I am sorry again. My name is Laurence San Damonio."

She arched a brow. "The same as the town?"

The corners of his thin mouth lifted ever so slightly. "The very same. My family has been here for a long time—-but as to whether we were named after the town, or it after us, no one can say. My mother, though, was English; as a child I lived in Kent; when I was old enough I came home."

"I see." She was repeating herself. What a dunce he must think her. "And you're a tour guide now?" she asked lightly.

He laughed, a rich sound. "Hardly. A businessman. A little of this, a little of that."

Oh, swell, she thought, a ne'er-do-well, and yet he hardly looked the part. His clothes, while casual, seemed expensive, and he was well-groomed. Maybe, one part of her said, he was a mass murderer—a local one—and he was waiting to get her alone before he stabbed her seven thousand times. Go ahead, another part of her said; who cares.

Who cares, indeed? Ceil wondered, and realized she did.

"Okay. When?"

"Tomorrow?"

"Fine." If she lived that long. Ceil, Ceil, stop it, she told herself. Stop, stop, stop.

"I'll meet you here around noon then." He stood and bowed ever so perceptibly, then returned to his table.

Ceil finished her *antipasti* and set down her fork, Signore Ventaglio approached, as if he had timed his entrance to that very moment.

"Signore San Damonio is quite a gentleman," Ventaglio said as he whisked her plate away. "Very charming, indeed?"

"Indeed," Ceil said, trying hard not to smile. "Very continental."

"*Si!*" He beamed at her. "And would there be anything else for you?"

Yes, a new life. Aloud: "Not today, *grazie.*" As she started to leave the dining room, she noticed for the first time a terra cotta medallion to one side of the door. The bas-relief appeared quite worn in places as though many fingers had rubbed it. "What's that?"

"Janus, the God of the Sun and of all portals, doorways, and thresholds," the innkeeper said.

A grotesque, she knew, was an architectural decoration, a fanciful creature or representation of a person...commonly found on old architecture. Did this date from some ancient temple? "Oh, yes, of course—Janus, the Roman God!"

"The *Etruscan* God," Signore Ventaglio corrected politely.

Of course. Rome's authority lessened the farther north she went. Here, the Etruscan influence remained strong.

Interesting. Perhaps there was a book about the Etruscan gods...if she could find a bookshop. All these books she was buying...when would she have time to read them? She had the rest of her life, and she nearly laughed aloud at the idea.

She could have gone to her room for a nap, but she wasn't tired, at least not yet; and besides, wouldn't she have time enough later on to rest....

It was close to 3:30 now and the shops were just beginning to reopen. Ceil nodded to an elderly woman sweeping the stoop in front of a grocer's. Several times she thought she was being watched, but when she turned around she saw no one—only another black and white cat. Or was that the same one? Always a magnet for animals, she wouldn't be surprised if this one adopted her. She'd seen few animals in the village, which was odd because in other towns she'd visited she'd seen dozens of roaming dogs and cats.

At a fruit vendor's, she selected several oranges. A few steps away she discovered a store filled with antiques. Much of the contents, she realized after she had stepped inside and greeted

the owner, weren't much older than a few decades. But still...
there might be something she just couldn't live without.

She paused, an ironic smile on her lips. Sometimes...for a
moment or two...she forgot. Briefly tears threatened to sting her
eyes; she bit her lower lip and moved away so that the owner
couldn't see her.

"What is this?" she asked, holding up a bronze object, one of
many on a table. It was shaped almost like a bowl, the center a
sun face, with an outer circle of moons.

"Etruscan lamp," the proprietor answered, her dark eyes
solemn. "Very, very old. From two thousand years ago. It comes
from the tombs. A sepulchral lamp. Very famous."

Ceil studied the lamp. Olive oil had filled the vessel, the wick
floating. The lamp might well date from the time of Christ; yet
if the lamp were a copy it was well done. She ran her fingers
along it, the bronze cool against her skin.

"I'll take it." She paid for the lamp, tucked it into her oversized purse, then stopped at the threshold—another terra cotta
medallion hung by the door. This one depicted a youth wearing
a cape and helmet, his right hand holding a lance. The carving
was so lifelike that she reached up to touch the rounded cheeks.
"Mars?" she guessed.

"Laran."

"The Etruscan version, I see."

By the time she arrived at the vineyard, she was hot, dusty,
and extremely thirsty. She traipsed into the winery's restaurant
and ordered a glass of wine. "On the house", the man said, prof-
fering a glass of Chianti. She thanked him and asked if it were
all right to wander through the vineyard. He nodded toward
another door.

Outside again, she strolled up and down the orderly rows.
She wasn't sure why she wanted to do that—she scarcely knew
anything about wine. Some wines were white, some red, some
sweet, some dry, French, Italian, Californian, New York. That
was the sum total of her *vino* knowledge.

Here and there olive trees intermingled with the vines.

The trees were gnarled, old, perhaps even ancient. How many decades—centuries—had they grown? she wondered. These trees would be here long after she was dead. She marveled at the age of everything in this town; Americans, with a history of only a few centuries, could not comprehend something a thousand years or older.

Insects buzzed around the fruit—the only sound. She paused under the shade of an olive tree. A dusty haze hung over one end of the vineyard; perhaps, she thought, someone was working there. With the heat of the sun and the droning of the insects, she felt drowsy now.

Suddenly something moved a few rows away from her; she'd caught a glimpse of it out of the corner of her eye. She stepped back into the sun and peered around a fat bunch of grapes. Nothing. Her skin prickled, and again she sensed being watched. Surely there were workers—pickers? harvesters?—out here. As she glanced around she saw no one.

She returned the glass to the man and thanked him. She checked for a terra cotta medallion—surely the winery had one. In the tasting room she found it: a man in middle years, his smiling face surrounded by grapes and grape leaves.

"Bacchus?" she said, pointing.

The man shook his head. "Fufluns, the God of wine. Of vitality." He winked.

"Ah." So, it would seem, at least in the townspeople's versions that the Roman gods could all be traced to the Etruscan Gods. That made sense; the Etruscans were the first to settle this area, and it was the tongue of Tuscany, after all, the basis of the language of the country.

She wondered if any of the shops sold the medallions. She would ask Signore Ventaglio about it; he would know. The lamp, the medallion...what would she do with all these things she was suddenly adding to her life? She could always send them to her husband...her soon to be ex-husband; the divorce proceedings hadn't started yet. Perhaps he would be curious as to why she wasn't there. Perhaps not. And she wished with all her heart that she could turn back the clock, return to when she'd met her husband and change that chance encounter—she'd find someone who would truly love her for the time she had left.

She shook her head sharply. Enough.

"You are sad," the man said. She shrugged. "You are so young yet, you must live."

"I wish," she said bitterly and left the winery. She took her time returning to the inn; it was all uphill now and sometimes quite steep. Exhausted, she paused only to wave to Signore Ventaglio and climbed the stairs to her room.

She wanted a bath badly. The minute she reached her room she started stripping clothes off. She ran hot water until the tub was half filled, then eased into the warmth, and almost immediately the aches of the day began to fade. She closed her eyes. She would rest for a moment or so.

When she awoke, the bath water was cold. She finished bathing, toweled herself dry, then slipped into a long tee-shirt that served as her nightgown. Checking her watch, she was shocked to see that it was after nine. She had been in the tub over an hour. She should go downstairs for dinner, but just the thought of talking to someone right now seemed too much of a strain.

She had her oranges; she'd dine on those. And perhaps if she got ravenous later, she'd ask if a tray could be delivered to the room.

She sat on the bed, peeling her first orange carefully, and flipped through the guidebook reading about all the places she hadn't visited yet. She finished the orange, then selected another, but when she realized she was doing more yawning than peeling, she put the orange down, and washed her hands. She wobbled back across the room, turned out the light, and fell into bed.

Almost instantly she drifted off to sleep.

It seemed like only a moment later that she opened her eyes, but she knew she'd been asleep for some time. Was that a noise that had awakened her? She listened hard, but heard nothing. As she moved her legs she touched something furry, and she yelped, leaped up and switched on the light. The black and white cat lay curled on the mattress. It blinked at her, then yawned.

She laughed nervously. "Just how did you get in here?" The window—wide open. She had forgotten to latch it. "I suppose you can stay!" She flicked the light off and crawled back into bed. The cat shifted, its head resting on her shin. She closed her eyes.

And woke again much later. She reached out to touch the cat, but it must have shifted. The air seemed thick, almost like velvet, and she could scarcely breathe. Sitting up, she shivered. The room was pitch dark, but outside there seemed to be a faint light. She rose and crossed to the window and saw a full moon in the inky sky.

Faint lights, like the flames of candles, dotted the slope above the town. In the street below a flame bobbed along. It paused beneath her window, and she saw a face—horribly disfigured— and then she realized it was a mask, one of a grinning youth, whose nose was so long and sharp that it nearly met with its equally pointed chin.

Whoever was behind the mask stared up at her. Quickly she stepped away from the window; surely she couldn't be seen. Her heart pounding, she waited until she thought it was safe, then sneaked a glance out the window. The man in the mask now stood farther up the street, but he had turned and was watching her even now.

She gasped, stepped back and latched the window, then drew the curtain across the rod. She fled to the bed, pulling the sheet up over her head. She was shaking, and she lay, too fearful to lower the sheet. After all, what if she peeked out and saw the masked man inside her room? Don't be ridiculous, Ceil, one part of her said.

She was being silly. It had probably just been a trick of light; that person couldn't see her. But still....

She closed her eyes, but all she could see was that hateful mask and the way it had looked at her.

When she finally did awake in the morning, she ached all over. The cat, seeing she was up, started purring and rubbing its head against her. The purring intensified as she scrinched it behind the ears. She didn't want to move, didn't want to get up and bathe and dress. She didn't care. She would stay in bed all day. She wasn't even hungry. She closed her eyes. Was this how it was to be? No, she wouldn't give up, not yet at least. She peered at her wristwatch. Almost 11:30.

Suddenly she leaped from the bed, startling the cat, who hissed. She was meeting that man at noon! She had almost forgotten! She jumped into the tub, scrubbed briskly, washed her hair, threw on her makeup and clothes, peered into the mirror at her pale face and the dark circles beneath her eyes, sighed, then grabbed the cat and left the room.

She arrived in the dining room just as San Damonio sat down. Breathlessly she rushed to the table.

"You've brought me a cat?" he asked, his tone droll. "How kind."

"It slipped into my room last night." She set the cat down, and immediately, purring loudly, it began threading its way around her legs.

"You have a friend."

"And I haven't even fed it. But perhaps someone in the kitchen could."

"Perhaps. Are you ready?"

"Yes."

"Do you want me to drive or do you want to walk?" he asked.

This was a test, she figured...let's see the lazy American in action. "Walk. It's not really that far, is it?"

"A few miles. Uphill."

"I'll manage." And she hoped she would.

"Good. I'll point out some sights along the way."

San Damonio set off briskly; Ceil hurried to catch up.

They encountered no one else on the rugged road, lined with tall cypress, and as for interesting sights, there were few. Once, he stopped by a ruin, only tumbled blocks now.

"This was the abbey," he explained. "It was abandoned several centuries ago." He kicked one of the blocks, knocking a sizable chunk off. It rolled down the slope a few yards, then stopped when it hit a tuft of grass.

"And the Church didn't rebuild?"

"The Church never cared about San Damonio."

"Oh." They started walking again. "I saw lights last night—up here, I think. Was there a festival or something?"

"Lights?" He shrugged.

That gesture could mean anything. He hadn't said no, there weren't lights; but he hadn't said there were. He seemed far less friendly than the day before, and for the first time she wondered at her eagerness to follow a man she didn't know to an isolated spot.

This is Italy, Ceil reminded herself, not the United States. But still...she wasn't being very careful.

And once more she had the sense of being watched. Pausing, she scanned the hills. Nothing. But of course it would be so easy for someone to hide from sight. She glanced back and saw a small black and white object.

"Oh, oh."

"What?" San Damonio asked.

"The cat from the inn is following me."

He glanced back at the animal. "Ridiculous beast."

A curious way of putting it, she thought, and more and more she felt uneasy. Yet they weren't that far away now; she saw the villa pressed up hard against the hill, almost as if the earth had tried to swallow it.

Overhead birds, dark against the sky, wheeled in lazy patterns. She wondered what kind they were, and when she glanced back at the cat, she saw it had flattened itself against the ground, as if it feared being attacked.

They reached the villa—once grand, it had obviously not been maintained for years now. Here and there Ceil saw missing roof tiles, and the windows all looked curiously blank. Like dead eyes, she thought with a slight shiver.

Instead of escorting her up to the double front doors, San Damonio led her around the side to a huge stone arch, under that and into a modest-sized courtyard, paved with slabs of volcanic rock. A marble fountain, long unused, sat in the center. Blue wildflowers grew now where water had once splashed.

"This is lovely. It's too bad it's fallen into disrepair. Is this yours?" Ceil asked.

San Damonio nodded. "I live here."

"Oh. I'm sorry, I didn't mean—"

He cut her off. "It's all right. The family has fallen onto hard times, as you Americans say. I've closed off most of the villa, and this is one part we haven't repaired yet. We'll get to it. Soon."

She studied the walls for the first time. Dozens and dozens of medallions—like those she seen in the town below, but of bronze—were set into the courtyard's walls.

"They're beautiful! The workmanship is marvelous! These must be worth a fortune."

"Or two," he said wryly. "There," he said, gesturing to one high up on the left. "That's Horta, the Goddess of Agriculture. That one is Losna, the Etruscan Moon goddess."

Losna's medallion reminded her of the sepulchral lamp, only the inner face was of the goddess, the outer ring showing the moon in its different phases.

"Who's this naked fellow?" she asked, indicating a bearded figure over San Damonio's shoulder.

"The God of Fresh Water—Nethuns." In quick succession he rattled off a dozen names that swirled in her head: Juventus, Menrva, Mlukukh, Picus, Summamus, Zirna, and more. Gods and goddesses...some of them long forgotten, some evolved into familiar Roman deities: Minerva and Diana, among others.

"And this?" she asked. This medallion had caught her eye even more than the others, for the goddess depicted was part animal, part human, part bird, with snakes entwined in her hair and along her arms. There was something about the fierce stare of the Goddess that alarmed her, and she took a step back, bumping with San Damonio.

"Tuchulcha. The Goddess of Death. There is no other Goddess like her anywhere in the world...even the Romans, who took so much from us, did not corrupt her. She's partly of the sky, partly of the earth...." Running his fingers across the medallion now, San Damonio traced the outline of Tuchulcha's visage, caressed the stone snakes.

Shivering, Ceil edged away. She rubbed her hands along her bare arms. It was hot today, but suddenly she was cold.

"The grotto?" she asked.

"Come this way." He led her through another arch, smaller than the first, and down a flight of crumbling steps. As she peered back toward the fountain she thought she saw something move. She was getting creeped out; perhaps they should postpone seeing the grotto. And yet they were almost there...and it *was* a long hike, one that she didn't want to repeat. She was so tired now.

Down and down the couple went until finally they reached an old wooden door. San Damonio pulled the door open, and they stepped inside.

The blackness swallowed the light from the doorway. It was indeed damp, as Signore Ventaglio had claimed. Again the skin on her arms prickled and she rubbed the skin hard, trying to warm up.

Abruptly San Damonio stopped. She couldn't see his face now. "What's wrong?" she whispered.

"You must go on by yourself now."

"I don't understand."

He pressed something in her hand. A sepulchral lamp, just like the one she bought. Or was it the same? Firmly San Damonio gripped her by the shoulder and pushed her past him. "Go on. You must go alone."

Inside her chest her heart fluttered like a panicked bird. "No, I think I want to go back now. Take me back to the inn!"

"It's too late."

"What?"

Ceil struggled to get away, but he held her easily, though not unkindly, and suddenly over his shoulder she saw the doorway crowded with other people now, all of them silent. She could never push past them.

She realized that they wore masks—or did they? There was so little light, and yet wasn't that Veive, the God of Revenge? Cautha, Janus, Summamus...all that she had seen in the village and out in the courtyard.

Who were they? The villagers? Something more? Wasn't that Signore Ventaglio with the Janus mask? And that had to be Marco, limping, under the Laran face? What were they doing here? Why had they followed her?

One of the watchers held the black and white cat which, seeing Ceil, leaped to the ground and ran to her. She scooped the animal up with one arm, and retreated as San Damonio and the others silently pressed forward.

She realized now that the lamp was burning—she nearly dropped it. She glanced back, saw those staring faces in the flickering light, and stumbled away.

The blackness pressed down on her, threatening to swallow her, and she tried not to whimper. She had never been afraid of the dark...until now. She prayed that the flame of her lamp would not be extinguished.

Deeper into the grotto she went, and it seemed that the walls, so confining here, were carved with strange animals and figures, all of them grotesque. They seemed to stare at her, to watch her, and she ducked her head.

From time to time Ceil glanced back, afraid the others were still behind her, but she was alone. She didn't understand what the villagers wanted...didn't know why they were acting so strangely. Perhaps there was another way out here. She'd find it, and she'd leave—with the cat, of course—and she'd run back to the village, and in no time at all she'd be back in Florence. She almost laughed aloud at the thought—it was so easy!

Overhead the grotesques faces acquired identity, and as she walked on, Ceil saw her father's face, her mother's, that of her sister and her brother. There was her friend from the third grade, Amy, who had died from a burst appendix. Peering over Amy's shoulder was Danny, Ceil's boyfriend from high school who had died during the first Tet offensive. Her grandparents were there, her great-aunt, the young man she had dated during college, students from classes she had taught, and ringing them all were the pets of her childhood: the abandoned birds she'd brought home to nurse tenderly, only to have them die unexpectedly; the stray cats and dogs...all of them dying after only a few years.

Dying...as everyone in her life had. Dying...as did everything—everyone—she touched. She wondered that her husband had survived; perhaps it had only been a matter of time for him.

The walls fanned out now, and above her she saw still more faces, more and more fanciful, some part animal. The cat jumped to the ground and trotted after her.

Ahead Ceil heard rushing water. The tunnel widened into an immense cavern with a fast and wide river. The grotto proper. On this side of the waterway a man in a boat waited; cautiously she approached him.

Charon. Or Charun, as the Etruscans knew him.

Wordlessly Charun beckoned to her and not knowing what else to do, she climbed into the boat and handed him the lamp. He blew out the flame, and yet Ceil could still see. The cat jumped in beside her, and Charun pushed away from the riverbank. From the tunnel the grotesque faces watched.

Ceil didn't speak to Charun, nor he to her. The cat, trembling, crawled into her lap; she tried to calm it by petting it, but her own hand was shaking. Silently they floated across the river, and there on the other side, Ceil saw a woman waiting... no, something more. A Goddess.

Tuchulcha, she recognized with a stab of cold fear. The Goddess of death. Tuchulcha was part human, bird, and animal, with snakes in her hair and curled around her arms. The Goddess looked at her, and Ceil felt the ice grow inside her. Above them the dark birds circled, their cries echoing in the grotto's greatness.

Ceil wanted to cry out; she wasn't ready; not yet, not yet. But would she ever be ready for death? Would she? She who had brought so much death in her life.

She hadn't meant to! she wanted to cry aloud. She hadn't wanted any of them dead. But they had all died, had left her... left her to die alone in this cold cavern.

Somehow Ceil found herself standing on the shore, still clutching the cat. Already Charun was halfway across the river. She tried to call to him, but the cold of the underground stole the words from her.

She faced the Goddess, who reached out to her with her long fingers.

Ceil squeezed her eyes shut as the fingers and snakes spiraled around her arms, drawing her and the cat closer. The animal struggled, and she murmured words of comfort to it. She shivered, feeling both hot and cold. Once more she saw her parents, her sister, her brother, Danny, all the others of her life, one face after another, their features melting to reveal the masks beneath...all grotesque.

It had been a long journey, she thought, but she had come home. Home to this underground grotto. And all of them here had known, had waited for her. A feather brushed her cheek.

Then abruptly the exhaustion she'd fought for so long was gone. She was no longer cold. She opened her bright bird eyes. She gazed down at the snakes curling and writhing around her arms, at the soft black and white fur stretched across her abdomen. And she finally cried, grief mixed with joy.

HAIR

The problem about body hair, Margaret Delon decided on Monday, was there was so damned much of it. And it grew back, no matter how often you cut or shaved it.

Maggie spent many hours each day devoted to maintenance of her body. She made a disgusted sound. It sounded like she was working on a car. An *old* car, at that. Except that she wasn't old. Not really. But she was about to turn the big Four Oh, and that made her feel positively ancient, even though most of the people she knew were much older than she and had no sympathy at all for her birthday pangs.

So she tried to stay younger than forty. She exercised in the morning before work, took a turn around the parking lot at lunch unless it poured rain, and when she came home, she would do another hour or so of exercise. She watched her calories, fat intake, dairy products, cholesterol, gave up beef, bacon, and barbecue, looked out for nitrates and salt, with the upshot being there wasn't a whole lot left to eat at that point. But that didn't matter—eating took precious time away from the hair.

In the morning before she got ready for work, she would peer at her face in the mirror over the sink. She'd pinpoint the fine wrinkles that had appeared in the last year on her forehead and at the corners of eyes. There weren't many, thank God, but they were unmistakably there. She couldn't do much them, except use cream on her face and not go out in the sun, which she never did anyway. Nothing aged a person—man or woman—more than the sun. Her mother never sat out in the sun, and look at her; over eighty now, she could have passed for a woman in her early sixties.

Her skin was dry in spots and oily in others, and she didn't know from day to day what would be where. She applied moisturizer to some areas, and just prayed the others would be all right as she spread her beige tone makeup across her cheeks and chin and forehead. At least, she'd never suffered from acne or been besieged by freckles.

Her lips tended to chap, even in the summer—she licked her lips, a nervous habit, far too often, but she just couldn't break herself of it—and applied Chapstick before she put her lipstick on. Lipstick dried her lips even more, but she wanted them to look nice, so she put the other as undercoat. Her mother always said a woman wasn't totally dressed until she put on lipstick.

Her nose was the same as always, long and narrow. If she believed in cosmetic surgery, she'd have it shortened. But she didn't dislike her nose all that much.

Ah, but the hair...she could do something about *that*. She had noticed the fine bristles around her lips darkening in the past few years. She'd always been thankful that she didn't have those horrible black moustaches that some women are cursed with, but lately...well, it wasn't a moustache, but it *was* unwanted.

She clipped it with cuticle scissors, and pulled out other errant hairs on her upper lip with the tweezers. Her eyebrows had once been thick and dark; now they were arched, thin. She peered at the smooth skin below her brow, searching for a hair that might be about to poke through.

She also shaved her underarms and her legs daily. The legs took a long time, because she shaved from ankle to the top of the thigh each time.

And now, lately, the pubic hair had begun bothering her. She told herself not to fret, but that was impossible. The more she tried not to think about it the more she *did* think about it. Stray hairs poked out beyond the legbands of her panties, and it looked, well, so *messy*. She cut off the excess that stuck out and that looked better although it itched a little, got dressed, took the baby to day care, and then went to work.

Mid-morning she got a call from Donald that his car had broken down again and he'd had it towed to the garage and the mechanic didn't know when it would be ready although next week looked good, and she'd have to come and get him at work.

She tapped her pencil against the desk as she chatted with him, and stared down at her fingers and noticed the fine hairs growing there.

She frowned slightly, put the pencil down, and when she hung up, she went into the ladies' room with her purse, slipped into a stall, and closed the door. Inside her purse she kept a cosmetic bag Donald had given her for Christmas, and she kept her other cuticle scissors in there. Luckily there was a light fixture just above her stall, and so she could see the hairs quite plainly now. They were a golden brown and weren't really noticeable until you looked closely. But they were there. She knew that all too well.

Carefully she cut them away until nothing remained but a fine fuzz. She ran a finger over them, frowned. Too much stubble. She'd have to do something about it. Tonight.

When she got back to her desk she glanced at the clock and was surprised to learn she'd been thirty-two minutes in the bathroom. It hadn't seemed that long.

She spent the rest of the afternoon, looking over policy papers and shuffling things from one end of her desk to the other. No matter how much she tried, it seemed she would never see the wooden surface under all this paper again. She would start to get things caught up, and then more orders would flood in, and more policies and more memos piled up, and the strata of paper just grew higher and higher. Her "in" and "out" baskets were crammed, as was her wastepaper basket. It wasn't as if she didn't get things accomplished; she did; she just didn't do it fast enough; no matter how well she did something, it wasn't good enough.

Somewhere along the way she realized her groin itched and she thought she must have left some stray hairs in her panties.

She'd fix that later. If she couldn't control her paper and life, she could at least take care of the hair.

She was halfway home when she remembered Donald's call, did a U-eey and headed back to his office. He was standing outside and looking perturbed when she pulled up. He always looked perturbed, she thought; as if *everything* that went wrong was her fault. He didn't say it, but then he didn't have to.

"Sorry," she said perfunctorily as he got in, slammed the door and said, "It's about damned time. I've been standing out in the sun all this time."

She glanced in the rearview mirror before swinging away from the curb. "Why don't you wait in the lobby for me? It's cooler in there."

"I don't like to. People come up and talk to me, as if I'm still in the office." He thumped his briefcase a couple of times, as if that settled the matter.

Maggie sighed. They had this conversation on the order of at least once a week. Donald's car was always breaking down. They couldn't afford to buy a new one right now, and so they had to make do. He'd wanted to trade cars with her, take hers, and let her have his, and she'd laughed. He had glared at her.

They didn't speak much on the way to day care. She waited while Donald went in to get the baby, and she wondered when he had begun to lose his hair; there was a bald spot at the back of his head. She'd better not tell him. He was sensitive enough about his appearance. God knows that would really throw him into a tizzy.

He returned a few minutes later with the baby, who was trying to tell him about her day. DeeDee was three, almost four, and would always be her baby, Maggie realized, even when the baby was thirty-three. She and Donald had been married thirteen years and had waited a long time for their daughter; God knows, they'd tried often enough, but nothing had clicked for years.

She smiled at DeeDee, who dimpled at her, and Donald buckled her up in the backseat. The itching in Maggie's groin had grown, and she shifted.

"What's wrong?" he asked as he slid into the passenger seat. He made it sound more like a demand.

"Nothing," she said, smiling.

"Then why are you wiggling around?"

"Just a momentary itch."

"God, I hope it's not your period again. It seems like it's always your period."

Like most men, she thought, Donald didn't understand a woman's cycles, nor did he care to understand. It was just some sort of inconvenience to him, particularly when he was in the mood and she just wasn't because it was the first day and all.

DeeDee chattered about what she'd had to eat for a snack after lunch and how they had played a new game. Sometimes Maggie asked her a question; Donald only listened.

When they got home, Maggie changed into jeans and a casual shirt, while DeeDee got into her jammies. She started dinner for them, and did her exercises while the food cooked, and then when they were ready to eat they settled down in front of the TV.

During dinner she reached over and squeezed Donald's hand. It was their special non-vocal signal, a sign that let him know she was ready for bed. Nudge, nudge, wink, wink. Donald belched. Maggie wasn't fazed; he did that a lot. He was a hard sell on sex, but she could usually wrangle him into bed. He was okay once he got there. She had been scared for years to take the initiative, but had decided there was nothing wrong with that. God knows, she couldn't always wait for him to make a move.

When the shows were over, she gave DeeDee a bath, and brushed the child's long light hair.

Such pretty hair, she thought as she ran her fingers through it. She had hair like that once, so baby fine and baby soft. Innocent hair; hair that hadn't been teased and sprayed and curled and permed. New and fresh and so sweet-smelling.

"Ouch, Mommy, a tangle," DeeDee pouted.

"Sorry."

She'd had really long hair once, hair so long it hung below her butt. Her mother said it made her look like a witch. Ladies, her mother declared, don't have long hair. And certainly, her mother said on more than one occasion, ladies didn't keep their hair long after they reached the age of forty. Maggie's hair was shoulder-length in defiance of her mother. Her mother tsked whenever she saw it. Her mother wore short uncomfortable-looking curls and as far back as Maggie could remember, her mother had had the same hairdo.

Maggie tucked her daughter into bed, and then went into the other bathroom—not the one off the master bedroom, because Donald would complain if she were in there more than three minutes—and locked the door.

She didn't take long that night because she was looking forward to some cuddling. When she finally went into the bedroom, Donald was already asleep, the remote control loose in his hand. She sighed and felt strangely relieved, took the remote from him, switched off the TV, and then the light.

It took her only seconds to fall asleep.

* * * * * * *

Tuesday she was late because she had to drop the baby off at the nursery and Donald at his office, and there had been an accident on the freeway. Her boss said he understood, but Maggie knew he just didn't, not really because the man was single and what kind of responsibilities did he have for God's sake and he always seemed to be looking at her and she didn't know why, and the company was being reorganized in the next few months, and not for the first time she began to wonder if there would be a place for her in the new set-up, particularly if she came in late or called in sick those times when DeeDee had to stay home.

Her groin itched all day and whenever she went into the restroom, she scratched and scratched, and the hair felt coarse and, well, peculiar. She tugged at a few hairs, winced at the pain. There was nothing she could do here.

Back at her desk her fingertips found the fuzz on the back of her hands. She placed her palms down on the desk as she read a report, anything to keep from playing with the hair.

All the way home Donald bitched about work. He had been chewed out by his boss; one of his co-workers had accused him of snitching on her to the company head; and there was a new comptroller coming in next week who was rumored to be a real ball-breaker.

The baby hadn't had a good day, either, and had the sniffles.

She didn't talk about her day, because she didn't think Donald would want to hear about it. Whenever she tried to tell him about her office worries, he cut her off, saying he had problems, too; she wasn't the only one. She never said she was.

Maggie's groin itched unbearably.

"What's wrong? You keep twitching? You got a bug down there or what?" Donald asked.

"No." She tried to smile seductively. "I'm just a little itchy for someone."

He glanced out his window. "Yeah, just what I wanna do, Mag. Get fucked at work, and then come home and get fucked some more."

She almost slammed on the brakes then and told him to get out, but the baby was in the backseat, crying and wanting to get home. So she just pressed her lips together and made a precise turn into their driveway.

Once inside, she told him he could get dinner ready while she got the baby ready.

"But I've had a hard day at work!"

"So have I."

She walked out of the room and got DeeDee ready for her dinner and then bed.

When she came back in, there was no sign of dinner, and Donald had left, taking her car. She hated it when he did that. She didn't like not knowing where he went. What if there was an accident? She supposed that in that case the police would get in touch with her, and she closed her eyes, not wanting to think about that.

She made macaroni and cheese, and they watched a Disney tape, and she read DeeDee a story and by then it was ten and still Donald wasn't home. She tucked DeeDee in, kissed her, then went to sit in the living room and wait.

By eleven he still hadn't returned, so she went into the bathroom. She stripped and looked at herself in the full-length mirror. She lathered up the soap, daubed it along her groin and took out her Lady Bic and began shaving. The pubic hair came off in brown curls. She gathered it up carefully and tucked it inside a tissue and then threw the tissue into the wastebasket, after putting a crushed Kleenex box on top.

Now her mound was smooth. She ran her fingers over the unfamiliar bare spot, and tried not to giggle. She almost looked like a little girl again. She got out some aloe cream and carefully massaged it into the shaved skin; she didn't want razor burn in the morning.

Then she sat down on the closed toilet and began trimming the hairs off her toes. There weren't many, and she'd never had any on top of her foot, like some of her friends, but still. This made things so much nicer...so much neater.

She shaved her underarms and her legs again, and when she looked at her wristwatch which she had set on the side of the sink, she could see that nearly two hours had gone by.

She spread more cream across her body, feeling its cooling gentleness.

Then she look at her part and along her temples for the white or gray hairs she knew were there. She plucked them as best she could. She knew one day they would get too many to pull out, and then she'd have to resort to dyeing her hair.

She remembered that in the Elizabethan days the fashion for women had been high smooth foreheads and they had tweezed the hair from the hairline back several inches to achieve that strange mode. She wondered what that would be like, and touched some of the hairs there.

Just a few, she told the worried image in the mirror, and

plucked a neat dozen hairs. Her hairline was faintly pink, but the soreness would go away in minutes, she knew.

Not bad. Maybe she could do more tomorrow.

She cleaned up the bathroom and put on her nightgown, and went into the bedroom.

Donald was in bed, his back toward her side of the bed. She slipped in.

"Do you want to talk about it?" she asked.

"Talk about what?" he muttered.

"Our fight."

"We didn't fight."

"Our spat then."

"I went out, okay? Let's leave it at that."

"Where did you go, Donald?" The light was off, and she was lying on her back, and she could see the lights of a car outside move across the ceiling of their bedroom.

"Just out, okay?"

"No, it's not okay. I was worried. I didn't know where you were. What if something had happened? To the baby?" She felt like crying, and she didn't want to, not now. She felt like she should apologize to him, but she knew she shouldn't. She hadn't done anything wrong.

"Well, nothing happened, okay? I got home, and I'm all right, and you're all right. Okay?"

Except, she thought in the silent darkness of the bedroom, we're not all right.

* * * * * * *

"Are you doing something different with your hair, Maggie?" Ryan, her boss, asked on Wednesday. "It looks good. Not that it didn't before," he hastened to add.

She almost smiled. She *was* doing something different with it; somehow he must have noticed she'd plucked the hairs from her forehead, but she couldn't very well say that, now could she.

"No, I don't think so, Ryan." She laughed a little nervously, and thought it sounded like a titter. Good, that ought to impress him, she thought sarcastically.

"I really like it." He leaned against her desk and watched her.

She shifted in her chair. He made her nervous. She liked him well enough, but he was her boss after all, not her friend. She wished he would go away and let her work. He was about five years her junior, with pale blue eyes and dark blond hair, and a tan. Sometimes she had wondered how far his tan went. Did he have tan lines? She didn't like thinking like that. He was her *boss*, for God's sake. A male boss, and they were always the worst.

"Well, gotta get back to the grind. Bring that Anderson account in when it's done, okay?" He smiled, waved and went back down the hall.

The Anderson account. Momentarily her mind blanked. The receivership. Oh, yeah. Now where was it? She sifted through papers and folders, not finding it. It had to be here. She never threw anything away. But where could it be? She checked her files in the drawers, then located it in the bottom drawer of her desk. She had actually filed it. Could it be that she was getting efficient in her old age? Hardly, she told herself. Must have been a mistake.

Old age. She shuddered, and glanced through the Anderson file. It looked fairly complete, but she still had one more action to complete on it.

She picked up the phone and made a call.

After lunch she took the file into Ryan's office. His fingers touched hers as she handed the folder to him. He smiled. She swallowed.

"Fine. Let me look it over, and I'll let you know."

"Okay."

She went back to her desk, and sat there for a long time not looking at anything.

Donald had the car that day so he picked her up and they went home. They didn't talk much. They didn't discuss the night before.

She made dinner again, and Donald complained. He didn't like to try different kinds of food, but he bitched about having to eat the same old thing time after time. Can't win for losing, she thought sourly, and scratched her forehead.

After dinner he turned on the TV loudly, and DeeDee helped her clean up. Actually, DeeDee made a mess, but Maggie would never criticize her when she was trying to help. It was important to encourage children. She had never been encouraged to do these things on her own. She wanted DeeDee able to do things for herself, not to depend on anyone...not to depend on a man.

When she went into the living room Donald was on the phone, but got off hastily.

"Who was that, hon?" she asked as she plopped down on the couch.

"Wrong number," he said off-handedly as he switched channels.

"Oh, yeah?" But the phone in the kitchen hadn't rung. He had made a phone call. And ended it quickly when she came into the room. She didn't want to be suspicious, but....

"Who is she, Donald?"

"What?" He didn't look away from the Weather Channel.

"The woman you were talking to."

"I wasn't talking to a woman. I told you it was a wrong number."

"You pig," she said and got up. In the bathroom she locked the door and stared into the mirror. She looked tired tonight. She *was* tired tonight. She touched the circles under her eyes. Bags, Donald would call them.

She stripped off her clothing and realized she hadn't exercised tonight. It was too late now. Tomorrow.

She'd never really noticed, she thought, as she peered into the mirror that there were tiny hairs along the edges of the aureoles of her breasts. Now, why, she wondered, do we have hair there? She took out the tweezers and quickly dispatched the hairs. It only stung a bit.

There was hair everywhere; she was as hairy as a gorilla, she thought, and shuddered. Now that was an attractive picture. No wonder Donald didn't want to sleep with her.

She shaved her legs and underarms again, and noticed that her upper lip needed trimming again; then she decided to check for gray. She didn't know why she did this because it just depressed her. She was finding more each session, but if she didn't keep doing it, they'd just get away from her. Her pubic area was stubbly, so she took care of that too. She used the tweezers. That hurt a little.

The pain of tweezing didn't bother her like it had when she first started plucking her eyebrows, when she was eleven.

She plucked some more hairs from her groin and rubbed cream on the offended area.

Then she yanked out some more hairs from her forehead, which was a little wider than it had been. But not that much, she decided. Not enough to notice. She wondered what Ryan thought he'd seen.

She shrugged and turned off the light and went to bed, and in the bedroom she could still hear the TV from the living room where Donald sat.

* * * * * * *

Thursday morning she got a call that her father was being rushed by ambulance to the hospital. She told Donald that he and the baby were on their own and that she was taking the car.

"How will I get to work?" he asked her.

"Call your friend for a ride," she suggested as she kissed DeeDee, grabbed her purse and went out the door.

"No, I'll drive you," he said, and he dropped her off at the hospital.

Her mother sat in the waiting room, looking very bewildered.

"What do they say, Mom?"

"What do who say, Margaret?" Her mother thought nicknames were vulgar, particularly for young ladies. Maggie wondered when her mother would realize she wasn't a young lady.

"The doctors, Mom, the doctors."

"Don't snap at me, young lady."

"I'm not snapping at you, Mom."

"You were too."

"What did the doctors say?"

"I don't know. They won't talk to me."

Maggie nodded. Her mother had just sat there and waited for Maggie to arrive, to take care of things, as she had done all of Maggie's life. She had always let Maggie's dad or Maggie do things. After all, a lady didn't dirty her hands.

Maggie glanced sideways at her mother. It wasn't quite seven in the morning, but her mother was dressed as if she was going to the opera. Had she, Maggie wondered, carefully applied her makeup while her husband got sick?

She asked the emergency room nurse about her father. He was being attended to, the woman said. Later she tried to talk to a doctor, but he couldn't because there'd been a car accident out on the highway and the injured were being rushed to this hospital.

It was nearly two hours later that Maggie learned her father had suffered a heart attack. He was being moved to the Coronary Care Unit; they would be able to see him later. The prognosis wasn't good.

Her mother broke down, weeping into her violet-scented handkerchief when she heard the news.

Secretly Maggie felt relief, then was appalled at her reaction. This man was her father, after all. And it was because he was her father that she didn't want him to have any more to do with her life. And yet...she thought she loved him. She did. Didn't she?

"It's all your fault that he's sick, that he's d-duh...."

Her mother couldn't say the word. Savagely for a moment Maggie wanted to shriek: "Dying, dying, dying, that's what he's doing, Mother, *dying*!" But instead she sat quiet, playing with the hairs on the back of her fingers.

"You don't visit like you should, and your father frets and it's been such a burden on his heart, and he misses Deirdre so. A grandfather shouldn't be deprived of the pleasure of seeing the only grandchild he'll ever have."

"He's not deprived, Mother. You both see us once a week. I can't get over any more because of my job. You know that."

"Your job." The words were a curse. "Is that more important than your father's health?"

Maggie bit down on her lip. Yes, she wanted to say, but she couldn't. She'd read somewhere that a woman's view of men were formed by the relationship a girl had with her father; she had known from early on that she was doomed. She was afraid of him, afraid of Donald, afraid of them all. She had prayed when she was pregnant that she would have a daughter; her prayers, she believed, had been answered.

"Margaret, you aren't listening to me." Tears had left pale streaks down her mother's powdered cheeks.

She wasn't about to get into it with her mother, not here, not about this. "I have to make a phone call." Her mother's weeping intensified as Maggie walked away.

She found a public telephone and called Donald's office. "I just thought you'd want to know about Dad," she said when he came on the line. "He's had a pretty bad heart attack. It's not good; the doctors say he could die anytime, but—"

"Look, Mag, I really can't talk. I'm late for a meeting as it is. Give your mom my love, and tell your dad I'm thinking of him." The line went dead.

"I will, if he lives," she said slowly and hung up the receiver. She turned and looked around the lobby, at the ladies in pink at the reception desk, at the neat stacks of magazines, at a man drumming his fingers on his knee.

It was times like this that she wished she smoked. Or drank. Or both.

She asked the ladies in pink where the restrooms where, and she went in, and stood before the badly-lit mirrors, and took out her cuticle scissors and began cutting her hair. As she sawed away at the strands, she remembered how her dad used to take her out for ice cream on Tuesday nights when her mother was at her ladies' club and how he would come into her room later, before her mother came home, and—she thought of how he would probably die, and she would be rid of him, and she would miss him, and she cried and cut and cried. She hacked off a good two inches or more, and then began the extended process of evening it. Snippets fell below her collar and made her itch, but she didn't care.

There, she thought when she was done, she looked much better.

She went back to where her mother sat, still weeping into her now soggy handkerchief, and she waited until the doctor told them they could go upstairs now, and the hair down inside her blouse itched, and her groin itched, and the hair on the backs of her hands make her itch, too.

* * * * * * *

Thursday afternoon she came into work and Ryan asked her how her father was doing.

"Not good. I'm going to see him again tonight."

"My dad had a heart attack about ten years ago; it can be rough. Let me know if there's anything I can do, okay?"

She nodded, aware that she was trembling, and thanked him, and when he had left, she stared at the papers on her desk, and felt trapped. There were so many papers on her desk, more than there had been the day before, and she didn't know what to do with them, not when all she could think about was her father and how close to dying he'd come, and now Ryan was so under-standing, and Donald didn't give a good Goddamn. It had been a mistake coming into work, but she hadn't known what else to do. She couldn't go to the hospital and sit with her mother for hours and hours. She couldn't stay home. She had to do some-thing. Or at least that's what she'd told herself.

As she began filing, she realized she hadn't exercised this

morning, and she hadn't exercised last night, nor the night before. She was slipping, she realized. Definitely slipping. And that was bad, real bad. She rubbed the stubble on the backs of her fingers and wondered if anyone could see her moustache through the makeup.

Later Donald called and said he wouldn't be able to pick her up; she'd have to get home on her home.

"What about DeeDee?" she asked.

"You'll have to do that, too."

"Just how the hell am I supposed to without a car?" she demanded.

"Call a friend," he said and hung up.

She looked down at her desk through a shimmering of tears. Now she was stranded. Like the time her dad had forgotten to pick her up after her piano lesson and she had waited until it was dark and so cold, and then begun the long walk home. She could call a taxi, she supposed. She looked through her wallet. She had six bucks. Not enough for a cab to the day care center and then home.

"Problems?"

It was Ryan.

"My husband can't pick me up tonight. And I have to get my daughter from day care."

"I can drive you home, Maggie. It's no problem."

"Ryan, I don't want to be a bother—" she began.

"What's the bother? It's not like you're demanding this. I'm volunteering."

There was probably some bus she could catch, although she didn't know the schedules, and she'd have to call the day care people and let them know she would be delayed, and just what the hell was Donald doing that he couldn't pick them up tonight?

"Well...."

"Come on. I'll get a chance to meet your daughter finally. I feel like I know her, but I want to meet the real thing."

"Okay."

"Fine. We'll leave around 5:30 or so. Is that all right?"

She nodded. That would get them to the day care place just about on time, she realized. She went back to work and ignored the itching in her groin.

They left just a few minutes later than they'd expected and picked up DeeDee and Ryan insisted on taking them to dinner. They went to a diner, and Ryan said he thought DeeDee was beautiful, just as beautiful as her mother, and he smiled at her when he said that.

Maggie smiled, but her face felt stiff, and the hairs on the back of her fingers seemed to crackle. She rubbed them, felt only stubble, and wondered how he could think she was beautiful when she was as hairy as an ape. Wasn't that was her father had called her once? His little monkey?

"Something the matter?" Ryan asked. He was busy showing DeeDee how to flip a packet of sugar across the table.

"No."

They had coffee, and DeeDee had a small bowl of vanilla ice cream and then he drove them home.

"Do you want to go to the hospital? I could take you," he said, when he saw the empty driveway.

"Thanks, Ryan, but I should get DeeDee in bed. I'll call and see how my dad is doing. If anything has happened, I'm sure Mom would have called." At least she would have hoped her mother would call. And where was Donald at this hour, nearly seven-thirty now? Out with some bimbo from his office?

"Thanks for everything. I really appreciate it. See you tomorrow." She gathered up DeeDee and waved to Ryan who waved back, and then she went inside.

She gave DeeDee a bath and tucked her in, then sat in the living room and told herself she ought to do her exercises, but she just didn't feel like it, and she realized she hadn't taken her vitamins either. She should get up and get them, but she just didn't feel like it. She rubbed the backs of her fingers, felt the damned stubble again, and wished that Donald would get home.

It was nine now. Still no sign; he hadn't called.

Ryan had been very kind to her today, she thought. Very

understanding. He would probably fire her next week.

No, she insisted, he wouldn't do something like that. He was too nice. He was concerned.

He was after something.

That had to be it. No one does anything for free, her mother always said.

And hadn't that been the way of all men in her life? Her father, Donald, Ryan?

Hadn't she seen how he had looked at DeeDee during dinner? He would take a bite of his hamburger and then he would look at the little girl who was chattering about the puppy that their teacher had brought to day care that day.

She didn't like the way Ryan had looked at her daughter, not one bit. It made her think of how her father had looked at her when they had the ice cream together.

She licked her lips, and went into the bathroom, and closed the door only a little bit. She wanted to be able to hear DeeDee if she should call out.

She shaved her legs and armpits, and her groin, and trimmed some of the hair on her arms, even though it had never bothered her before. For a few minutes she stared into the mirror and shuddered at all the hair she saw. She decided that her hair wasn't quite the right length, and she got her hair scissors out and cropped away until her hair was chin length.

Better, much better, she thought. She plucked her eyebrows, and decided they could be a wee bit thinner, no, thinner than that even, and the hairs around her lips were coming back again. She took care of them.

Then she discovered some fine hairs on her tummy, around her navel, and she plucked them. That sort of tickled, and she almost laughed aloud.

She touched her upper arms and realized she had hair there as well, hair so fine she had never really noticed it, but tonight it bothered her, and so she took out her electric shaver and switched it on and sheared the hair from her arms.

She looked at her bobbed hair and thought she could do better than that.

She cut more off, and it fell in chunks to the bathroom floor. Then she turned on the electric shaver. When she was done, she rubbed her hand over the unfamiliar skin and thought how good it felt.

Then she went into the baby's bedroom and bundled her up in her arms, and brought her into the bathroom. DeeDee rubbed her eyes and asked sleepily what she was doing.

"We're going to make you pretty for daddy when he gets home," Maggie said.

She turned on the electric shaver and the long blond curls fell to the floor and DeeDee began crying and Maggie told her to hush, young lady, because there was nothing to worry about any more.

THE HOME

"This is it," Jeannine said aloud, "this is my last *ever* summer in Greystone Bay."

The words sounded good, yet she knew it wouldn't be the last. The previous year she'd vowed *that* would be her last summer, and the year before *that* summer would be her final one here. Only it wasn't; it never was. Somehow. Yet it would be nice if she'd find another job elsewhere, pack up her belongings, and move away from Greystone Bay and all the memories and this terrible summer.

Memories....

Summer....

From where she lay in bed she looked out the window and saw the humidity hanging in the trees like moist gray shawls. Birds sang disheartened songs; somewhere a cricket chirped. Beneath her the sheets were damp.

God, how she hated summers here. And winters, too.

But the summers were by far the worst. Jeannine had lived here all her life, but yet had never grown accustomed to the summers with their high temperatures and high humidity rates, the way the air became absolutely still, until you struggled to breath; sometimes it felt like something was sucking the air out of your very lungs.

Or the spirit out of your very soul.

No wonder Greystone Bay had such a high suicide rate. There was a saying among the natives, "If the winters don't get you, the summers will."

True enough.

Glancing at the clock, she saw it was 5:30. Almost time to begin another exciting day.

Be still my heart, she thought and giggled aloud. The giggle turned into a choking noise and she squeezed her eyes shut. She forced herself to take a long deep breath, to slowly release it... and not to think, to think, to think.

Maybe, just maybe, the problem was her attitude. If she viewed it—the summer, the heat, the humidity, her job, EVERYTHING—more optimistically, maybe it *would* be better, maybe things would work out for once, maybe she wouldn't feel this rotten all the time.

Maybe.

She didn't have to push the top sheet back to get up; that had been off her since midnight. The backs of her legs seemed to stick to the sheets and she almost expected her skin to pull away with a wet ripping sound.

She padded into the bathroom, stared at herself in the mirror. Her blonde hair stood up at all angles; to avoid snarls, she'd had it cut to chin length. Not short enough, she mused. She yawned and wished she didn't have all the silver in her mouth. She had smudges under her eyes from the mascara she hadn't removed last night and her face gleamed from the sweat on it.

Swell.

She washed her face, brushed her teeth, then stepped into the shower stall. The curtain kept touching her, a clammy mildewy feeling and no matter how much she shoved it away, it clung to her. Exasperated, she jerked the curtain back on its rings. Finally, she turned off the hot water and forced herself to stay under the cold water. This morning ritual never failed to wake her up completely, and to cool her off, even if it were just for a while.

She reached for the towels hanging on a wooden rack on the opposite wall just an arm's length away, and an earwig tumbled out. She wrinkled her nose and watched it scuttled away. The bug wasn't poisonous or anything, just disgusting. And *everyone* had seen that old *Twilight Zone* episode with Lawrence Harvey and the earwig. Or was it *Night Gallery*? *Outer Limits*?

Carl always claimed—

No.

Didn't matter; earwigs didn't crawl into your ears while you slept; all they had to do was just scuttle nearby and you were disgusted enough. Better an earwig than a centipede, although she had plenty of those in the damp weather. Damp weather. Meaning: every day, every night of the year practically. She didn't see them in the winter—maybe they went south to Florida—but she saw plenty of them other times. She hated it when she caught some movement out of the corner of her eye, and there creeping across the carpet would be an earwig or a centipede. She'd kill it, then find another one on the wall, and after that, she'd sit back on the couch, and every time she had an itch or the hair on her arms was ruffled or *anything* just touched her, she'd think it was something crawling on her.

Disgusting, simply disgusting.

And then there were the flies and mosquitoes that buzzed around outside and—all too often—inside. She hated those, too. Sometimes with all these creepy-crawlies around her, she wondered if she had simply died and someone had neglected to tell her.

She shook the towel, wrapped her wet hair in it. Then she reached for another towel, shook that as a precaution, and started drying herself. Only it didn't feel as if she was dry; it felt like she had simply moved the moisture from one spot to another.

Jeannine dressed, then ate a quick breakfast. She grabbed her purse and car keys, and left the ground floor apartment. She waved to Mrs. McDonald who waggled her fingers as she tended her roses. They didn't look too good this year; the blight had got them, as the old woman put it, but she was valiantly trying to save them. Usually the flowers were an exquisite deep red, a sunshiny yellow, a dainty pink. This year the petals all looked gray, as if they weren't getting enough sun.

She glanced overhead. That wasn't surprising since the sun

was obscured by a haze. The haze had held on all month long, and she was beginning to wonder if the sky really was blue beyond that. Maybe there was nothing...maybe there was just night...blackness...waiting to swallow them.

She shivered, despite the heat, and got into her car. Although the sky was hazy, it was still bright and she fumbled to put on her sunglasses. Local weathermen had been predicting for some time—and so far erroneously—that the area would be getting big storms one of these days. They muttered something about high pressure systems and a build-up, the meeting of cool air and warm...and one of these days...shazam, down it would come, the heavens opening up, the possibility of tornados and downpours and vicious winds and baseball-sized hail and God knew what else. It's coming, it's coming, the weather forecasters said, and after a while, people started calling the radio and the TV stations to say, yeah, and so's Christmas. She'd never done that, though she often thought about it. It was the sort of thing Carl would have done.

Quickly the stab of pain and then it was gone.

Even this early she turned the car's air conditioning on, but she could still feel the trickle of sweat down the middle of her back, under her bra strap, and the skin between her thighs was already moist, despite the hose.

She drove along Foster St., past the closed up buildings that had made their shuttered appearance this last year—their proprietors all having given up—past the tacky fast food restaurants that seemed part of any urban blight now, past the youths hanging out on the street corners, watching her with empty eyes. She turned down Crescent with its small frame houses and tiny front yards, and followed that until she reached Port Blvd. That was the fastest way to get to work.

From Harbor Rd. she swung north, taking the road over North Hill, past the elaborate houses and painstakingly-tended estates—the gardeners all out despite the earliness of the day clipping and mowing and sculpting—and all those people with all that money burning holes in their pockets, until she was in what was euphemistically referred to as "wetlands." Swamps. Northern-type swamps. No live oaks or alligators or Spanish moss here, but nonetheless it was a swamp, an area where water stood nearly hip-deep more months than not, where strange vegetation poked out of the still waters, where unusual birds and animals found some refuge.

Following the small road through the swamp she reached the bridge. She paid her toll—absurd, she thought in a city the size of Greystone Bay—and drove across the old bridge.

Originally Harborview—the Greystone Bay Nursing and Convalescent Home—hadn't been on an island; but through the years the thin spit of land that connected that area to the shoreline had eroded through storms and tides.

In years past if you had come this far out of town you could have walked, or driven your horse and buggy or old Model A, on the connecting land to Harborview, or the Home, as most residents called it. Now you'd have to swim, and be an excellent swimmer because the currents and tides here were some of the roughest along the entire coast. So the city fathers, back in the '30s or so she read once, had reluctantly constructed the bridge. It was old and desperately in need of repair, and it was just one more thing that the city government had put off fixing.

So five years ago they'd set up the toll booth at the city end of the bridge.

The revenue from the tolls, the wise leaders dwelling in city hall declared, would help pay for the bridge's repair. Right. What these learned leaders hadn't counted on were the cheapskates living in Greystone Bay, who had once thought it annoying enough to have to drive *all the way* out of town and across the Hill to go to Harborview, but who then decided that paying a whole buck one way was just too much and so didn't come out as often to visit old Mom or Dad, the decrepit, and even the once-loved spouse who'd had been forced there because of Alzheimer's or Huntington's or something equally incurable.

Now, thanks to the marvelous toll, the Home was nearly empty except for a few fossils, the only sound being some days the footsteps of nurses and aides, the occasional doctor who remembered he had patients out here, the cry of a sea gull, and the shuffling and hacking of the old inmates.

Inmates, she thought, negotiating across the narrow bridge, and feeling, as she always did, the wobbling of the bridge beneath her car's wheels, that's more apt than residents. They're patients, but more like prisoners.

Jeannine parked in the diminutive lot, and paused before going in. She sniffed the air; the smell of brine never failed to amaze her. There was no place, she thought, like the ocean and its environs. Overhead a sea gull wheeled and screeched at others posed on rocks along the shoreline. She sniffed something else in the air, but couldn't identify it. With one hand she shielded her eyes against the sun and gazed out across the dazzling water, wondering if there might be a tanker heading north to Boston or down to New York City; but she saw nothing but the ocean, not even the white triangles of sailboats. She shrugged and headed for the door.

The building was old, made of granite they'd hauled from some quarry from Vermont a century ago. The granite had darkened over the years, and in some places the stone appeared nearly black, while other places were simply dirty-sheets gray. It was three stories high, immense although most of it was no longer used—the back wing, for instance, was used simply as storage these days.

In the old days, a century ago, when the Home had been constructed it had served first as a hospital, then as a mental asylum, and it was from the former that it had earned its unsavory reputation. There were gruesome tales told of the things that had gone on here decades ago; she had heard them all in nursing school. Some were obvious fabrications, but too many, she knew, were closer to the truth.

Gradually the asylum had given way to an old people's home, but the conditions hadn't improved substantially. When she had first come there years ago as a trainee, she had seen old men and women tied down in their beds all day and night, aides beating some old patient who refused to eat his gruel, another being kicked, patients laying in sheets soaked with urine and feces, with bedsores the size of saucers on their backsides. She had protested, and been told to mind her own business; she was just a student, she was reminded.

She hadn't minded her own business, after all. She had complained to her supervisors, and when they hadn't listened, she'd gone to the hospital, and then to the hospital board, and then all the way up the ladder of authority until the scandal had reached the State Capitol. Butt had been kicked, heads rolled, and conditions changed.

And in the end after she'd had some years experience nursing, she'd been put in charge. She was the Head Administrator.

Not bad for someone this side of forty, for someone who was the first in her family to go beyond the eighth grade. Not bad at all.

It was her Home now, and she was damned proud of it. Oh, yeah, it had some problems, most of that related to money (wasn't everything? she wondered), but she had a skilled staff, even though it was too small. Too bad there was such a lack of interest in the Home.

Every year they organized a summer picnic for the residents and their families, and every year they were lucky if half a dozen family members in all showed up. And there sat the old men and women, in their best short-sleeved shirts and best dresses with the bold flowers on them, with red and blue and green balloons tied to the handles of their wheelchairs, and bright paper hats jauntily set on their gray heads. And she and the other staff moved among them, and spoke to them, kneeling or crouching down so they could look at the residents eye to eye—never over them as if the residents were somehow inferior—and she and the staff would sing songs..."you are my sunshine, my only one"... always the old favorites...and get the oldsters to clap and maybe one or two quavering voices would join in, and they would have hot dogs and hamburgers and cole slaw and some cake that some bakery had donated—happy birthday could still be seen in faint icing letters—and sometimes she just wanted to cry.

She tried so hard; the whole staff did. No one cared. No one.

Carl had cared, though, and he had come out as often as possible and helped. He had a marvelous singing voice, a silly grin and told wonderful jokes and they all loved him out here and—

No, no, no. She knew where that would lead; and today she didn't want the tears. She didn't want to feel that way. She was feeling good, feeling whole, she told herself. And that was that.

Only she knew it wasn't.

Every chance she had she invited children's singing groups to come out and entertain the old group. Sometimes one or two kids straggled out to sing in off-scale innocence. Occasionally a woman from the local library wandered in with an armload of books and proceeded to sit and read to those who listened eagerly. The holidays were worst, though, with the trappings of cheerfulness strung across the halls and walls of the commons room and the individual rooms, and the residents with their red paper hearts clutched in gnarled fingers or their mother's day corsages purchased out of her pocket pinned to their dresses, or the meager turkeys with slim trimmings set out on the dining tables for a Thanksgiving feast. And always, always waiting.

Mostly, though, no one came.

Mostly the old people sat in their wheelchairs parked by the windows, and they stared out over the rolling waves, mile after mile of gray nothingness, or they watched the swamp and pointed out the birds to her as she walked by. She never failed to stop to watch with them and to chat to the resident. Then she'd pat the person's hand and touch them on their shoulder, and more often than she liked to admit the old man or woman would simply sigh. Glad to have some human contact. Something...in this lonely cold remote building.

City fathers had been promising for some time to build a new home within the limits of Greystone Bay, but she and all those who worked here knew that wouldn't happen, not while they were still breathing. And so in the summer they simmered; the building had many windows, but not nearly enough, and some had window air conditioners in them, a bequest by someone who had felt guilty that he hadn't visit his mother enough. Of course, he'd only left enough money for five, when at the time they could have used closed to forty. But it helped.

So they simply opened all the windows and hoped for some sea breezes. And usually they got it; too, the limestone was cool, and that kept the residents from overheating. Besides, most of the old people had such sluggish blood flowing through their veins that they didn't suffer until it really got hot. And most summer days it didn't get *that* bad in Greystone Bay.

Most days.

She went through the glass front doors and into the lobby. She wrinkled her nose at the faint odor. Normally all you smelled was the disinfectant and the fresh cut flowers that usually sat on the front desk. Today, though, there was something else. She tried to identify it, but couldn't. Yet it was familiar. She'd have to talk to someone about that.

Inside it was darker than she liked, but they'd had to turn out some lights; the utility bills were running too high, and given the budget—or what there was of that—it was better to keep some rooms slightly dark than to cut back on the residents' meals. The old dinosaur was too expensive to run; it would be cost-effective in the long run to construct a new facility, but the wise town fathers couldn't see that either; oh, how they hated that phrase, "new construction." Unless, of course, it was another string of condos or high-rise corporate offices, neither of which anyone in the world, much less in Greystone Bay, needed more of.

Ah well, she told herself, another day as the home's supervisor.

She called hello to Frances, the receptionist and telephone operator, who mostly sat idle these days; there were few visitors, even fewer phone calls. The older woman had brought a stack of paperbacks to read at the beginning of the month, and was now nearly finished with it.

"Looks like you're going to have to restock," Jeannine said, nodding at the purple plastic bin against one wall that held the unread ones. There were only a handful.

Frances looked up from the slim book about giant lizards and nodded, the roll of flesh under her chin wobbling. She was dressed, as always, in a sleeveless white top, which Jeannine swore most of have been purchased thirty years before—after all the blouse buttoned down the back.

"Yeah, there's gonna be a friends of the Library sale next weekend startin' early, and I'm gonna go down with a wheel-barrow. Me and Walter plan to get our next year's reading that way. They got pretty good prices—half, and even a third of the original sometimes."

"Certainly is better than tossing them out. I never could stand seeing a book in the trash."

"Yep. Me neither. And me and Walter trade them with our friends, although I gotta tell you, Miss Walker, sommet his friends got pretty bald tastes."

"Ah," she smiled. "Bald" meaning "risqué" meaning some of Walter's friends went for the sort of short novels that where churned out by publishing houses with names like Racy Tales Publishers and Hussy House.

At least, she told herself, they were reading *something*. On the other hand, did they really understand what they were reading?

What a snob she thought as she headed down the hall. Her low heels tapped with slight echoes on the linoleum floor. Today she thought the place sounded completely empty. She stopped; listened. Nothing. Not the sound of telephones ringing or voices or even some faint throbbing of machinery. It was as if there was no one here but her, left alone in this out-of-date colossus.

She forced herself to look down at the floor and keep walking. She thought it had once been white and black, but now it looked more gray and yellow, despite the morning and night scrubbing it got from Mr. Wextner, their janitor. Or was that custodian? Or custodial engineer? Supervisor? Of what? He was the only one left in that department. He wasn't particularly young; and neither she nor he could lure any younger men out to Harborview. Better wages could be made in town. So Mr. Wextner did the window cleaning, and the floor polishing, and he cleaned mirrors and bathrooms and tried to maintain the grounds. It was a lot of work for a man his age, but he worked diligently, and when she could she slipped him some extra money.

She smiled to herself. Was it any wonder she was still living in the three-room apartment that her mother thought a disgrace for a "person as important as yourself."

And yeah, try taking that to the bank.

Originally the ground floor had been all administrative offices; now half of it was shut down. No personnel. No funds. The second floor was all residents, and the third floor was closed. She passed Mrs. Denilli, the nurse, who looked efficient, but who Jeannine knew had a drinking problem. She couldn't bring herself to fire the woman, at least not yet, because Mrs. Denilli still worked hard and she had never harmed a patient. And she thought the woman deserved a second chance; she had spoken with the nurse, who swore she would be going to AA soon.

She nodded to her secretary, Mrs. Gómez. The woman was just about twenty years her senior, about a foot shorter, had huge brown eyes always carefully outlined in heavy eyeliner, and had the most placid disposition of anyone she'd ever met. Nothing ruffled Mrs. Gómez; Jeannine liked that.

"Hot enough for you, Miss Walker"?

Mrs. Gómez always greeted her that way—during the summer; in the autumn and winter, it was "cold enough for you, Miss Walker"?

They all called her "Miss," too, even though she'd tried to get them to address her as "Miz." Greystone Bay—and its residents—was not always with the times, though.

"Anything going on, Mrs. Gómez?"

The woman picked through a stack of manila folders and handed one to Jeannine. "Dr. Ranolf called a few minutes ago."

"He's up rather early. What's the matter—his conscience won't let him sleep?" She always thought of him as Ranolf the Werewolf. Why she thought that she couldn't imagine; he wasn't huge and hairy or even the least bit threatening. He was short, pudgy, wore thick glasses and more than once she thought he bore a passing resemblance to that mad scientist on the old Muppets Show.

The secretary tried hard not to smile. "He says he won't be able to come out today."

"Oh, swell, what did he do, screw up his golfing date?" Exasperated, she blew on the hair already straggling down into her eyes.

Mrs. Gómez chuckled. "He says he's not feeling well, has some sort of bug going around."

Yeah, the golfing bug. "Physician heal thyself," she muttered.

"What?"

"Nothing. Anything else?"

"He said to tell you that he's sending a replacement out. Today. Maybe."

"Well, let's hope he gets more done than Dr. Ranolf usually does." On a weekly basis Dr. Ranolf the Werewolf was supposed to make this incredibly arduous trip out here—of 3.2 miles from his house; she knew because she had driven there to check the distance once—and check blood pressures, and sore throats, and slight temperatures, and some other minor complaints that had arisen during the week. More often than not, he simply "couldn't make it today." It played havoc with their scheduling at Harborview, but he didn't care. Obviously he had more important things to do—and richer patients to bill.

God, she was so cynical. When had that happened? Where had that innocent girl who went into nursing to change the world and make it a better place gone? Left. She left, long ago. But at least she was still doing something positive, even if it were in a small way. She hadn't given into the bastards, not like Dr. Ranolf and all the other people she knew.

Years ago she had petitioned for a special van adapted to wheelchairs so that several of the staff could take the residents to the hospital for check-ups, and for outings beyond the Home.

She was still waiting.

Always waiting.

"Miss Walker?" Mrs. Gómez was staring at her.

"I'm sorry. What was that last?" God, her mind had been drifting.

"I said here's a list of people you promised to call today."

She accepted the piece of paper with names and numbers neatly typed on it. The people she would be calling to ask—beg—for money. It never ended.

She went into the inner office, leaving the door open as was her habit and sat behind the old desk. Her chair squeaked as always. She set the file and paper down and pulled the phone to her and began making calls. As she listened to the phone ringing at the other end, she gazed out over the ocean and saw the darkening clouds far off in the distance. Well, maybe, there would be a storm after all. Good, they could use the rain.

Some dark flashed along the floor, but when she turned around, she saw nothing.

She swung back to her desk then and concentrated on her pitch.

Later before lunch she made her rounds upstairs. She always made an effort to go up at least two—and sometimes three—times a day to see the residents. Surely they must feel better to know she hadn't forgotten them.

"How are things going, Sandra?" she asked the floor supervisor.

The woman, pale and rather frail-looking, shrugged. "Same as ever."

Sandra wasn't much of a talker. In the years Jeannine had known her she hadn't heard more than a few sentences from the woman at any one time, but that really didn't matter; Sandra was damned good at her job, and the other women liked and respected her. She was about Jeannine's age, married with two sons and a husband who drank too much beer. But she never commented on her personal life; Jeannine heard things from the other aides.

"How are you, Mrs. Emerson?" Jeannine asked a little woman in a wheelchair at one of the tables in the commons room. Mrs. Emerson cradled a rag doll in her arms and was crooning to "her baby." Mrs. Emerson looked up and smiled, revealing a mouth bereft of teeth. For someone her age—a year or two shy of ninety—she was remarkably unwrinkled. She always smelled of lavender and rubbing alcohol.

"Just fine, sweetie. Just fine. You tell your father it's time for dinner, and he's got to set the table. You tell him now."

Jeannine patted her hand. "I will." Sometimes Mrs. Emerson would have a second doll with her, one in each hand, and the dolls would be holding conversations. It was rather unnerving, especially at night, Jeannine thought, when the only sound on the floor was the raspy whisper of Mrs. Emerson's two voices.

She greeted Mr. White next and complimented him on his new shirt.

He rubbed his dark hand against the soft blue material. He smelled of talcum powder, and he was one of her favorites. He was so even-tempered, such a gentleman; she couldn't understand why his daughter had put him in the Home. Probably because Mr. White just didn't fit into the daughter's extensive schedule, Jeannine thought bitterly.

"My daughter got this for me. 'Member she was here last week?"

"Yes, I do." Mr. White's daughter hadn't stepped in the Home since 1982. The woman, she'd explained to Jeannine in a phone call two years ago, just had *so* much to do—you understand, don't you—what with PTA, and after school activities of her four children, and her husband was a *very* important man on the town council, you know, and there was all that social entertaining to do, of course, because her husband was thinking of running for the state legislature, and surely, you know *how* important that is—

Jeannine had hung up on her.

It was Jeannine's money that had bought Mr. White his shirt, but she had signed his daughter's name to the card. She didn't want to shatter any illusions he might yet have.

She waved to some other residents, and stopped to chat with others. She glanced around the commons room. It was painted in what was supposed to be a cheerful color—a pale yellow—but sometimes, like today, when the light came from the ocean through the large windows—she thought it was rather a bilious color. Still, it was better than white. It was always kept spotless. Yet she had a feeling something wasn't quite right. She studied the player piano along one wall, the line of orange and yellow chairs, the tables with their paper tablecloths and little vases with straw flowers, the large-screen TV in the corner. Nothing seemed out of place.

And yet—

She shook her head. She didn't know what was wrong with her. She'd been feeling out of sorts since she got up. Must be the weather. She smiled faintly. Something else the natives here said. No matter what happened or was happening or about to happen, its source was traced back to the weather. "Must be the weather." No one seemed to want to admit that there might be something else involved, the hand of Fate or God or some cosmic jokester. No, "must be the weather." Very convenient.

She counted heads—twenty-two left. Once there'd been several hundred in the Home, but death had claimed the majority of them. Several had been taken out of the Home and moved to different nursing homes in different states where their children or other loved ones had moved.

Twenty-two. That was all. And even now she knew they waited, waited for death.

Don't we all? she wondered. A voice dragged her thoughts back.

"Say, Mrs. Pulnockski, see, lunch is here now."

Tina wheeled in the large cart on wheels, its shelves containing the trays of food.

"About time. Been waitin' all day." The woman next to Jeannine sniffed.

"Oh?"

"Yup. Hope it's not that pot roast." She leaned closer to Jeannine. "They make it terrible, and they *always* serve it to us."

"That's a shame."

"Yup."

Tina placed the tray in front of Mrs. Pulnockski and pulled off the lid. Chopped ham and mashed potatoes and a Jell-O cup and a slice of bread.

"Pot roast. Again." Mrs. Pulnockski shook her head and made a disgusted sound.

Tina and Jeannine smiled, and Jeannine helped the girl deliver the rest of the trays. Tina's duty, among many others around the Home, was to help some of the residents eat; some could barely hold their forks or spoons. Others just need to be reminded that their meal was set in front of them. A number of aides had called in sick today, so they were more short-handed than usual, and Frances had come upstairs to help. She was delivering the trays down the hall to those few who couldn't sit in the common rooms with the others; there were only a handful of them now. Mrs. Denilli was helping out, too, though this wasn't part of her nursing duties, and when Jeannine passed the nurse, she could smell the alcohol on the other's breath.

Briefly their eyes met, and then Mrs. Denilli turned away.

Jeannine helped Miss Hurlbut spread her paper napkin across her lap.

"Thank you, dear."

Miss Hurlbut was a retired schoolteacher; in fact, Jeannine had her in sixth grade and had never forgotten the woman nor the lessons she taught. Miss Hurlbut had always been a good teacher, devoted to her students and they had all loved her. No one forgot her.

And here Miss Hurlbut had ended up. Jeannine always thought the woman had deserved better, but the teacher had no family and when she'd had a stroke that prevented her from walking she'd been forced to enter the Home. Miss Hurlbut was one of the more lucid residents.

"There's a storm brewing." She pointed with her fork to the

back windows.

Jeannine glanced over her shoulder and saw that the sky had darkened considerably since she'd last looked out her office windows. She thought she saw a glimmer of lightning, but must have been mistaken. Well, it looked like the weathermen had finally been right.

"It sure looks like you're right, Miss Hurlbut."

"My favorite barometer told me so." She saw the other woman's puzzled look and indicated her legs. "They always ache when the weather's changing. And this one is going to be big. I saw green sky for a while. Not a good sign. If the storm had been brewing on land, I'd say we were in for a tornado. I don't know what this means. Probably just another squall."

Jeannine smiled reassuringly. "We've certainly had our share of those."

Miss Hurlbut nodded and speared a chunk of ham. She gazed at it. "I do wish the kitchen would realize that some of us still have our teeth and don't need to have everything blended to baby food consistency."

"I'll remind them."

"I believe you already have, dear. I just think they're a little dense down there."

"I suspect so."

They chatted for a few minutes more, then Jeannine left and went downstairs.

"Any sign of the doctor?" she asked Frances, who was busy rearranging objects on her desk in the lobby.

"Nope."

Jeannine sighed and went back upstairs. She took her lunch out of the refrigerator, and was about to sit down when she saw an earwig on her chair. Wrinkling her nose, she swept it off and sat. She pulled the sandwich out of the plastic bag and paused. She thought she had heard something.

The crashing of the waves, the whistling of the wind and— there, something more. A moaning? A whispering? She checked to see if her intercom was on; no, so she couldn't be picking up anything from another office.

The sound stopped now.

Puzzled, she began eating, and was just finishing her tuna sandwich when Mrs. Gómez buzzed her that the doctor wouldn't be coming out. He was sick, too.

"Likely story," she muttered. Probably he didn't want to come out because of the storm, she thought, as she swung around in her chair and surveyed the ocean. This area could be pretty bad during stormy weather, and in fact, a storm was now upon them.

The clouds had crept up on the Home and it was much darker than before; it looked like dusk, and yet sunset was hours away. She'd had to switch on her desk lamp a short time ago. The wind was blowing hard—she could hear it groaning through the cracks in the building—and when she stood and looked out the windows she could see the waves smashing against the island. The Home was set slightly up, so they didn't have to worry about flooding.

Still....

The storm today made her uneasy. She glanced at her watch. Only 2:14. It was going to be a long day. She watched as a fork of lightning sprang from the clouds; a rumble of thunder a moment later, then lightning...flickering, flickering, flickering....

She kept at her paperwork, although once in a while she looked up. Once she buzzed Mrs. Gómez. "Did you call me just now?"

"Just now?" The woman sounded clearly puzzled. "No, Miss, I didn't."

Someone, though, had called her name. She tapped her pen against the paper. "Where's Mrs. Denilli?"

"Downstairs, with Frances, I believe."

"Drinking?"

"Well...."

"Drinking." She sighed. "Will you call her up here please."

"Sure thing, Miss Walker."

She continued writing, and after half an hour, Mrs. Denilli finally showed up.

"Yeah?" Mrs. Denilli's eyes were bright, her face flushed.

"Mrs. Denilli, I know things are not going well today, but I would appreciate it if you don't drink. You know that I can fire you, and if you continue to—"

"I don't need this job; I don't need you," the woman said, leaning across the desk. Her breath was rancid. "I'm quitting. All night my husband beats me, and then I come in and hear crap like this." She stormed out of the office.

Jeannine leaped to her feet. "Mrs. Denilli!" She hurried after her and shouted to the woman across the parking lot, but the nurse had ripped off her cap and thrown it down where it was caught by the wind and blown across the lot, and was climbing into her old sedan. She watched as Mrs. Denilli backed into a red car, Frances's she believed and nicked some paint, and then slammed her car into gear and peeled out of the parking lot. Jeannine watched as Mrs. Denilli took the bridge at too fast a speed; but she made it. Jeannine breathed a sigh of relief. She would prepare her leaving papers in the morning, and her final paycheck. She had wanted to help the woman, really; but some people just didn't want to be helped. They wanted to continue living in their own private hells.

She glanced at the clouds, thought she smelled moisture, then smiled. Of course, she did; they were right by the ocean. More lightning with the thunder much louder now, much closer. She rubbed her arms and went back inside.

Slowly, she went past Frances, who was intently studying a cover of a book, and climbed the stairs and went into her office where she went back to work.

Some time after three Sandra called down to say that someone had heard a noise up on the third floor and some of the residents were agitated. The rain and wind lashed against the windows, and she wasn't sure some of the screens would last. They'd pulled down some of the windows, but it was stifling hot up there.

"Bring them down here. I'll be up in a minute to help." She got up and asked Mrs. Gómez to find Mr. Wextner and tell him that he was needed on the third floor.

Then Tina and Sandra and Jeannine and finally Mr. Wextner slowly brought all the residents down to the first floor on the elevator; it groaned and creaked and took its own time. Once Jeannine thought it was going to get stuck between floors, and she shuddered at the thought. Mr. Wextner or she would have had to climb out of the escape hatch, and then what? Please, let's not say we do, she thought.

Several of the patients, those in much poorer mental and physical conditions and confined to their beds, were mewling, one screaming; they were brought down in their beds, and settled into empty offices where the staff could keep an eye on them. Other residents wept; one man prayed, fingering his rosary, his words just audible. Miss Hurlbut's face was a little pale, but she flashed a brave smile at Jeannine. She put away her work for the day and helped the others with the residents.

Somewhere along the way the rain had grown almost vertical, slashing so hard against the windows that they couldn't see anything outside. The wind rose to a shriek and one or two residents clasped their hands to their ears to keep the unearthly sound out.

A little after four Jeannine was wondering about the possibility of evacuation when the electricity went out. Someone—she thought it was Mrs. Emerson—screamed. Mr. Wextner labored for an hour to bring the electricity on with the back-up generator, but that wasn't working, either.

Jeannine also found that the phone lines were down, too. They were cut off from Greystone Bay, from the world.

They all went hunting through desks and cabinets to find candles and flashlights, and Mr. Wextner produced a Coleman lantern from the basement.

"Just like a camping trip," Miss Hurlbut said, taking one of Mrs. Emerson's hands and squeezing it. "It's all right, dear. We'll just sing. Can your dollies sing?"

Mrs. Emerson, sniffling although no longer weeping, nodded.

Miss Hurlbut began to sing, her white curls bobbing as she

moved her head in rhythm to the music. Mrs. Emerson joined in, and held up one of her dollies. Mr. White's quavering voice could be heard, and that of Tina's and Mrs. Gómez's, too. "You are my sunshine...."

Jeannine would have liked to sing, but she couldn't. Her throat felt paralyzed, as if she tried to open her mouth and nothing would come out, and no air would come in or out, and she would suffocate, slowly, ever so slowly.

She had to do something. She stood up and took a flashlight and explained that she was going to take a look around.

She climbed the stairs up to the second floor, the singing growing fainter until she could no longer distinguish the words. She would check to see if there was anything she should bring down to the others. The hall echoed with her footsteps, and that was all she could hear besides the pummeling of the wind and rain. And yet there was a faint creaking, too. But she couldn't place the sound.

A centipede hurried across the tile, and she brought her shoe down on it.

They always liked to come inside when it was wet or humid, which meant just about year-round in Greystone Bay, she figured.

The second floor was eerie, deserted as it was, and once she thought she saw someone move in one of the room. She directed her flashlight in there, but all she saw were two single beds, the spreads tucked neatly under the pillows, and a large number of stuffed animals arranged by the pillows. Nothing. Only the rain lashing at the window. This one had been left open, so she crossed to it and pulled it down. No need to soak everything in sight.

She checked each room. She wasn't sure why. She just knew she had to.

Slowly she took the stairs to third floor. Here the staircase curved, and her flashlight cast strange shadows on the walls. When she reached that floor, she sneezed. Dust was fairly thick here; she had Mr. Wextner gave it a cursory cleaning at least twice a year, but still it gathered dust and cobwebs from disuse.

Heavy cloths covered some of the furniture, and they cast lumpish shadows in the faint light. Here now she could hear more clearly the drumming of the rain on the roof. It was a good thing none of the residents was up here, she thought; that incessant sound would drive them crazy. Would drive her crazy if she had to listen to it all the time.

Something brown darted from one table to another. A rat. Mr. Wextner also sprayed for those up here, but she supposed the spray wore off after a while, and the dead rats' relatives just moved back in. She'd have to mention it to him again; they were due for a spraying.

Something crashed behind her and she whirled. Nothing. Nothing but dust and shadows and some rats. Still, she walked down the hall to take a look. She wanted to make sure no rain was getting in. That could leak down to the other floors, could get to the electrical wiring, and then they'd really be in trouble.

Something—someone—touched her cheek. She brushed at it absently.

Jeannine.

"Carl?" It had been his voice. She was sure.

No. Carl was dead these four years. Dead here in the home. Carl.

She fought against the tears; they won, and spilled down her cheeks. She loved the Home, and she hated the Home, and yet this was the very place where her love had come to die. There had been the accident, and a wreckage of body and mind, and she had looked at him as they had brought him to the Home after those long months in the hospital, and she had cried because he could no longer recognize her, because all he could do was stare off into space and drool, and she couldn't help but wonder what if his mind were undamaged, what if his mind were trapped inside that wreck of a body. And she cried each day and each night, and for a year he lived that way, slowly worsening, the flesh receding until his skin seemed like a film pulled tautly over his bone, until his breathing grew labored, until the man she loved became a frail pitiful creature. Until one night, with her sitting by his bed holding his limp damp hand, he had breathed deeply and then died.

She had cried. From relief, sorrow, emotions she couldn't even put into words.

And she had come back to work because she had no other place to go.

Each day, though, brought back memories.

Carl.

Jeannine.

She followed the sound down the hall, and heard strange sounds...moaning and weeping and voices from the past. In the semi-darkness she thought she saw the white-clad bodies of people from another time, a time when this was a madhouse. She heard the screams, the angry voices, the whimpering, saw the rats poking among the limp bodies on the dirty floors, saw a woman tied to a wall begging to be let loose she would be a good girl now, saw and heard and smelled the horrible stench of unwashed bodies and vomit and feces smeared on the walls and—

The creaking noise beat a pattern, and half dazed, she approached a window in a long-deserted room. The sound intensified. She glanced out and saw the bridge, the old tumble-down bridge, swaying violently from the gale-like wind. Even as she watched, horrified, the bridge creaked once more and then *twisted*, and bucked upward, and buckled, and slowly, ever so slowly, crumpled into the waters below with the sound of a thousand thunders. Cable dangled from the towers on both shores and blew in the wind as if they were nothing more than threads, and in the middle...nothing.

She could hear shouting from below, and she ran down the hall, ran down the two flights of stairs to the lobby.

Some of the residents were sobbing and shrieking, the employees talking in loud voices.

"Did you see it, Miss Walker? Did you?" Mr. Wextner's voice was trembling as he pointed out the front door. His hair was plastered against his forehead; his clothes soaked. Obviously he'd gone out to check on the racket. Mrs. Gómez stood behind him and was staring outside, her eyes wide.

"I saw it." She was calm now. No more ghosts. This was reality. The bridge had just collapsed, cutting them off. She had things to do. "Now everyone be calm. This not the end of the world, you know. Once the storm dies down, and I'm sure it'll do that sometime tonight, the hospital and authorities will be sending helicopters to help us get back to the mainland."

Francine nodded. "That's right. I read about things like this happening. Once these people were on an island for the summer and there were these wild dogs—" She saw Jeannine's expression and stopped talking.

"Now we don't know how long it's going to be, so we need everyone to cooperate. All right? Think you can do that?" Miss Hurlbut nodded as did Mr. Wextner, and Mrs. Emerson made her two dolls nod, and Mrs. Gómez said, "That's right." The others—Tina, Sandra, Mr. White—said nothing.

"Now, Mr. Wextner," she said facing him, "I know we've never discussed this before—we didn't think it would be an issue—do you think you can find an old radio in the basement? What about something you can send signals on?"

"Don't know. I'll take a look. And I'll take a look at the generator again."

"Good." She swung back to speak to Sandra, just as someone said, "I'm hungry."

Jeannine peered at her watch in the faint light—she had told them to conserve candles and flashlights, and only two candles flickered now—and realized she'd forgotten all about that.

There was a crash of thunder that seemed to shake the building. Conversation stopped, and someone whimpered.

She looked at Tina. The help in the kitchen had long been gone when the electricity went off. She hoped there'd been food deliveries yesterday or today. If not, they were screwed.

"I'll check for something to eat, Miss Walker," Tina said, jumping to her feet.

"Thanks."

She spotted another centipede, not far from Mrs. Emerson's wheelchair, and slowly she moved across and stepped on it.

One of Mrs. Emerson's dolls peeked over the arm of the chair.

"What's that?" asked a squeaky voice.

Jeannine forced a smile. "Nothing."

A few minutes later Tina came back to report that there were quite a few loaves of bread, boxes of saltines, jars and jars of jelly and peanut butter, and tons of canned soup, but no way to cook the later.

"Nonsense," Miss Hurlbut said. "We'll cook it over the open fire for the others."

Tina and Jeannine exchanged glances.

"Open fire?" Tina asked. "I'm sorry, but I don't understand."

Miss Hurlbut pointed to a candle. "Open flame, open fire. It'll be slow, but at least the others will have some warm food."

"Of course. Are you sure you weren't a boy scout in another life?"

Miss Hurlbut shook her head. "Just camped out a lot with my father and sister when I was a child."

Mrs. Gómez and Frances went to the kitchen to help and they had lukewarm soup that night, along with a few crackers. Jeannine poked at her soup with a spoon and tried not to think of Mr. Wextner down in the basement by himself. Rats and cobwebs and earwigs, and God knew what. She left her meal and went to the basement door and called down to him.

"How's it going?" Her voice echoed.

"Guess it's all right. Didn't find a radio. Knew there were some things I should have picked up in town before this. I'm working on the generator right now. Keep your fingers crossed."

"We will."

Briefly around eleven or so the lights came on, and there was a ragged cheer, but just as quickly they went out, and finally around two in the morning Mr. Wextner climbed upstairs to say he couldn't do anything more. Jeannine thanked him, but inside she felt a dark coldness.

They had no end of beds, having brought more down from upstairs, so everyone had some place to spend the night. Jeannine couldn't sleep, though, and listened to the rain and the thunder and watched the glimmer of the lightning. Occasionally she would go to the front door and stare out into the darkness. There were still no lights on in Greystone Bay. For a minute she wondered if it were still there. What if it had been swept away like the bridge? Not a pleasant thought.

Surely by morning the storm would die down, and the power would come back on, and someone would be contacting them from the mainland.

Surely.

She thought she saw something dart past the door, but she knew she was tired and seeing things?

Like those things upstairs? one part of her asked.

That was different; how, she didn't know. Just different.

She had taken off her shoes so that she wouldn't wake the others and now in her stockinged feet she padded down the hallway. She didn't know why she was so restless. She just had to be up and moving, had to be—

Jeannine.

"Oh, Carl. I wish you were here, the way you were. I need comforting." She knew she sounded childish, but she didn't care. She knew he couldn't make it any better with his presence, but she didn't care. She missed him. She wanted him. She remembered all the nights she lay awake, just wanting his arums around her, wanting the press of his body against her.

No more. No more.

She didn't hear anything else, and returned to the lobby and her bed, and even though she lay with her eyes closed, she did not sleep.

The storm raged all night and into the new day. In the morning they all had more lukewarm soup, and for lunch they all—those who could eat it—had peanut butter sandwiches with jelly, and a bonus of cupcakes that Mrs. Gómez had found in one of the cabinets. Jeannine had brought medical supplies down from the nursing station on second. Some of the older patients were not doing well, and she feared she might lose them if they didn't receive more advance medical attention within the day.

Frances, who had been pacing back and forth along the hallway all day, kept saying they had to do something. And Mrs. Hurlbut kept telling her that they were trying, but that they would all have to be patient. Frances continued pacing, until finally Mrs. Pulnockski yelled at her to sit down because she was shaking the floor. Frances just stopped and stared at the woman and then went to look out a window. She hadn't spoke in over an hour.

Somewhere along five Frances said she couldn't stand it any longer, Walter was waiting, and this was getting ridiculous, and went outside. She didn't come back in. No one knew what happened to her. Mr. Wextner went to look for her, but he couldn't see her. Her car wasn't there, either, and Jeannine bowed her head, wondering what could have possessed the woman.

That night it was more lukewarm soup. Jeannine had never been crazy about tomato soup, and she realized she really disliked it, especially made with water and just this side of cold. Not a gourmet meal. On the other hand, at least it was food. They had plenty of water, thank God; they had their own wells on the island, and she didn't think they were in danger of running dry any time soon.

She looked up from her plate and grimaced as she saw another earwig. She shifted her foot and crushed the insect. Surreptitiously she swept it up into her napkin and disposed of it.

Mr. Wextner looked her way. "Nothing kills them, does it? They've got the best survival system, all those bugs. Sure makes me envious."

"Me, too. If only I weren't so disgusted!"

They laughed and finished the remains of their soup. Miss Hurlbut entertained them with stories about some of her students, and they laughed, because that was the only thing they could do.

That night she and Mr. Wextner stood at the front door and stared out into the great darkness that was the Bay.

"This much rain," he said, "makes me glad I never lived in Seattle."

She chuckled, realizing it sounded a little ragged. "I don't think Seattle gets this much all at once. Lucky dogs." For a while they were silent, then: "Do you have family, Mr. Wextner?"

He shook his head. "Just a sister in Canton. Ohio."

"Sounds like a nice place to be just about now."

"Sure does."

He wandered back to the others shortly after that, leaving her with the blackness outside, and the blackness inside as well.

She still couldn't sleep that night and heard the whisperings and moans and cries of those long gone, and when she raised her head from the pillow, she saw that everyone else slept. Apparently only she had heard anything. Or imagined it, she told herself.

Jeannine.

She forced herself to keep her eyes shut, and insisted that she had to sleep. Had to, had to, had....

The next morning she found she'd lost the first of her residents. There was nothing that could be done and so she and Mr. Wextner and Tina wheeled the body in the bed to one of the back offices. A second soon followed, and ended up in the back office. They would have to wait, like all of them.

On the third day the lights in Greystone Bay came back on, blinking on all at once so that Jeannine wondered that they didn't overload the system and make the city go black again. They could just see the gleaming lights from the city and those along the harbor. The lights looked so reassuring, so warm.

Bet those people out there aren't having lukewarm tomato soup, she told herself.

"It'll be all right," Miss Hurlbut said. "You'll see." She nodded and munched a saltine, crumbs dripping onto her chest.

"Think so?" Mr. Wextner asked.

"Yes. I'm an old optimist from 'way back. We die hard."

It was an unfortunate choice of words, Jeannine thought.

"You don't have a family to worry about," Mrs. Gómez said tearfully. "I have a husband and a son and a daughter, and what must they be thinking?"

"I know, I know," Miss Hurlbut said, patting the other woman's hand and leaving cracker crumbs on it.

"You don't. You never married! You didn't have children."

For a moment Miss Hurlbut said nothing, then she sighed deeply, the crumbs on her chest shifting. "I may not have married, Mrs. Gómez. But I had children, dozens and dozens of them, and I felt for each one of them. I remembered each one of them."

"It's not the same," Mrs. Gómez muttered, and Jeannine looked away, feeling the ache of both women, and knowing that it wasn't the same, remembering the children she and Carl had talked about, the children she would never have now.

Mr. Wextner brought out a pack of cards he'd found in a box down in the basement, and although they were missing the eight of diamonds and the two of spades, they played card games long into the night.

They waited in the Home, but the electricity didn't return. The phone service was still disrupted.

They waited for another day. Still no one came.

Ignoring the rain that continued pounding the island until she thought part if it might wash away, Jeannine walked out onto the parking lot and stared across at the Bay. Within seconds she was drenched, and she shivered. The rain was too cold for this time of year. Mr. Wextner came out after her.

"I can swim," he said.

"No, it's too dangerous. Look at that choppy water." She pointed to the channel where the bridge had stood. Whitecaps smashed against the island. "Besides, you might get snagged on some of the wreckage. Plus, and I hate to say this, you're too old, Mr. Wextner."

He looked at her, his face creased into a sad smile. "I suppose you're right, but I have to try."

"Please no."

"Someone's got to."

"No!"

But he ignored her, and all she could do was watch as he walked to the craggy shore of the island, slipped off his shoes and dived into the water. His head bobbed up, he turned and waved and struck off with sure strokes toward the far shore. She watched as he grew smaller and smaller, and then a huge wave crashed down on him, and when the wave receded, he was gone.

She watched until it was dark, but she didn't see him again.

She went inside and Mrs. Gómez found her a blanket to wrap around her shoulders, and she sat and thought of poor brave Mr. Wextner.

"A fire," Miss Hurlbut said.

Jeannine looked up. "What?"

"You could start a signal fire. Away from the building, of course." She laughed a little nervously.

"Maybe."

"You have to, honey. It's the only thing you can do."

It was, and Jeannine knew that. She hated feeling helpless, she who had been in charge for so many years. She looked around at those left. They were waiting, depending on her. She had to act.

A signal fire to let the others in town know about them out here.

She and Sandra and Tina dragged wooden desks and chairs and curtains out into the rain while Mrs. Gómez went searching for some lighters. They set some papers afire—ones they kept the rain from soaking until the very last moment and then set them among the curtains. Time after time the water squelched the flames. Finally, on another try, the wood, old and dry, caught, and they stood back as the flames roared up into the night sky. They worked feverishly to bring out more furniture. They had stripped the third floor of everything that could burn, and still the fire burned bright yellow and red against the blackness.

Jeannine watched, ash flicking onto her face and sodden blouse. She watched the fire, then turned to look at the Bay. She waited for the flashing lights that would indicate a rescue was underway.

Nothing.

Life seemed to go on as usual in the Bay.

The fire burned out and she returned to the others inside, and wrapped another blanket around herself, and no matter what she did, her teeth chattered. The cold had seeped down into her bones, her soul.

The earwigs and centipedes crawled across the floor, and something inside the walls made scratching noises. It kept her awake.

The next night Mrs. Emerson's heart gave out and she died. They moved her body back with all the others.

The Coleman lantern burned out after that, and not long after that the candles and flashlights began flickering out one by one, until they sat in the darkness, listening to the wind and the rain and the thunder.

Miss Hurlbut tried to lead them in songs, but no one had voice, and so hers was the only sound in the night, the only sound beyond the whistling wind and pounding rain, the heart-beat thunder.

Still, through the glass doors of the Home, they could see those bright lights of Greystone Bay. They could imagine the people going out to dinner, heading to a double feature, or glancing out their windows occasionally in their warm, comfortable homes and commenting on all the rain they were getting this summer, but wouldn't it be great for the lawns and flowers?

Sandra left the Home the next day and tried to swim across the channel. A piece of steel from the bridge bobbed up and pierced her instantly. She sank below the waves.

Jeannine knew she should try. She was in charge, wasn't she? Or was she any longer? Was anyone? But what if she died? Yes, but what if she made it?

She couldn't; she didn't know how to swim.

The old ones died hour after hour, after that, until only a handful of people were left in the building. The sounds of squealing and moans and whimpering were louder now, and sometimes she thought she could feel earwigs and centipedes wiggling through her chest and neck.

Jeannine.

She squeezed back the tears. Tina sat in a chair and cried most of the time now. Mrs. Gómez tried to help Jeannine, but she could see the other's heart wasn't in it. Was anyone's?

"Sure is hot," Mr. White said and blinked at her.

"Sure is," she said with a faint smile and tried not to feel the pain. His new shirt was ruined, the sweat stains darkening it, and here and there were the darker stains of blood when he had hurt himself somehow. She brushed an earwig off his arm.

The air was close, the smell of urine overwhelming. They hadn't eaten in a while. The food was running out, but no one wanted to get up and make a meal. No one wanted to do anything.

She sighed long, and felt the hollow ache under her breastbone. Sometimes she thought she saw people moving around the room, but when she looked she saw no one. Once a hand touched her cheek, or maybe it was a hand. Maybe it was a cobweb or a centipede.

Mr. White smiled at her and patted her hand. The sweat trickled down her cheeks.

She blotted away the moisture on the old man's face. Miss Hurlbut slipped her hand into Jeannine's, and Jeannine squeezed it. Mrs. Gómez said nothing, while behind her Tina sobbed, choking, and Mrs. Pulnockski lay in bed, neither dead or alive. And they waited.

Waited for someone to come, on this summer's eve.

Waited. But she knew no one would come to help them. That wouldn't happen, though. She knew.

No one cared.

The Bay had been forgotten them.

Jeannine.

LIVING TO THE END

"He really is a mean old man," a youthful voice whispered fiercely from somewhere in the grayness. "He deserves to die."

"Emily!" A flutter of material, an old-fashioned handkerchief, perhaps. The scent of roses, flowers on the table.

"It's true, Mom," the girl said. "He never did anything good in his life. You know that. He never says anything nice about anyone—just last week he called you a bitch—after all you've done for him."

"Don't say that word, please."

"But he called you that—I heard him, the neighbors probably heard him. And that's not right. He should be more appreciative of you. You've done so much for him."

"I'm not looking for anyone to thank me. I did what I had to do, Em. I've told you that before."

"I know. But it's still not right. Not at all." An impatient movement, a hand slamming down on a jean-clad thigh then.

"Well, no, dear, it's not. I'm sure he didn't really mean what he said. After all, you know how it is when they get older. They don't remember things as clearly as they once did, they aren't as patient as they used to be; things seem so different—"

"Mom."

"Well, they aren't!"

"I know, but it doesn't excuse the hell he's given you these past five years."

Silence from the older woman.

Then the girl: "We'll all be glad when he dies. You, me,

everyone. I hope it's soon!"

"Emily, you're talking about your grandfather!"

"I don't care. I don't! He doesn't love me, or you, or Grandma. None of us. And he never has."

"Hush, child, he might hear."

"I hope he does."

Weariness in the woman's voice. "Leave, Em, please, for a while, honey. You're just making things worse than they already are."

"All right, Mom. I'm sorry I upset you. But it's the truth."

There was the sound of a door closing, distant, aloof, and then through the grayness—

* * * * * * *

Remembered: the incredible surprise that this was even happening, then falling out of the immense tree, feeling the branches scratching him as he fell through them, stinging his skin and ripping his work clothes as he plummeted, the soil and earth rushing at him, smashing onto the ground, smashing, and smashing, and the explosion of white hot pain.

Oh, yes, he remembered the pain. He remembered that when he recalled nothing else. There was nothing but the aching and throbbing inside him and outside him for days and weeks now. The pain so agonizing that it drove everything from his mind and memory.

Casts entombed his legs and arms, while something solid held his body firm, motionless. He was as helpless as an infant, dependent upon strangers, strangers who loomed at him out of the grayness.

He blinked in and out of consciousness occasionally to see the pallid faces of those people he knew had come to see him one last time, and they talked to him in those falsely cheerful tones he loathed, and spoke of everything they and their busy family were doing—why, it was a wonder they'd managed to even squeeze in this hospital visit—and of the weather, which he could care less about, and the sports season, which he'd never liked anyway, but never once did they mention his accident.

Later he listened to his visitors outside in the hallway when they thought he couldn't possibly hear, and they said that he had been a foolish old man, that he should never have been pruning the tree up there, not at his age anyway, and there had been sobbing and the sound of a soothing voice.

And the old man knew. He was dying. He would never go home again; he would never leave the alienness of this damned hospital. Not now. He would stay there in the antiseptic white-ness, living to the end. He would breath and eat and...live?

Could this be called living, he wondered, when each one of his bodily functions was monitored by a quietly humming machine, whose red and amber eyes peered out of the curtained gloom of the hospital room at him? At his elbow loomed some-thing vaguely shaped like a metal tree—the tree from which he'd fallen, he thought for a moment, then realized that was a delusion—and from its cold metallic branches hung four bottles trickling liquid into his collapsing veins.

Fruit for the dying, he thought wryly. Fruit of the glucose and antibiotics and painkillers and whatever else these modern doctors thought they should pump into his tired old system in their grandiose effort to keep him alive one more hour, one more day.

"Heroic efforts" these healers called it, unaware of the irony.

He saw his bruised wrist, grotesquely over-swollen from the seeping of intravenous liquids, where the tubes pierced his skin. He had been grafted, had become one with the tree now.

And there was a cold tube that thrust up into his nose, that wormed its way down into his old lungs, pumping out the fluid, dark and yellow, that filled them and obscured his breathing. And a tube had been inserted into his groin, the waste fluids flowing into a plastic bag hanging at the side of the bed. He couldn't even have the privacy of that any longer.

His throat hurt. He couldn't touch it, because he couldn't move, but he suspected he had had a tracheotomy to allow another tube to be shoved into his body. He saw an obscenely thick blue plastic hose snake away to a machine in which what looked like a small inverted accordion rose and fell. That kept him breathing.

Another heroic effort.

He coughed, a wracking liquid sound, and watched the needles on the monitor jump, the accordion pump up and down. He pulled his dry lips back into a smile.

He had pneumonia. He knew that now.

Elderly people usually got pneumonia when they went to the hospital. But then the doctors and nurses would cure it with their wonder drugs—usually—and the elderly people would get well eventually, and they would go home, more feeble than before, and they would live their lives until they got something else, something that hurt more, something more fatal than pneumonia.

In the old days, when he had been young, if he'd fallen from that tree and hurt himself this way, his family would have simply moved him into the front bedroom, and the family physician would have visited, and shaking his head sadly, would have pronounced his impending death. And there would have been no visit to the hospital, no effort to prolong, because nothing would have helped, nothing could be done. And maybe that was the way it should have been. Within a few hours, maybe days, he would have died, dignity intact, a whole man, not whittled away until he was something less human, something slightly more than a machine.

His uncle had been injured on the farm, had fallen into a piece of the machinery, and when the hired hands had found him, hours later, the man, only in his forties, had still clung somehow to life. They'd carried him back to the house, and the old man remembered visiting that very day. To say good-bye to his uncle, who was conscious to the very end. The man had been surrounded by those he loved and those who loved him, amid his own house, on his own farm. And he had died. Whole. With dignity.

His uncle had given him his watch, one of those old gold pocket types that hung from chains no one wore any more, and the old man had always cherished it, for it was the one thing that he had of his uncle, the one thing that would always recall the man's cheerful face and good-natured laugh and wonderful long-winded stories about the land and the animals. He'd had that watch in his pocket the day he fell out of the tree. When he landed, he had heard it crunch underneath him, and he knew then that after all this time it had finally been broken, and that had saddened him even more than his accident.

His accident.

The old man couldn't blame his wife or his daughter or even his granddaughter. Not really. They had just thought they were helping him when they called the ambulance and the emergency squad had picked up the bloody pieces and rushed him to this hell. They didn't know the agony he would be in. He didn't blame them. Not much.

He wished he could cry, but he was unable.

He had never thought he would die. Not really. Not consciously. He had always been so strong, so fit. Never been ill, not really, except for that one time in the sixties when he'd come down with that damned Hong Kong flu or whatever was going around then and had been laid up for nearly two weeks. Had never been to the hospital; he even had his appendix and tonsils yet. Not many old-timers could claim that, he thought proudly. He'd watched the others around him die, first his mother, then his father, aunts and uncles and cousins, his older brother and sisters. All gone before him. He lived on and on, and he knew that there was nothing to stop him.

Until now.

He heard a cheerful feminine voice, a youthful voice that had never suffered excruciating pain, and he knew it was time for some damned procedure that the hospitals insisted upon inflicting on sick people, like taking his temperature or his blood pressure or his pulse. And what did it matter any more, these silly things, he wondered, when he was going to die.

She left, and it was quiet again, except for the machines, the harshness of his breathing.

He hated the cards that the nurses read to him in their syrupy every-so-bright voices. "Get Well Soon" and "Hope You're on Your Feet Soon" and "Heard You Had an Accident!" some of them said. He would have laughed at those feeble sentiments, had he been able to. In his life he had sent many of those cards; how meaningless they had been, since all he'd done was scrawl his name under some patently syrupy sentiment. Far better if he'd sat down and written a personal note. But he hadn't. And now in a long life of few regrets, he regretted that.

He hated the phone calls—didn't everyone know they brought bad news? Phone calls which he received daily, even though his family and friends had been informed he couldn't talk. He heard his wife speaking in a low tone, and he hated it because he couldn't understand what she was saying, yet he knew it wasn't good.

But most of all, he hated the flowers. Especially the roses, because they reminded him of his mother. And he had not thought about her for a long time. He couldn't recall her face as well as he once had; it was more a shadowy form than anything solid. He couldn't remember her voice, either, except that it had been soft. After all, he had been only a small child when she died. But he did remember standing by her bedside and looking down at her wasted form and smelling the roses, their reeking perfume churning his empty stomach.

It was soon after that his father began spiraling downward into his own grave with the help of the bottle. And it was after his mother's death that his father began to beat him, and his older brother. And it was only a year later that his father had struck his brother too hard, once too often, and even though they rushed him to the hospital right away, the boy never came out of the coma. Dead at the age of thirteen. Dead by his own father's hand.

The drinking worsened, and every night his father came home from work and drank and shouted and cursed. He and his sisters kept to themselves. He did for himself; he would not ask his father for anything—not now. His younger brother retreated into a dream world, where no one could reach him, unless he allowed it.

He left home, then, at seventeen. His sisters and brother cried, but he couldn't stand it any longer. He had to be on his own. And that was the way it had been all his life, even after he married, even after he had children. Up to the end.

And now he was dependent upon someone else, upon something else for life, and he hated it. How he wished he could pull these hated tubes out of his body and fling them as far away as possible, but he couldn't. He could only lie there, and blink and think, and pass the time until his death.

And the days passed in a daze, a blur brought on by his medication and the extent of his injuries and all-consuming pain. He could mark the passage of time by the dripping of the fluids into his veins, by the smell of the dying flowers, by the malfunctioning of his body. Sometimes he saw his uncle in the room, and they would talk, sometimes the shadowy form of his mother, who would weep, and sometimes the old man would see his father. But for him the old man had no words.

The grayness seeped into him, even as the life-sustaining liquids did, and he dreamed, and woke, and didn't know the difference.

And now his family were all coming to bid him a farewell. They didn't say that, of course, but he knew. He wasn't dumb. He wasn't senile. He wasn't dead.

Yet.

There was his wife, and she was being absurdly brave, although her eyes were reddened; he could see that; and she sniffed a lot into her handkerchief. He wished he could hold her one last time, say that he was sorry for all the times he had yelled when he hadn't wanted to. But he couldn't. And his daughter, that pitiful bitch was there—she married a man weaker than herself—and her sassy brat. The girl's face was grim; he knew she wouldn't miss him. He grimaced at her, but because his teeth weren't in, it weakened the expression. She turned away. No doubt disgusted with him. And yet she was the most like him, of all the family. She would have hated to hear that, he thought. She would have denied it vehemently, but it was true, nonetheless. But what did she know yet? She was only fifteen; time enough for her to learn.

His younger brother, reeking of alcohol and who'd never said much in his entire life, but who now just clasped his hand tightly, while his sister-in-law, with her damned forties hair-do and heavily mascaraed eyes and prissy lips, couldn't meet his eyes. She kept blowing her nose. The hypocrite. He'd never liked her; she's always detested him for his independence, his non-need of the family. At least his good-for-nothing son wasn't there; had the good sense to stay away. The boy—no, the man— was too much like his grandfather.

They were a reassuring lot, the old man thought. No one spoke to him, no one reassured him that he would make it, after all; he supposed they had nothing left to say to him.

Well, he certainly didn't have anything left to say to them.

He endured. Day after day, long night after long night. One hospital shift after another, one cheerful nurse after one cheerful orderly. He saw the passing of light and dark through the oblong window across the room, and sometimes he thought he saw it raining. Days were passing. His life was passing. Trickling away with the seconds and minutes.

In and out of the grayness, voices like the humming of over-head wires.

He didn't know what he wanted. He wanted to live, he thought; he didn't want to die. But if he had to live like this, only half a man, if he couldn't be himself and get up and around—

If only he had another chance. Even with that, he wasn't sure.

And all he heard was the rasping of his breath, the thrum-ming of the machines, the harshness of the accordion. Up and down, *pause*, up and down, and up and—over and over until he hated the sound.

And the day had come, and the light in the room had flickered briefly then dimmed, and his wife's face had been floating above his own as she gazed with tears down at him, and he heard her first talking, almost pleading, then weeping, and beyond her in the grayness, he thought he saw someone else, a woman, but he couldn't be sure, couldn't see very well, and then:

He *escaped.*

* * * * * * *

When David Farrister woke up, he knew he was dead. He had died. Was gone. Passed over. Was no more.

Dust to dust.

And yet here he was in his all-too-familiar silver and maroon bedroom, in his own twenty-year-mortgaged home just a few miles north of Philadelphia, and not in the whiteness of a sterile hospital. Here he was surrounded comfortingly by the memorabilia and junk and incredible accumulation of all his thirty-seven years. Here he was.

Slightly dizzy, he got up, feeling the scratchiness of the faded carpet under his bare feet. One wadded sock stuck out from under the bed. He looked around the room, taking in the hand-made bookcases along one wall, the numerous framed diplomas flanking the door, the nude drawing in charcoal that his mother had done once and which had shocked his grandmother. He grinned at the memory. The window was open and a brisk cool breeze caressed him and ghosted the sheer curtains back and forth. And he realized he was nude. Where were his pajamas?

Frowning, he moved across the room, and jerked open the top drawer of the oak bureau. There they were. Tan with the blue trim, neatly folded up as he recalled. His fingers brushed the monogram. But he remembered putting them on last night. He had showered after Sammantha left before midnight, and come in here, still dripping slightly, and pulled them out—

But here they were, fresh from the laundry, crisp and clean.

Frowning slightly, he scratched his side and stood there, looking down at his pajamas, then at his toes, and remembered nothing at all.

Slowly David walked into the bathroom, flicked on the overhead light, and stared at himself in the full-length mirror.

The face there, with its taut skin and wrinkleless smoothness, and the day's growth of dark beard, that face there was of a young man. The body was that of a man in his prime. The eyes blue and bright, clear, unhazed with pain and death.

Why did he remember an old face: One with grizzled beard, and pouches, and sags, and seams? A body with broken bones? A hospital room filled with strangers who stared at him with sad eyes? A room filled with the scent of dying flowers?

Why?

Slowly, not understanding what had happened, he shaved, methodically, as if doing it for the first time. He splashed on his after-shave lotion, crisp and clean and *alive*, and rolled on his deodorant, smelling the almost medicinal freshness of it.

He dressed slowly, so slowly, so methodically. He selected each article of clothing carefully, and held his shoes as if he had never seen them before. They were expensive leather ones from Italy. He ran a finger along the gold-tipped toe. He frowned again. He was savoring, tasting all the activities he took for granted, all the day-to-day activities.

As if—as if— He grinned.

He knew what had happened.

He had cheated death. He had escaped. He had left one life— but entered another.

Smiling, he padded out into the sunny kitchen with its white laminate cabinets and Italian tile counters, and made a breakfast of dry cereal and cranberry juice and strong black tea, and as he sat in the tiny breakfast nook, he sipped and ate slowly, and stared out into the garden in the backyard, at the robins pulling up worms from his garden, at the starling nibbling at the tender young plants that struggled to live.

To live.

That's what he would do, again. He'd been given another chance.

Whistling, he picked up his leather briefcase from where he had tossed it on the couch the evening before—a lifetime ago, he told himself with a slight chuckle—and walked out the door of his house, past the rosebushes that were just beginning to bud. He glanced at them from the corner of his eye. He didn't like roses; he would have to have them dug up; would replace them with azaleas or something.

He walked down the street, and caught the bus into town and walked, taking long energetic strides, aware of the buildings for the first time, walked into his ad agency and nodded to his employees and talked to them and went to his office.

His secretary had a single white rose bud in a cut crystal vase on her desk. He smiled at her, and she smiled back.

"From an admirer?" he asked, nodding toward the rosebud.

Her overly plucked eyebrows drew together slightly. "Don't you recall?"

He smiled, forcing the expression. "Of course." He winked.

She grinned.

He closed the door behind him and sat down behind the cluttered desk.

He began working.

And during the long hours of the morning none of the men or women in the agency noticed anything different. They treated him the same as always. But of course, he had seen them only the day before.

The day before. Before his death. He laughed softly to himself, then picked up his pen and began scribbling a note.

There was the usual amount of work, and new accounts to be reviewed, and an old client to take to lunch because she was thinking of leaving the agency after all this time but wasn't really sure she wanted to do that, and he needed to sweet-talk her into staying. The silly old bitch. He'd had a lot of trouble with her since he'd taken over, and he'd really preferred letting her go, but there was the money to consider. A hell of a lot of money.

And he did all this.

And at six-thirty he left the office—early finally, his secretary said with a smile—and napped as he took the bus back out to his street, and he was walking around the bus, and he was thinking ahead, thinking of the next day and all the appointments he knew he would have to keep even though he'd like to take some time off, when he heard the sound and realized something was *wrong.*

There was the squealing sound of brakes slammed on, the sound of something big skidding, and a long high-pitched shriek that seemed to be coming from his own throat—a throat that hurt because of the tubes, he could feel them, feel them snaking down his throat—and he saw the twin headlights bearing done on him, glowing red and amber, and then....

Darkness and the smell of roses.

* * * * * * *

When Mary Mike woke up out of the grayness, she knew she was dead. She had died. Was gone. Passed over. Was no more.

Dust to dust.

It had been a strange dream. She had dreamed she was a young man, a man in a strange city, who had— She did not want to remember any more. She did not understand her dream, and it disturbed her greatly. She did not have many dreams.

She rose slowly, and still in her nightgown, said her prayers, facing the small silver crucifix on the white wall, and then crossed herself, and slowly, so slowly because the rheumatism was coming into her knees these days and she was always so stiff in the morning, she got to her feet and washed her face and her hands. She dressed and shuffled to breakfast.

She did not talk to the other sisters of her dream, for they were an order vowed to silence. During the meal, though, she watched the faces of the other women, almost twenty of them, and their faces were peaceful, serene, and very intent on the breakfast before them. Surely they did not have dreams such as hers.

She returned to her room for her missal and walked to the chapel, and there she talked to her confessor, just as she had done the day before, and the day before *that*, and each day she had been here.

And the priest said much the same thing he had that day before—that her sins were very small and thus only a tiny penance must be done, even though she knew he was wrong for her sins were great—and she knew that she must tell him of her strange dream, but she was afraid. Afraid that he would condemn her for dreaming of being in a man's body. Was this a sin? Mary Mike asked herself, confused. A sin to dream that? But, how much control did someone have over one's dreams?

In the end she did not tell the priest. She would keep it to herself and in time, in time, the dream would fade, for it really wasn't a sin, she insisted, and she would forget.

Forget about that young man. Forget about the car hitting him. Forget about her death. *His* death.

She was not in her thirties, but rather sixty-three years of age. Not so young any more. But not so old, either. She had many good years ahead of her. Didn't Sister Catherine say that all the time, and wasn't Sister Catherine—so close to a hundred years now and eighty years a nun—always correct?

Always. Mary Mike would live on and on and on. Forever living.

Until she died, said a small voice, pious in tone. But she shrugged that off.

She had escaped, one part of her said. Escaped from death, glorious death.

Mary Mike shuddered, then hastily crossed herself, and glanced around, as if fearing someone had heard that voice speak.

She walked out to the garden, along a line of trees, and strangely they bothered her. She lowered her eyes until she was past them, and then gingerly dropped to her knees and picked up the trowel from the gardening box she had left it in yesterday...a lifetime ago...and thrust it into the soil and turned it over, looking at the fat earthworms as they wriggled in the light. She smiled and pulled out the roots of a weed and tossed in into the weed pile.

Behind her the roses nodded in the breeze, and the scent of roses blew on the wind.

She had always been sickly, and was pleased when the nuns took her. She couldn't work long hours, and the Mother knew that, so she had been assigned to the garden because she so enjoyed seeing the plants grow. She sat back and wiped her forehead with the back of her hand, then began troweling again.

She closed her eyes and through the red and amber light saw a hospital room and the starkness of the white walls, and she saw a ring of people standing. Waiting. A death watch.

She frowned, then swiped at a trickle of sweat beading down her cheek.

She worked on and on in the sun, oblivious of the hours, oblivious to her rapid breathing, of the sweat pouring down her forehead and her back now. Worked on and on, because she really must finish working on the herb garden because Mother expected it before the end of July and that was only a few days away. Worked so that she would forget the young man and everything associated with the dream.

Worked and worked until the garden tool dropped from her numbed fingers, worked until the earth whirled around her, and she saw a blue accordion and tubes snaking around and twisting up a tree, and she tumbled forward to lie, her cheek pressed into the soft warm soil, to lie in the sun, to rest just a few minutes, that was all.

To rest. To escape.

She tried to call out, even though speech was forbidden. Tried to, and she shouted and yelled, because this one time she knew they surely wouldn't mind just this one time.

But no one heard. No one came. And finally there was nothing but....

Darkness and the smell of roses.

* * * * * * *

He opened his eyes into the grayness, and he knew he was dead. He had died. Was gone. Passed over. Was no more.

Dust to dust.

He was no longer in the hospital room. But neither was he the young man, nor the old nun.

He was himself, the old man who had fallen from a tree and broken himself into so many pieces that none of the doctors or nurses could put him back together.

He had a great fall.

He had not escaped after all.

He would have laughed...had he been able.

The scent of roses was very strong, and he tried to move, but could not. The roses were very close—he realized they had been laid across his chest, and he wrinkled his nose in disgust. He hated their very touch on his cold skin. And distantly, he heard a man's voice droning, and the sounds of sobbing. *Ashes to ashes, dust to dust*, the man was saying.

Dust to dust, the old man thought, and he smiled.

Smiled wildly as the first clod of dirt pelted down upon the coffin.

Smiled and screamed into the grayness, where there was no escape, where he would lay, awake, unable to escape, for all time.

DEAD POSSUMS

It was raining and nearly dark and already beginning to get foggy. Damn, how he hated the fog. Hank Strasak was dead-dog tired after a workday that began at five a.m., and now all he looked forward to was kicking off his shoes and lying back on the lumpy couch in the living room until Mary-Ann called him for dinner.

That was, if Mary-Ann was home.

They'd been having a few problems lately. Big problems. What an understatement. He tried to grin and caught a glimpse of himself in the rearview mirror. The gray light of dusk washed out his normally dark skin color, and he looked like he had rictus. He relaxed his facial muscles, and the frown that formed looked far more natural on his heavy features. A curl of untrimmed hair flopped into his eyes and he blew at it.

The car veered slightly, forcing his attention back to his driving. Damn, he'd better watch what he was doing. He'd nearly gone off the road back there.

Something gray flashed against the darker gray of the street, and without thinking he tapped the horn, then realized it wouldn't do any good. He applied the brakes, but the creature was already under the wheels. He felt the sickening thump, slammed on the brakes. The car fishtailed to a stop alongside a deserted orange traffic cone, and he sat there for a moment before getting out and walking back to the animal.

A possum. And it was about as dead as it could be. He stared down at the blood-flecked fur and felt a little sick. It was the first time he'd run over anything. The first time. He walked around to the front of the car and stared down at the splash of blood already beginning to wash away in the rain.

He got in the car and drove away. He would be home soon. Home.

* * * * * * *

"I'm home, hon!" he called as he walked into the house on Ashley St. He was careful not to slam the door; Mary-Ann had told him many times before that she hated when he slammed the door, and since then he'd been very careful not to do it. Except, of course, when he was pissed at her and didn't care what got her angry.

Nothing. The house was silent.

No Mary-Ann. No Heather. Where was she? She should have been home from school by now. Christ, she should have been doing her homework. He knew she had a math test tomorrow, and they'd planned on him quizzing her the night before.

So where were they?

He walked through the hushed house, alien with its emptiness. He glanced in Heather's neat bedroom with its pictures of horses and cats, salvaged from magazines and pinned on the walls, in their bedroom, in the kitchen. No one. Shrugging, he returned to the bedroom to get out of his damp clothing. As he changed, he realized how long it had been since he felt her presence there. Too long. Once in dry jeans and shirt, he returned to the kitchen to look out the window over the sink at the backyard. He could barely see it now in the early darkness, but that didn't matter. He knew each inch of that yard.

He was proud of it, that little space of greenery. He'd worked long hours on weekends to put in the lawn and the flower beds along the neat wooden fence, and almost every Sunday he was out there raking or trimming or just admiring his work.

At work they called him a farmer.

They also called him a Pollack. Czech, he repeated he didn't know how many times. I'm Czech—Bohemian—and they just laughed and called him a Pole. And told him another insulting joke about a Polish couple on their wedding night.

God, how he hated them and that miserable job. The glass factory had been founded by his grandfather, who'd come to this country from Bohemia in the last decade of the previous century. He'd brought with him the fine technique of glass-making that made Bohemia glass so famous.

Grandfather Heinrich Strasak had built the factory from the ground up, and it had become well-known throughout the country, and then his father had inherited it. That's when the problems had begun. His father had no head for business, and by the time Hank was old enough to know what was going on, his father had lost the factory, and now the grandson of its founder was working in it, just like any other guy in town.

It wasn't fair, Hank thought, not for the first time; but that was the way it was, and there wasn't much he could do. Still, it galled him. Particularly as it remained the Strasak Glass Works, and each day when he drove under the wrought-iron arch proclaiming the name, he flinched.

He pushed away from the sink and sat down. Nearly six, and they weren't back. He made a sandwich of ham and cheese and drank a beer, and by the time the last crumb was wiped up, he was still alone. He hadn't bothered with the light, and sat in complete darkness watching the rain as it splattered down the windowpanes, and thought of the possum.

Poor thing.

He sighed and rubbed a hand over his face, then got another beer and trailed into the living room. It was dark here, too, and he wondered what Mary-Ann would do if she came home then and found him in a dark house. She'd know he was brooding again, and why had she married him when he was just a grumpy ol' Pole.

Czech, he would reply wearily, and wonder why she couldn't remember that after twelve years of marriage. He remembered that she was German and English. It wasn't hard.

But Mary-Ann, he knew, didn't have much time for him or for remembering such things as his birthday or their anniversary, or for sitting down in the evenings and just talking with him. Not since she discovered her new religion. When they were first married she'd worked in an office, but after Heather was born, she'd stayed home. He didn't mind, although it would have been nice to have two incomes. Still, he liked having her here for Heather. And she never complained, so he supposed she didn't mind, either.

But when Heather was four, Mary-Ann got interested in some really weird stuff. Restlessness, he thought. She bought those screaming-headline tabloids at the supermarket and read them to him at dinner. He laughed and said they were all made-up stories, and she got mad, and threw a plate at him. Luckily it missed. But it didn't stop there.

She took yoga lessons; that didn't last long before being replaced by est, and in turn by Gestalt, water therapy, Scientology, and nirvanaism. A few years ago she announced she was "going" vegetarian and she refused thereafter to touch any meat—not only wouldn't she eat it, she wouldn't prepare dishes with meat in them. So he shopped after work and bought the hamburger and hot dogs and pork chops, and at Thanksgiving, when they weren't going to her folks' house, he fixed the turkey. Again, he didn't mind.

The beer can was empty, so he tossed it into the garbage and fetched another one. He sat down in the living room.

One day last year he got a phone call at work. He listened quietly, then went down to bail his wife out of jail. By the time he got back, everyone knew where he'd been and why, and they were laughing at him. Oh, not always outright, of course, but he could tell. As he went by his co-workers, they'd fall silent, as if they'd been talking about him, or a moment later someone would giggle. That's when he'd told them to stuff it, and Old Man Marsh's widow called him in and reamed him out on his attitude.

It was even harder on Heather, though. Her classmates laughed at her, called her names, and said her mother was a criminal and a nut and that she was just as nutty. She cried at night when he tucked her in and asked why her mother was different, and not knowing the answer, he said she was just being kind to animals. How could he say that her mother really was a nut?

The animal-rights group Mary-Ann had joined wasn't just any ordinary humane group, he had realized then. It was a militant organization not content in simply writing letters to senators and congressmen. It wanted action. Immediate action, and it didn't care how it got it. And it sure as hell didn't mind the headlines it got along the way. The group, Mary-Ann informed him, was prepared to take up arms in defense of the animals— and even to die in that defense.

Sure, he liked animals. He had a dog as a kid, but he wasn't about to treat it like a human. This group thought they were. Mary-Ann and her friends had gone to a medical laboratory just below North Hill to protest the use of animals in experiments. She was busted by the police for spray-painting "Thou shalt not kill" on the outside of the building, while her buddies were busy inside letting the rabbits and rats and cats and dogs out of the wire cages. Her friends got busted, too. "Liberating God's creatures," they'd claimed, and they chanted biblical verses from their cells. That's when he learned they were mixing religion with their politics.

He didn't talk to her on the drive home nor all of that night, and it was then he realized how far apart they'd grown. He thought once or twice about divorce, but wasn't sure he was ready for it. Most of the time everything seemed to go all right.

There was, of course, that time when they were at the Fletchers and their daughter Jill wanted to show the new trick she'd spent all week teaching her golden retriever. Before the little girl could start, Mary-Ann stood up and coldly announced that she didn't want to see the trick because it was cruel to force animals to do something they obviously didn't want to do. Jill's face darkened and she ran crying from the room, and that's when Hank stood and said they better be running along.

He yelled all the way home, and so had she, and Heather, crying, huddled in the back with her hands over her ears.

All that time he put up with the multitude of booklets strewn across the table at breakfast time and the stacks of photocopied flyers that the group put up in markets and on utility poles and under windshield wipers of cars in parking lots, but which had to be stored someplace, and somehow his house got volunteered. He even put up with the occasional meeting held there, and when he knew the group was coming over, he'd take Heather out to a movie or to walk or to a special snack at one of the restaurants on the harbor.

They no longer made love. She lay on her side of the bed, and he on his, and whenever he rolled over and touched her, she flinched. Soon he stoped that. She didn't call him by name anymore, either, and strangely that bothered him more than the other. She called him "he" or "your father" when she talked to Heather. Never "Hank," and sometimes at night, when he couldn't sleep, he would think he had become a nonentity to her.

She stopped taking care of the house, and he would come home to find not only the breakfast dishes still in the sink, but those from the previous night, as well as an assortment of ants and roaches. He endured unmade beds, and mildewed towels and tiles, stacks of paper everywhere, a film of dust coating everything, and with Heather he made it an adventure on weekends to see what they could clean up next in the house. They managed to keep up with the housework most of the time, and if Mary-Ann was aware, she gave no indication. She continued her phone calls and pounded away at their old Olympia typewriter by the hour, drafting one letter after another.

And he tried to understand. But he couldn't; not anymore. It was as if she'd crossed a line somewhere and was moving ahead, while he was standing still, watching her as she faded into the distance. The farther away she got, the less he understood. He didn't like the idea of experiments; no one did, but to actually destroy laboratory equipment worth thousands of dollars...to disrupt research...to get violent...that was incredible.

And to upset a little girl because she taught her puppy a trick—he couldn't forgive her for that. Not ever. Nor had the Fletchers, apparently, because they were never invited back, even though he saw Jack at work almost every day.

And then there was the time the group started petitioning the City Council to outlaw the annual winter dogsled races because they were cruel to dogs. He'd blown up then, too, as he reminded her that dogs had always worked for humans—that's why they'd been domesticated, for God's sake, and one of their tasks had been to pull sleds across snow and ice. She'd countered that that activity was no longer necessary, and if a dog had a choice, it wouldn't pull a sled.

He argued; she countered. They got nowhere, and finally parted in silence. Silence kept them away each other the next week, too, and that was when Heather began sucking her thumb again. Ten years old and she had a habit like that. Disgusted, he tried to stop her, but Mary-Ann told him to leave the girl alone. She was simply expressing herself.

He and his pillow and a ratty old afghan his mother had crocheted when he was nineteen moved out onto the couch that night and remained there.

Sometimes he thought he was living a nightmare. Sure, he knew he didn't have it as bad in some ways as other guys at work—like the guy who'd lost his family in the fire—but why had his life turned out this way? What had his marriage become?

He got another beer and clasped it lightly in his hands. Against his skin the cold metal tingled, awakening him, and he stood. He couldn't wait here all night; not when it looked like Mary-Ann wasn't coming home. She'd left him, then. But gone... where? He drained the can, then tossed it into the garbage and wondered with surprise where all those other cans had come from. The garbage can was completely full.

It didn't help, of course, that he suspected she was seeing some guy in the group? Suspected? Hell, he was pretty damned sure of his fact. And he bet right now she and Heather were over there.

And he was gonna get his family back.

* * * * * * *

It wasn't all that hard to locate them, after all. He just looked in her address book and when he found the name of the group's leader, he knew he had the right guy. He checked the address, then drove over there.

The rain sluiced over him as he got out of the car and went up the walk. The doorbell was one of those with a tiny light in it, and it stared like an orange eye at him. Grimly he thumbed it. The door opened, and a man he'd seen several times at his house stood behind the screen door.

"Oh, hi, Hank. I didn't expect to see you here."

"I bet not."

"Want to come in?"

"Yeah." Hank jerked the screen open before the other man could make a move. "Richard, isn't it?" he asked as he eyes searched the living room. The other man nodded. Hank didn't see anything out of the ordinary there...no hint of them.

Almost as if Richard had read his mind, he grinned. "The others are downstairs."

"Downstairs?"

"Basement," Richard called over his shoulder as he led the way. "Made it into a den a few years ago. Thought I'd need that for the kids to play in, but when my wife left me, she took the kids. So I just rattle around in this big house."

Yeah, until you rattle around with my wife.

He could hear the voices now, and knew that even now they wouldn't be socializing.. Not these people. They were fanatics. They didn't have time for anything but their Cause. This was Business, after all.

They were there, both Heather and Mary-Ann. His wife looked up. Her blonde hair was neatly pulled back, her face bereft of makeup. That was another thing he blamed on the group. She didn't style her hair now, or wear lipstick or eye shadow, and she wore dowdy clothes. She looked like she'd aged fifteen years.

The group members paused in their heated discussion as they recognized Hank. Heather, whose dark head had been bent studiously over a jigsaw puzzle, waved at him. He smiled at her.

"What are you doing here?" It was Mary-Ann.

No greeting. Hank repressed the belch he felt spewing up from his stomach, even though he wanted to let it out so it would shock these people.

"I gotta talk with you."

"Can't it wait?"

"No."

She saw he meant it and excused herself and followed him back up to the stairs. She glanced back once, and he knew Richard was watching him.

"What's this all about?" she demanded once they were in the living room. "How did you find me?"

"Why didn't you leave a note? I was getting worried. Something could have happened."

She folded her arms across her chest. "Well, nothing did, so what do you want? I don't have time to stand here. I've got to get back to work."

"I want you to come home with me."

"That's impossible."

"I want us to go home together and make love, and then talk afterward."

She stared at him coldly. "I can't."

"Hank." His voice was pleading. "Can't you even say my name?" She didn't answer and he moved away.

"You've been drinking again."

She made it sound like he got drunk regularly. Sure, he enjoyed a few beers after work, but he never drank the hard stuff. She knew that. But with her conversion, she'd also given up alcohol and smoking. He wondered when she would be nominated for sainthood.

"Just a few beers."

"You smell like an old wino."

"You on speaking terms with winos now?" The humor was lost on her; on him, as well. Her foot tapped. A bad sign. "Come on, Annie, come home now. We'll put on some good music, snuggle a little."

"Don't call me Annie. You know I hate that."

"What does he call you?"

"What?"

"I said what does he call you?" He jerked his chin toward the stairs. "I bet he doesn't call you Mrs. Strasak. Are you having an affair with him?" He held his breath.

Her gaze met his. "Yes."

He released the air. There, it was out in the open, and surely now he would feel better. Why, though, did he feel a knot twisting inside his guts, like the beer had gone sour or something? Why did he feel like he wanted to explode and yell and scream?

Instead, he shifted his weight from one foot to the other, then said: "How long has it been going on?"

"A year."

"That's all?"

"Yes."

"Yeah, you wouldn't lie. You might get struck down by a lighting bolt."

"I'm going back."

"No, you're not." He grabbed her arm before she could turn around.

"Let go."

"No." His fingers tightened.

"You're hurting me."

"You've hurt me for years now, Annie, and you didn't give a damn. I wish I could hurt you, but I don't think there's any way." He released her arm just as Richard walked into the room.

"Is everything all right here?"

The perfect host, Hank thought, and felt his head begin aching, as if a band were tightening around it. She was probably right; he had drunk too much.

"Go on back," he said wearily. "I don't want to keep you away from your little fuzzy critters any longer."

She left. Without a backward look.

Hank let himself out quietly, and when he got in the car, he sat in the front seat, staring at the house. He didn't see the car door open or close, and was startled to her Heather's voice.

"I'm lonely, Daddy."

"Oh, baby." He pulled her to his chest and stroked her rain-dampened hair. And knew what he could do to hurt his wife.

He kissed the top of his daughter's head, then started the car and drove home. He told her to sit in the car while he was in the house just a minute. Inside, he first packed a little suitcase with some of her clothing and favorite toys, then pulled a large case down and began tossing his things into it.

When he was done, he turned off the last light and left. The house stood black in the fog.

* * * * * * *

He took the curve wide, the car swinging over the solid yellow line into the left lane of what in the town one mile back was Port Boulevard, and Heather squealed with fright. The windshield wipers squeaked as they scraped an arc across the glass.

"Daddy, please," she pleaded, "slow down."

For answer, he pressed down on the accelerator, and the car leaped ahead in the wet darkness, its twin lights raking the dense forest that pressed closely on both sides. A wisp of fog curled around some of the tree trunks; leaves, plastered by the rain, slipped silently to the forest floor. Something thumped under the tires, and Heather twisted around on the seat to look back at the dead creature, painted a hellish red by the taillights.

"Daddy, you ran over an animal."

"It's just a possum," he said to the accusing tone, and tried not to feel guilty. "Sit down, and put your seat belt on like I told you."

Quietly she obeyed, and in the faint greenish light from the dashboard he saw the tears on her cheeks. She lifted one corner of her Sylvester and Tweety tee-shirt and rubbed her eyes.

He shook his head, then jabbed at the cigarette lighter. She really liked animals; loved them, that is, and that was beginning to worry him. She cried over the horses getting killed in the westerns; didn't care if the good guy got it. Just the goddamn horses. And she'd leave the room if an animal on TV got hurt or killed. That was too much like her mother. He lit his cigarette. She was the only good thing that had come out of his marriage, and he wondered if it was too late for her. Had her mother already poisoned her?

Another thump under the tires jerked his attention back to the road. That had to be a pothole, didn't it? They would be reaching the interstate in a bit and when they did, he would—they would—be leaving Greystone Bay behind for good.

Rotten town, rotten job, rotten wife. Worse...a rotten life.

It would be different up north. He'd go to Boston, maybe, and look around. Boston would need good workers. He'd had a lot of different jobs in his lifetime, so he was qualified. God knows, he could learn quickly, too. Ash dribbled down his shirt front, and he coughed, then wiped the back of his hand across his mouth. His stomach was sour from all the beer he'd drunk earlier, and he was beginning to feel pressure in his bladder.

"Daddy, slow *down*."

That was the tenth or eleventh time, and he was getting tired of it. He knew she was right, but he wanted to get as far away from Mary-Ann tonight as possible. And the faster the better. He hunched over the wheel, shifting his weight from one buttock to the other. He was already stiff and they hadn't been on the road for ten minutes yet. It was gonna be a long night.

He tried not to think about what he'd done. He knew the fault wasn't all Mary-Ann's. Two made a marriage; two unmade it. He knew he'd said and done things that had only made the situation worse, and sometimes he'd just baited her so that she got angry, and yet...was that just the end of it after all this time? Not a farewell? Not even a handshake? And she still hadn't called him by name. He felt tears at the corners of his eyes.

He glanced at Heather, saw she had her favorite toy, the blue rabbit, tucked under one arm. He didn't remember her bringing that with her. She was looking out the window, her forehead pressed against the glass, but he knew she was sucking her thumb.

He glanced left and saw the small bloody carcass on the shoulder of the far side. Another possum. Jeez. It was about the fifth one they'd passed so far. What was it with these dammed animals? Why did they feel obligated to throw themselves under a car's wheels? Why didn't they just stay in the woods? Why were they running out in front of him tonight? God, the first one had been that afternoon and since then it hadn't stopped.

He looked back at the slick length of the road and decided he'd better slow down. The alcohol had slowed his reflexes, and it was hard to see now. The fog—that blinding sound-sucking fog wouldn't be missed, that was for sure—was creeping in from the sea, only a few miles to the east, and he didn't want to end back up at Bay Memorial Hospital and then have Mary-Ann come in and demand to know just what the hell was going on. Or even worse...what if she didn't come at all?

Silently Heather pointed to something up ahead, and too late he saw the tiny pinpoints of light that meant the eyes of some animal that had just strayed out onto the road. He tried to brake, but once again the car ran quickly over the animal, and Heather screamed, as if it had been her own body he'd hurt.

The car slipped to one side and as he straightened, he saw the possum ahead on the wet tarmac, the animal sitting in the middle of the road just staring at him as if it had nothing better to do, and he jerked the wheel around to avoid the damned animal because he didn't like the way it was looking at him. The car went into a spin; he tried to bring it out, but the wheels locked on the slick surface, and the car skidded, then heaved itself off the road, crashing into the wide trunk of an oak with a sickening smack.

* * * * * * *

When he woke, he could feel the rain splashing on his face. And from nearby he heard the undulating wail of an ambulance or a patrol car, or maybe both. He grinned, tasting the saltiness of blood on his lips. He and Heather wouldn't be out here long, that was for sure. Someone was coming for them.

He saw the lights now strobing into the dark fog, and saw a stretcher being lifted into the back of the ambulance. Heather, then; God, he hoped she was all right. Kids generally were; they were young, healthy, she'd spring right back would his little Heather. There was nothing to worry about, was there?

He watched, though, in puzzled silence as the cop paused behind the ambulance to talk to one of the attendants. Why weren't they coming to get him? He wanted to go with Heather to the hospital. She was probably scared, probably crying, and he wanted to hold and comfort her.

"—not yet," the cop was saying as he tried to light a cigarette in the rain. Frustrated, he finally gave up, flicked the sodden mess to one side.

"—happened?"

"Looks like he might have gotten disoriented—maybe hit his head on the steering wheel—and crawled off into the woods. We're calling off the search tonight because of the fog. Can't see a thing. Hope it lifts by morning. See you back in town."

The cop slapped the attendant on the back, then they got back in their vehicles, and with sirens and lights flashing, they drove off. The only sound now was the drumming of the rain on the black pavement.

I'm here! Hank screamed, and only the wind soughing in the branches heard him. He struggled to move, but couldn't as pain like hot irons jabbed through his body. I'm here, he whimpered. Here. Alive.

The rain fell through the blinding fog, and it was only when the car was a few yards away that Hank saw the head-lights glowing. He screamed for it to stop because he was lying stretched across the highway, but the driver didn't hear him, didn't see him.

Not in the fog.

* * * * * * *

The fog and blood wetly kissed his skin.

He screamed again when the second car came speeding down the highway, and the third only minutes later. He screamed long into the night, but no one heard. Not in the fog.

RIDEAU

"Ride the Rideau," someone joked, and jostled my elbow. I tried to shift away but there were too many people around me.

Usually I avoided crowds, and while this technically didn't qualify for what I considered a crowd—it was just about a dozen people—we were crammed together by the canal. A bunch of us had come up from New York to Ottawa for the week for a computing services convention, and this being the first night of the con and thus slow, we'd gone out to sightsee; after today, we wouldn't have time for anything but countless dry computing seminars, practically from dawn to dusk.

We'd walked up Wellington to check out Parliament Hill—very impressive with its three huge buildings and copper roofs, although we didn't have time for any of the really touristy things such as the Changing of the Guard or one of the free tours. Systems Analyst Bill Fanta had muttered that it looked just like England's House of Parliament; his comment had earned him a poke in the side from Eddie Asidro's elbow. The leaves were turning color on the swaths of trees cutting their way through the city. Afternoon sunlight glinted off the cars on Pont Mackenzie King Bridge to our left, and overhead we watched a vapor trail of a plane headed for Montreal. The air was crisp, a little on the cool side, perhaps, but once you got moving you really didn't notice.

As we strolled back toward the hotel, someone—one of the Ottawans, I think—suggested that we might like to see the Rideau Canal. Of course, you couldn't go anywhere downtown without seeing it, and in fact, we could see the waterway from our hotel, but this would be up close and personal, as it were.

"The Canal," Jamie Leventhal, one of the Canadian programmers, said as we walked toward it, "is actually a chain of lakes, rivers and canal cuts, stretching for some 202 kilometers. That's about 120 miles for you metrically-challenged folks." It rose in a series of locks from the Ottawa River, and I thought it was altogether pretty impressive.

Jamie smiled. "If you'd come up in February, the Canal would be frozen over and you could have gone skating on it. There's a big winter festival here every year now."

The last—and first time—I'd ever gone ice skating was in high school. I had been with some schoolmates, and we'd skated for hours. Or rather they had stayed on the ice for hours, but I kept falling down and so gave up and sat on the side of the rink watching the people who were supposed to be my school friends. No one seemed to notice I wasn't with them any more. After a while, I had just gone home.

We decided to go for a ride, and so we paid our fares and scrambled aboard the boats. The really big ones were reserved by a trade delegation from Japan, so we had to settle for smaller craft—unless of course, we wanted to paddle our own canoes. We all declined; none of us being that adventurous.

There were just enough seats in two boats for everyone— except me. I held back by a third one, not sure what to do. I could try to shoehorn myself onto one of the already crowded vessels, but I was sure there were pretty strict regulations about how many people those boats could handle.

"I guess I'd ride in this one. Have it all to myself," I said.

While my co-workers smiled and waved, no one offered to join me.

That was only fitting, I thought a little sourly. I had sort of attached myself to their group when they'd announced back at the hotel they were going out sightseeing. No one had invited me, but then no one had precisely *not* invited me either. It was the sort of occasion where anyone could tag along. Even me.

Except I'd been uncomfortable doing just that. I was new to the office and to these people and wanted them to like me. Like? I would have settled for noticing. Back in the city I drifted through the offices and hallways on our floor like a ghost. No one spoke to me. No one dropped by my office. I worked and saw people, but people didn't see me.

I sat down. It was ludicrous—me alone in the boat. Tentatively I smiled at the canalman. He didn't smile back. He was probably French Canadian, probably from Hull across the Ottawa River, probably hated my guts because I didn't know the metric system. Trying to find the hotel today when we drove in, we'd ended up in Hull, and it was one of the accounting guys who pointed out all the signs were in French; we'd hightailed it out of there fast enough, believe me. There wasn't a French speaker among our whole group; vaguely we were all embarrassed at our reaction.

I almost laughed aloud. I was acting like this guy had seen us trespass or something.

This is ridiculous, I told myself. I didn't mind sitting here all alone. Really.

"Thanks for being my boatman, I mean, I really have to thank you for doing this...I mean, there's just the one of me, but you're probably paid the same no matter how many people are in the boat, right?" I was aware that I was babbling. Alone.

But then, no surprise here—I'd always been on the outside looking in. So, really, me by myself in the boat...I should have expected it somehow. Not for the first time did I regret coming on this trip.

I had taken this job because I knew I would have to work with people; it would, I reasoned, force me out of my shell. Only it turned out I didn't have to face the public, and only occasionally did I even have a phone call from outside.

Isolated wasn't even close to describing how I felt at work. Or at home. Or among crowds at malls, or even at the grocery store.

Sometimes it seemed I was able to step back and examine myself, and I wondered what it was that made me so different, or seem so different, and why it was that I attracted such apathy. I had tried hard throughout my life to please people, to get them to like me, but so far nothing worked.

The boats began to move, and I looked down into the water, caught a glimpse of some golden fish.

"I don't even think my own parents much liked me, although I'm not sure that 'like' is the appropriate term." I reddened when I realized I'd spoken aloud. I looked away. I think I might have understood more this benign neglect if I'd come from a huge family—say, one with twelve or fourteen kids. But I was the middle child of three. My folks had been very involved with my older brother, and my younger sister, born frail. There never seemed to be time for me. If I tried to crawl on their laps for a story, they always pushed me off and said, "Not now. Alice needs her medicine." Or else they were rushing off to Tom's soccer match or his Little League practice. Occasionally I caught them at some meal staring at me, as if to say, "Who's this?"

There was the one Christmas, too, when all the cousins and aunts and uncles had been gathered in Vermont at my grandparents'. We decorated the tree and drank hot chocolate afterward as my Grandfather solemnly passed out the presents he and Gram had gotten for the grandchildren. Each one got something...except me. They had forgotten me. I was stunned. Grandfather, to give him credit, was shocked too, and tried to recover by saying that my present hadn't arrived in the mail yet; he smiled and thought that would make the hurt all better. But I was ten and knew better. I just nodded, and watched him look at Gram under those bushy white eyebrows. Later that night as my mother tucked me into bed, I asked her why everyone always forgot me. I was feeling argumentative; I wanted to *know*.

"That's nonsense, dear," she said briskly. "No one ever forgets you."

"Gramps and Gram did tonight."

"Your present didn't arrive in time."

"Then why didn't they at least put an envelope under the tree with a note about that. It would have been *something*."

"Don't make such a fuss, Jenny. It's just a present."

But it was a *Christmas* present.

"It was supposed to be special," I whispered aloud, and for a moment I didn't know if I were in the past or the present. But the lapping of the water against the hull of the boat brought me back. I blinked, somewhat unsettled, and stared hard at the boatman. Had he reacted? Had he listened? Did I care. I shrugged.

"She forgot me at my music lesson once, too."

I had finished my piano lesson, watched as my teacher pulled away to run some errand, and I had sat outside her locked house until the sun went down. I had always been instructed to wait for my folks, not to try to walk home because we lived miles away and in between lay some fairly rough neighborhoods. I had been sitting at the curb, my arms wrapped around my legs to keep warm, when she came back four hours later. Appalled, she'd promptly driven me home to my mother, who when accused of forgetting her daughter, acidly replied that she hadn't forgotten, but hadn't had a minute to herself all day, she was behind in her errands, and she had called the teacher's house and gotten no answer so she assumed I was on my way home. I knew better, though. There had been no phone call. Mom had just forgotten.

Shortly after that I stopped the lessons. It was, I knew, too much bother for my parents to drop me off there, even though they managed to find time for all of Tom's sporting events and for all of Alice's many after-school activities. I would finish the school day and simply ride the school bus home.

Each day as I watched kids rushing to their waiting parents, I told myself I really wasn't missing anything.

In the distance I saw the spire of a church, brilliantly white against the sky.

"Church...that was my only activity, you know," I said, my tone almost apologetic. Had the boatman raised an eyebrow? A tacit go-ahead for more conversation? Or was this more confession?

"The only thing I did outside of school was go to church

each Sunday; even my parents and brother and sister didn't do that; they all liked to sleep late. In church each week I prayed that things would be different. I even talked to my priest about it, but he said I was being difficult—after all, didn't my parents provide for me, give me a wonderful home and a safe place to live? Didn't they watch out for me, and make sure I had enough to eat? He said there were thousands of children who had far less than that and would have gladly exchanged lives with me. He was right; I was being selfish. So, I started going to Mass on Wednesday. I prayed really hard."

But when I was sixteen I stopped going to church. Nothing had changed. My parents were just as neglectful. So my prayers hadn't been answered. Or even heard, I figured. Probably God had forgotten about me too. And when a lightning bolt didn't strike me for such thoughts, that simply proved what I'd believed all along.

I tried to be cheerful, tried to be responsive to other people, but it was difficult at times. They would look at me, and sometimes I wondered if I'd become transparent, if I were made of glass. If I said something, their eyes would refocus, and they would see me...for the moment.

I went off to college, one I had chosen by myself, because my parents were too occupied with getting Tom back in school after he'd been kicked out and with Alice's latest medical crisis.

"In college, I decided to change myself. Maybe, I figured, it was the way I looked, maybe that's what kept people from noticing me. My hair had always been short, so I let it grow long, and dyed its natural auburn a deep purplish red. That ought to make people *see* me. I wore red lipstick that clashed with my hair, and always tried to dress in shades of pink and red—if I'd worn black, I would simply have blended in with all the other students.

"But it was no good. I was the upraised hand consistently ignored by the professor; I was the one late with a project who was never questioned because the prof had forgotten she'd even assigned it to me. I let my natural hair color grow out, and stopped wearing the garish makeup."

Had the boatman shifted? I studied his face, but could see only shadows from the hat he wore. The sun was lower in the sky now, and things seemed to have dimmed a bit. I blinked. Sounds from the streets floated over the water in an almost disjointed way, and I could hear a group of kids on bicycles laughing as they whisked down the Promenade.

After college I'd drifted through jobs, never staying at any one too long. All were incredibly dissatisfying, or perhaps they really weren't bad; perhaps it was just me. In whatever I did, I did okay. I didn't excel, but I wasn't the worst. On yearly reviews my bosses always said I did my job satisfactorily. That was it. There was never any criticism, but then there was never any praise either.

Once I had thought about having breast implants—really incredibly *huge* ones. That, I thought wickedly, would make people notice me, but I feared that after all that expense and pain, I'd still be just as invisible as before.

As years went by I lost touch with my family. Or maybe they lost touch with me. I stopped writing to friends I made in high school and college.

More and more I felt isolated. Which is why I moved to New York, to start anew. Maybe in a different state, a different job I would do better, I would be more visible.

There's just one problem with that reasoning—you can never run from yourself.

But I'd figured out something from all this—I didn't have a really bad life; there *were* worse, far worse, I told myself, thinking of the latest crisis in the newspapers and on television. I should enjoy what I had, no matter what.

This job was turning out much the same as the others. I forced myself to talk to people, forced myself to participate in office things like football pools and holiday parties, forced and forced and forced...for what good? I couldn't expect more, could I?

And yet now all these years of neglect and being overlooked had brought me to this beautiful place. Maybe, I should move here. Maybe things would be better in Ottawa than in New York.

Maybe, maybe, maybe.

Reflected in the water were the trees and buildings close to the canal, and I raised my head to look at the sights. I could hear chattering from the two other boats, the laughter and talk drifting back to me. In my boat silence reigned. A tendril of mist curled around the boat's prow.

I wanted to ask so much about the sights I was seeing, but I feared the boatman wouldn't answer. He hadn't before; why should he now?

So I kept silent and told myself to enjoy the beautiful day. I was having a great time—wasn't I?

"Don't get me wrong," I said, this time directly to the boatman. He turned his head in my direction. "I'm not feeling sorry for myself. Not really. I have a good life, and maybe it's not all that I could have—would have—liked, but it's not bad. Not really."

Overhead the sky remained blue, and the sun, sinking slowly, burned red. I wished we had started earlier in the day. We would have had so much more time to see things; this afternoon I had felt kind of rushed.

I watched the others as they chatted, and some of the Ottawans pointed out sights. I looked at each attraction and wondered what its special story was.

Water slapped against the hull, the sound somehow reassuring.

I sat up with a jerk of my head—I had nodded off—and looked around. The mist was thicker now, and through its wispy fingers I could see the two other boats far ahead of us; there was no other traffic on the waterway.

I started to call out for Bill or Jamie, but something kept me silent. I couldn't hear any cars now, no more children laughing. Not even the sound of birds.

Shouldn't we go back? I wondered. We hadn't really discussed how long we would be out on the canal. What if they had all made dinner plans at some stop along the way? I could pass them by and never know it.

Or maybe they wanted it like that. I shrugged, and tried not to feel the pain that still went through me each time something like this happened.

Wouldn't it have been better for everyone if they had simply said to me back at the hotel that they didn't want me coming along? It would have been kinder. But people, I knew all too well, weren't kind.

"We should go back," I whispered, not wanting to raise my voice in this mist. I was tired now and wanted to go back to my room for a nap before dinner. Or maybe I would just lay down and not bother to go down to eat. I would call room service. I would sit in my room and eat by myself and watch television in a city of wonderful museums and restaurants and theatres and galleries.

I would sit. Alone. I would—

"It's too late."

Startled, I realized the boatman had spoken for the first time. "What?"

He said nothing.

"What do you mean, 'too late'?"

The mist swirled around us, licking damply at my skin, and I shivered. The sun had paled so that it was hardly a glimmer. I shifted, and realized I couldn't see either side of the canal.

The boat, the boatman, and I were all alone in this horrible grayness.

I wanted to shriek at him, then, wanted to scream for him to turn around, to stop at one of the docks so I could get off.

But it was too late then.

It's impossible now.

I should have fought back. I should have demanded the attention. But instead all I did was settle.

And now, as I ride in this boat, in this fog, I know that this is all that's left to me now.

For the rest of forever, invisible to all.

The water, and the mist.

My silent boatman....
...and me.

SKINNED ANGELS

Jim didn't want to go into the shop, but his wife insisted. "We're tourists, and we should be doing tourist-y things," she said.

He relented. After all, it was his vacation—their vacation—and they were out to have fun, or at least that was the theory. Poking around in old shops was his wife's idea of amusement; it wasn't his, but he wanted to please her. They'd had some problems recently, and this trip to Santa Fe was one of the things they'd thought might start to help.

The bell clanged over the door as Jim pushed the glass door open. Immediately he wrinkled his nose. Old dust, dried herbs, perfumes and spicy incense assaulted his senses, and beneath it was the smell of something he couldn't quite put his finger on. He wanted to sneeze, but managed to control it.

Bev was already across the room, examining some rugs heaped into mounds along one side of the store. They had a handful of Indian rugs in their house, and he hoped she wouldn't insist that they buy some more. He didn't know why he resisted everything; if wasn't as if buying one more rug would break them financially, and he actually liked Indian rugs quite a lot. "You're so negative," Bev accused him, and she was right. He *was* negative, but he couldn't seem to help it.

No, he amended with a faint smile, he was *positive* he was *negative*.

He ambled over to the ramshackle bookcase that all these stores along this little Santa Fe street—hardly more than a burro lane really—seemed to have and scanned the titles. Most were in Spanish, which he didn't know despite having lived in New Mexico for over thirty years. He had avoided learning the language, although he didn't know why because he spoke German and French, and could make himself pretty well understood in Italian. Spanish should have come to him so easily. But he hadn't wanted to learn it, hadn't seen the need, despite working with Spanish-speaking men and women ever since he got out of college.

You're just being stubborn, his mother used to say. And she was right.

Stubborn *and* negative, he thought, and wondered how anyone stood him.

He took a look around the store and saw some leather goods—boots and saddles mostly—in one section, some bright clothing hanging from a few racks, a chest that looked like it had numerous little perfume bottles on it, and all around the room stood case after case of jewelry.

If they ever outlawed jewelry in Santa Fe, the city would go belly up, he thought. That's fairly uncharitable, he realized. He could add that to his long list of growing sins.

The autumn light filtered in through the dirty window and he felt warm standing in front of the bookcase. It was a comfortable feeling, and for a moment he didn't want to move, didn't want to do anything, and it was as if he'd gone into another dimension because he couldn't hear anyone, couldn't smell anything, not even the too-sweet perfumes and incense. It was just him and the bright sunshine, and—

"Jimmy, come look at this!"

The sound of his wife's voice was like the ripping of a membrane, and he shook himself, almost more a shudder. He left the mildewing tomes and headed across the room. At first he couldn't locate her, then he saw her standing at a counter. She was being waited on by an old man.

He became aware then that there were two girls—excuse me, he chided himself, that was *young women* these days—standing not far from Bev, pointing at something in the glass case; one was talking while the other giggled. He came up alongside his wife and smiled automatically. If he did anything else, she'd want to know what was wrong, and he would say nothing was wrong, but she wouldn't believe him, and they'd go back and forth like that until something *was* the matter.

"Look, Jimmy, aren't they great?" She dangled a pair of silver earrings from her fingers, while the clerk smiled expectantly at him. She was waiting, he knew, for his response. His *positive* response.

"They're nice, honey. Really nice." Actually he thought they looked like a dozen or more other pairs of earrings she had pawed through in the dozen or more other shops they'd stopped in today.

There you go exaggerating, his teachers said, that's very unprofessional and unnecessary.

These earrings, though, had inlaid turquoise in the silver triangles, and were pretty in an unflashy way. But still....

She was watching him, waiting for him to speak the magic words, although she hardly needed permission.

"Well, Bev, if you want them, go ahead and buy them." His smile widened, and it seemed like his face was about to crack open. There, he'd said it. She had dozens of earrings in her jewelry cases, maybe more, and she had her own income and didn't need his permission to buy anything, but she always waited for him to say that.

She looked at the old man and shook her head. "Not quite right. What else do you have?"

Jim never understood that, either. He said the so-called magic words, thinking she wanted to hear him say it was all right to buy whatever, and then she always put the item back. As if she no longer wanted it. He wondered what would happen if he didn't say go ahead and buy it/them/whatever. He wasn't sure that he wanted to find out, at least not now. This was, after all, their reconciliation trip.

For the next half an hour Bev examined all the silver earrings in the three trays the old guy put up on the counter. She held one from each pair up to an ear and asked Jim for his opinion, and he smiled, his face now feeling frozen into that expression, and she'd sigh and put the earring down and pick up the next one. She went through a fourth tray, then decided to look at rings, trying each one on. The minutes ticked by, and Jim shifted from one foot to another. Behind him the warm sunshine tugged, and he wanted to stand there in the golden light and pretend to read the titles of the books even though he wasn't cold or anything, but he knew the minute he did, Bev would call to him.

And he would go to her, like an obedient dog.

He sighed.

The girls were still there, and now they were talking louder, or maybe he was listening more carefully, and the brunette was examining a strand of pale coral. It was more white than pink, and he'd never seen coral that color. She was talking about how the coral was formed from the bodies of dead sea creatures. The other girl interrupted.

"You've got it all wrong, Trisha. Actually, you see, angels die, and their skins just sort of *slough* off and drift down from Heaven into the seas, and the coral forms from the skins."

Next to him he sensed Bev crossing herself, and he felt a surge of annoyance at the gesture. She didn't go to church, hadn't been in one since before they got married—at least she couldn't blame him for that—but she still crossed herself. She still had her rosary, and he always wondered why when she'd turned her back on the church when her faith seemed so strong. His faith had left him years ago; one day he had it, the next it was gone, and he hadn't stepped inside a church since, hadn't felt the need, didn't know why anyone did.

You just don't understand. That was Bev's voice, and his mother's, and maybe that girl back in high school, the one he had dated in junior year.

It occurred to him that all the little things that annoyed him about his wife were probably what bothered her about him. Only more so, since he'd been told enough by her and his parents and everyone else that he had numerous faults. Sometimes at night as he lay next to Bev and listened to her wheezy breaths he wondered why she had married him if he possessed all these character flaws. It wasn't like he'd changed radically after marriage. He was basically the same as when he got out of college. Marriage hadn't made him any better or any worse. He thought. He was sure there were others who could tell him different.

Maybe Bev was one of those women who see a flawed man as a challenge and think that once they've married him they can change him, as if he were so much clay to be molded by her perfecting hands.

Or perhaps she liked the thrill of marrying a man so far from perfection.

Or maybe she married him, despite what everyone counseled her, because she was the type to defy everyone's good intentions.

Or maybe she just hadn't seen any of these flaws.

"Let me look at some coral," Bev was saying now.

Well, there was white coral and red coral and blue coral, and God knows what other colors waiting in other velvet trays. Out of the corner of his eye Jim could see dust motes swirling in the rays still streaming through the window. They drifted downward, and he remembered what the girl had said. Skins drifted downward. He felt the pull of the light, and yawned lazily.

Of course, there were single strand necklaces, and double strands, as well as triple. There were smooth beads, hardly larger than the thread used to string them; there were chunks of coral, and there was the branch coral that looked like so many fingers and toes hardened into bizarre angles.

Bizarre angels, he thought, and chuckled aloud, then looked away as he saw the old man and Bev staring at him.

You always laugh at your own jokes, she had once accused him after they'd argued about God knows what, and he always wondered what kind of vice that was. If that was the worst he'd ever done...laugh at his own jokes...then.... But unfortunately, it wasn't the worst of his sins. His sins were many. Sometimes they seemed to go on and on, page after page.

Sins of stubbornness, and negativity, and insensitivity, and pride. Could one be proud of the number of sins one carried around?

Probably.

Mea culpa.

"What do you think, Jimmy?"

"It's nice, hon," he replied and realized he hadn't even looked. He stared down at the necklace she'd clasped around her neck, and he imagined his hands around her neck, and how it would feel. Her skin so warm beneath his, and he shifted one from one foot to another, feeling the response in his body.

Swell. Add another sin to the list.

He moved closer and dropped a kiss on top of her head. Okay, that took care of the sin. She looked up at him, her thin lips pressed together, as if he'd goosed her or something.

"My hair...it'll get mussed," she said.

Good God. He'd just kissed her; he hadn't vacuumed her damned scalp, and if you asked him, her hair always looked the same, no matter what she did to it, no matter what color she dyed it, and why she always asked him—

No, he thought and blinked hard and turned around to look at the light. It was fading now, the sun having shifted since he'd last looked, and sadness enveloped him. He wanted to go stand there, and let the dust drift around him, like little skins, drifting downward ever so slowly, drifting, drifting...drifting....

"What do you think, señor?" the old man asked.

"What?" Jim turned around.

"The necklace," Bev said, impatient that he hadn't been attending every nuance of the deal going on, and she thrust a strand at him.

He took the necklace, and it was as if something at once both hot and cold touched him; he stared down at the white coral, and thought of skinned angels. He felt the warmth of their skins seeping out, the coldness of the water creeping in, saw the agonized looks, saw—

He shook his head.

"No?" Bev said. "What about this?"

The next necklace thrust into his hands was a double strand of reddish coral, and he saw the blood swirling through the water, felt the coldness of the skins, and yet they were so soft, so pliant beneath his fingers, and he caressed the coral, and heard the screams, and he looked up to see the old man watching at him intently.

"This is nice," he said hoarsely, and the old man nodded as if he'd expected all along for Jim to say that.

"I don't know," Bev said. She grabbed another strand and put that into his hands, and now he had another soft buttery skin beneath his fingertips, and as he stroked the supple skins, he groaned inwardly.

"Well, Jimmy?"

"Well?" He stared at her, feeling befuddled. His senses had dulled, and he couldn't smell the intense perfumes and spices as he had before, couldn't hear much of anything as well as if even the girls standing so close to him had stopped talking loudly and were now whispering.

He closed his eyes and thought about Bev and how their marriage was falling apart and how they didn't have the good sense to admit it, and how he wanted nothing more than to make the marriage...to make *something* in his life work, how he wanted to make everyone realize they were wrong when they said he was stubborn and negative and callous, and all he wanted, really, was to stand in the sunlight and be left alone and not be told that he was this or that, all of it bad.

When he opened his eyes again, he was standing in the warm sunlight, looking out the window. Outside he could see Bev crossing the street at the corner, and at her side, but one step behind was a man that he dimly recognized, and it hit him after a vague minute that the man with Bev was *him*.

Jim tried to move, but couldn't. All he could do was stare out the window and feel the dust motes settling on him, like little dried out angel skins, like the dried out husk that he'd become, that Bev had turned him into.

He would have laughed, but he couldn't. Nor could he weep. All he could do was feel the sunlight, and realize that the underlying smell of the place hadn't been perfume or incense at all; it had been that of dusty dying souls.

THE LAKE

"It was so cool, hon—I saw swans flying over our house yesterday," Maggie Stevenson said to her husband, who was busy stirring green peas into his mashed potatoes.

"Those weren't swans; they were white geese," David replied without looking up, fork halfway to his mouth.

"You don't know that!"

"I do. Why would swans be flying around here?" His tone faintly mocked.

"There's a conservancy down the road, and I've even seen swans on the lake there."

"Swans. Yeah, right." David dropped his napkin on his plate and stood up, the legs of his chair scraping across the brick floor.

The noise knifed through her. She watched as he stomped out of the kitchen and into the living room. Seconds later canned laughter blasted into the room. He had the TV turned up really high—high enough that she wouldn't be able to say anything more to him.

Gritting her teeth, Maggie gathered the dishes. As she washed up, she gazed out at a bird splashing in the birdbath in the backyard. Another typical night. A meal where they barely spoke, and if they did, he sneered at everything she said; then afterward he buried himself in a newspaper or magazine or cranked up the TV so loud they couldn't talk.

Somewhere in the last year or so their marriage had begun failing, Maggie knew now, but she'd missed all the obvious signs. He came home late from work; they never went anywhere together; he barely spoke to her with any amount of civility, much less affection.

As for lovemaking...that had ended months ago. She almost chuckled aloud with each excuse he offered when she put her arms around him and whispered she wanted some loving: "I've got a headache," "C'mon, Mag, we just ate a big meal," "I've got to get up early in the morning," "I'm not in the mood tonight."

David was never in the mood, though; not for sex, not for cuddling, not for talking, not for...anything.

It wasn't like she was unattractive. Only weighing five pounds more than when they married thirty years ago, she worked out regularly; she kept her graying hair nicely coifed and dyed; she was always ready with a laugh or a word of encouragement. She never nagged. She never did this or that, or anything she thought would somehow repulse him. And yet....

The signs had been there, but she'd been too busy with her job as a sought-after architect, too preoccupied with her own problems to see the strains. Plus it had not been a good year for her: her mother had died after a prolonged illness, her father had gone in a nursing home, a childhood friend had stopped talking to her without explanation, and she'd entered that natural state of the older woman, menopause.

Any one of these would have proved stressful enough, but combined...sometimes she'd had to focus on just forcing herself to get out of bed and get dressed in the morning. But she had persevered, and now she was through the worst of it. Or so she thought until she realized their marriage was in deep trouble.

So, if he was so unhappy with her, she wondered, why didn't he ask for a divorce? For that reason, why didn't she? She wasn't sure she wanted one. But then she wasn't sure she *didn't* want one.

She finished the dishes, wiped her hands on a towel, then opened the sliding glass doors to the patio. She stepped outside, pulling the screen door shut behind her; no sense in letting in any insects. David would be screaming about the moths or some poor late season bee buzzing around harmlessly.

She didn't understand what had happened, either. During her mother's illness, Maggie had turned to David, supportive as ever. He'd helped take her mother to the various doctors month after month, had sat with Maggie in the hospital room that final night. He had gone with her to half a dozen different nursing homes to interview the staff when it was apparent her father could no longer care for himself.

It wasn't all the strain of the past year, was it? They'd been through strains before—God knows, their friends used to joke about the ups and downs of their lives. Shortly after their wedding, David's father had died, and then not long after that his sister died, followed within two years by his mother. A few years later David had been fired from a job he'd held for years. In their tenth year together, they moved cross country, uprooting after decades in the same place. Up and down, up and down...a regular roller coaster...that was their history together, but most couples had ups and downs. That was the way marriage was—hell, that was the way *life* was.

It was a childless union, but that had been by choice. Once, early on, she'd gotten pregnant, a mistake, and panicked, not knowing what to do. Did she want the child? Did she want an abortion? Before she could even make up her mind, she'd suffered a miscarriage, and she had mourned for the child she'd lost, the child she hadn't wanted—and yet somehow did. After that, David and Maggie had been particularly careful about birth control.

Now, she was nearing sixty; birth control wasn't something she had to worry about. At least she didn't think so, she told herself wryly. But that concern had been replaced with another: the feeble state of her marriage.

A faint breeze had sprung up, and she shivered, wishing she wore a heavier top or one with longer sleeves. She rubbed her forearms. She was damned if she would go back inside right now.

Even so, for mid-September, it was a bit warmer than usual, the trees just now being touched here and there with scarlet and gold. Everything was winding down...the flowers fading, leaves slowly drifting down.... It was her favorite season.

Something rustled behind Maggie, and she glanced over her shoulder. David stood there, on the other side of the screen. He wouldn't come out onto the patio, even though she'd designed it for him. Too many bugs, he said; he preferred staying within the house's sterile confines.

"What did they sound like?" he demanded.

"What?" She blinked.

"The swans," he said impatiently. "Those swans you thought you saw."

"Well, I heard this honking, and I stopped—I was bringing the groceries in—and looked up, expecting to see Canada geese—but I saw three swans overhead. They were so close, too, and honking."

"Geese then, just like I thought. Swans don't honk."

"Well, you don't know what they sound like while they're flying." She hated that slightly indignant tone creeping into her voice. She sounded so defensive. She doubly hated *that*!

"They hiss."

"I *know* that, David. I've read about swans, but they don't hiss while in flight."

He practically glowered at her, and had she not known it was David she wouldn't have recognized him. "Geese. You saw geese, not swans. Damn it, Maggie, can't you get that through your fat head? Why do you have to be so Goddamned stupid about some things? Can't you just admit you're fucking mistaken?"

She stared at him, then tears stinging her eyes, walked across the yard and out the gate. She didn't look back. She didn't want him seeing her crying. She dashed at her eyes with the heel of her hand and took a deep, ragged breath.

That was new, too—the swearing at her—something she'd noticed within the last month. David had never been a prude when it came to cursing, but he had never *ever* directed those words toward her. Now, he did. She was a "damned fool," "stupid bitch," "fucking idiot," and worse.

Sometimes Maggie thought she didn't know her husband any more. It was like the man she loved for so long had been snatched away by aliens one night and replaced by an imposter. Preposterous, of course, but....

She realized then she'd walked past the convenience store on the corner and circled back. She had several bucks in her pocket to buy some day-old bread. She'd go to the lake and feed the waterfowl. Maybe she'd feel better doing that.

As she headed down the road toward the lake, she tried to figure out why her husband had changed.

David had a tumor. Something malignant pressed on his brain, making him say things he didn't mean. Except that when they were around friends, David was just as nice and affable as ever. He was unpleasant only with her. In fact, their friends had noticed; she could tell from the way they looked at him, then her.

David was going through male menopause. Could be. He was her age—fifty-eight. He was ready to retire from his corporate job in a few years. He went to the doctor regularly, and surely the physician would have said something, given him something to take. Surely.

David wasn't really her David. He was someone else, a stand-in, an evil clone, an alien. She muffled a giggle at that one.

David had simply gone nuts. It did happen, could possibly happen. Some chemical imbalance occurred or something snapped inside the brain or....

Or David was having an affair.

Oh, Maggie, she told herself, that makes absolutely no se—

She stopped abruptly, puffs of dust rising up from the road, and her cheeks flushed as she realized the truth.

He arrived home late most nights. He made numerous phone calls from his corporate cell phone—calls that he had to make from another room. One day while doing laundry she'd found a handful of calling cards in his pants pocket. With calling cards there'd be no incriminating record on the monthly phone bill.

He had no time for her, for the things they had done together. He had no desire—nothing—for her. One plus one equals...two having an affair.

Maggie found it hard to breathe right then. She forced herself to relax, to stay calm. She didn't want to have a heart attack here in the middle of the road. She didn't know for sure David was having an affair. She wasn't 100 per cent sure. Just ninety-eight per cent.

That had to be the explanation, and yet she couldn't completely accept it. David had never strayed throughout their long marriage.

Never.

Or at least he'd never been caught, one tiny voice inside pointed out.

At the lake now, she found a large boulder near the water and sank down onto it.

Wrong, wrong, wrong, Maggie told herself. David wasn't having an affair; he had never had affairs before. He had been completely faithful to her.

Then why had Fiona, her longtime friend, stop talking to her? Why did David stop mentioning Fiona?

All those so-called business meetings throughout the years... all those times when he came home late...drinks with the guys...a late-night client...a phone call from overseas that he had to wait for...In the beginning he'd been careful, late only here and there. It was recently, within the last year, that he'd grown sloppy. Or perhaps he just didn't care to hide things from her any more.

Maggie put her head in her hands. Yet no tears came. She was dry, a husk, with no tears left. She told herself she must be mistaken, but she knew she was right. He was having an affair, had had others. And she was the absolute last person to know.

A splash nearby made her look up. A brown duck had landed in the water and was swimming toward her.

She remembered the loaves of bread she'd dropped on the ground when she sat down. She got up and retrieved one.

The birds must have smelled food, because suddenly she was

surrounded by a handful of Canada geese and several ducks and smaller birds, too—robins who hadn't fled south yet for the winter, several kinds of sparrows, a few talkative bluejays, and a cardinal couple. She was amazed at the variety of the birds back east; when she and David had lived out west, she hadn't seen many—sparrows, crows, hummers, a couple of others. Here she'd spotted dozens of species: flickers, red-winged blackbirds, goldfinches, catbirds, juncos, mourning doves, red-tailed hawks, more. She had feeders scattered throughout the yard, making it a veritable avian smorgasbord, as well as a few hummingbird feeders at the kitchen windows for those rare appearances by the tiny birds. Every morning she made sure the birds all had clean fresh water to drink and bathe in.

Originally David had delighted in the creatures, just as much as she, but lately he'd been making wisecracks about them as well.

In fact, she thought nothing in her life was safe from his sarcasm now.

He ridiculed her job—even though she made as much money as he did and was a respected member of an old architectural firm. He made biting comments about her friends. He sneered at her hobbies, at anything she did now or said.

When had he become such a disagreeable person?

She tossed several pieces of bread toward the birds, and there was a great commotion as they eagerly snatched the morsels. She started tearing apart another slice of bread and noticed her hand trembling again. She clamped down on it with her other hand and closed her eyes, willing the tremor to go away.

That was something she had noticed during the summer— how her hands trembled ever so slightly. The shaking had grown more distinct since then. Nerves, she'd told herself, but now she wasn't so sure. She had to go to the doctor, but was afraid of what he would say. Afraid it would be Parkinson's, afraid it would be worse. She hadn't told David; now she'd be damned if she'd let him know.

She fed more birds, then watched as a pair of majestic swans glided across the lake.

"Ah, the royal couple approaches," she said aloud, nearly laughing when a cardinal backpedaled at the sound of her voice.

The trees around the lake remained mostly unchanged, although here and there red and yellow peeked out from behind green. Sunlight glinted on the surface as she watched a few dragonflies hovering nearby. She caught the scent of wood fire from somewhere. A camper or hunter perhaps.

It was so serene. She should come here more often. Maybe this was what she needed: a place to get away from it all. It didn't matter that she lived only a mile or so away. A retreat. Where she could sit and look around and think or not think, as the case may be.

A place to heal.

Something nipped at her jean-clad leg and she looked down. The brown duck, grown impatient for more bread. It hadn't broken the skin or drawn blood; in fact, it had just pulled at the material.

"You guys sure are greedy." Somewhere a mourning dove cooed in response.

She tossed more bread to her circle of feathered friends, making sure the swans got some, too.

The sun hung low on the horizon now; it would be dark within the hour. They'd eaten early today, what with both of them being home, and no doubt she should go back. But why?

It wasn't like David would miss her. In the past he would have been concerned, worried if she went away for hours without telling him. Now she didn't think he would even notice she was gone.

She felt a heaviness in her chest at that, and her hands trembled more. She tore bread apart, flinging it as far away from her as she could.

Suddenly the male swan hissed.

"I thought I'd find you here."

Her teeth clenched, and her shoulders hunched upward. David. The bread bag still clasped in one hand, she turned around.

"Feeding your little feathered friends? Telling them your little sob story?"

The sun was at Maggie's back so she could see his expression all too well, while David had to squint to see her. He edged closer to the water, so he'd be at a different angle.

The second swan hissed.

"Well?"

"Well, what?" she asked, crumbling more bread and feeding it to the birds. Another duck grew bold and swiped a piece from her hand. She smiled and held out more.

"Oh, isn't that precious? Saint Maggie of the birdies."

"Are you trying to be funny or what?" She was nearly finished with the one loaf; time to open the second one. Overhead a raucous seagull, miles inland from the coast, wheeled in tight circles.

"I thought you'd want to talk about things. You always do. Talk and talk and *talk* and rehash and run things right into the ground until I'm sick of you flapping your gums. You're become a real motormouth, you know."

The hand inside her chest squeezed, but Maggie forced herself to look into his pale eyes. "Talk about what, David? You're having an affair. You've had them before. You'll probably continue to have them until your pecker falls off inside someone's slimy hole."

He looked absolutely stunned. Good! She'd shocked him; he'd never heard such language from her. He had expected her to confront him; no doubt he imagined she was completely ignorant of his peccadilloes. Well, she had been until this afternoon. And in truth, she was also surprised by her own language and tone.

A Canada goose honked, and Maggie flipped a piece of bread its way. She dropped more crumbs by her foot, and the sparrows fluttered around.

David recovered quickly, as he always managed to do. "So, what do you want to do, *sweetie pie*?" He smirked at her. She'd never heard an endearment sound so obscene.

Pressing her lips together, Maggie pitched bread at her husband. The slice landed at his feet; instantly a bluejay pounced on it.

"Watch it!" David said, stumbling back slightly. "That bird almost touched my shoes!"

"Afraid those expensive shoes might get messy? Gosh, we can't have that, can we? Those leather loafers are so much more important than your wife's silly feelings, right?"

Maggie hurled a piece of bread at David, and it bounced off his arm. Another bluejay flew up, grabbing the scrap before it hit the ground.

"Don't!"

"Oh, David, stop whining." She half-smiled to herself. She knew he'd rehearsed this in his mind on the way down here, and these were *his* words; *she* wasn't supposed to say them. "Be brave. Keep your chin up. Everything will work out." She laughed now.

"What's so funny?" he asked, scowling.

The birds gathered around David as she tossed more morsels toward him. He backed away, and she watched in amusement as he slipped in a patch of mud and suddenly his shoe was underwater.

Cursing, David leaped away from the lake. His actions startled the birds, causing them to fly away. Only the swans remained, softly hissing.

"Look what you've done now!" he said, taking his shoe off and shaking the water out. "You've ruined it!"

"No, David," Maggie said calmly, "you've ruined it. It's time you take responsibility for your actions. You've ruined your shoe. You ruined your life. You ruined mine."

"My life isn't ruined."

Maggie's smile widened. "It will be by tomorrow when I call your boss."

"And tell him what?"

"That you're screwing his wife." A wild guess, and by the

way David's eyes opened she knew she'd hit the target.

"You don't have proof."

"I don't need it, *sweetie pie*. Think Bill is going to be thrilled at seeing you toddle into work tomorrow? I'm sure he's had some suspicions all along. My phone call will only solidify those fears."

"You don't want to ruin me!"

"Wanna bet?"

The birds were flying back now, looking for more handouts. Maggie fed some crumbs to a robin, then gave more to several ducks and a Canada goose. A handful of crows squawked for a handout, while just beyond David grackles and starlings fought over a crust.

"Oh, Maggie, c'mon, honey, you know it wasn't anything serious," he said, his tone wheedling. "I promise to walk the narrow and straight from now on. Really. You can depend on me!"

She shredded more slices and flung them at David as hard as she could, her anger and frustration boiling up. The selfish bastard hadn't changed, wouldn't change, she knew, and that he was trying to con her infuriated her. He backed away. He was so upset, she noted, he didn't realize water lapped at his heels.

"You're not the woman I married," he said accusingly.

Maggie sighed. "No. I'm not. Nor are you the man I married. The man I exchanged vows with loved his wife, behaved honorably, and would never have gone sneaking around her back and lived a lie for God knows how long."

A duck plucked at David's pants leg. More startled than anything, he yelled, stumbled, falling back and down into the water. There was a cracking noise as he landed on a submerged rock, and David screamed, clutching his leg. The swans hissed as they moved closer.

Maggie spread more bread around for the gathering birds.

"Help me up, Mag. I'm stuck in the mud here, and I've hurt myself." Tears of pain ran down his face.

Maggie smiled at her husband, then opened the third loaf,

ripping up the slices and throwing them toward David. A chipping sparrow with its little copper cap hopped onto the man's knee to peck at bread there. A starling swiped the bread from the sparrow, its wing grazing David's chest, and he recoiled.

"Sorry, David. I'm all out of help today."

She loomed over him now and dribbled bits and pieces of bread on him. He was trying to get up now, but it was obvious he couldn't maneuver into the right position with his hurt leg. The mud sucked at his hands and feet, keeping him mired. He swatted constantly at the birds, but they kept coming back to him to eat the bread.

Three robins and a solitary catbird perched on his knees and head now. The starlings paused at the edge of the water and gazed, unblinking, at him. He slapped the robins away, and a grackle dive-bombed him. He ducked his head, just missing being pecked.

David glared at her. "C'mon, Maggie, this isn't funny any more."

"Really? When did you finally realize that, David?"

The ducks waddled closer and grabbed his pants leg, shook their heads when they didn't taste bread. One leaned forward and quacked, while a goose responded noisily.

Suddenly Maggie thought of a phrase she'd heard years ago: "nibbled by ducks." It described all the little things getting at you, bit by bit...the way she had been feeling lately. No, the wording wasn't quite right. Nibbled to...nibbled by...what was it now?

The swans skimmed closer, hissing louder now, and she thought how mysterious they looked in the light of dusk—those dark eyes and black masks. But they were so beautiful with the long graceful necks, the elegant wings. Incredibly wonderful creatures. As David fought to get out of the mud, the swans lunged and bit him.

David howled. Maggie dropped more bread on him, and watched him struggle frantically against the starlings and waterfowl, while the crows, like black arrows, aimed for his head. He struck the birds with his flailing hands, and that enraged them even more. More birds attacked.

As the birds pressed around her husband, biting and nibbling and tasting, Maggie remembered the phrase.

"Nibbled...nibbled to death by ducks," she said aloud and laughed, although she doubted David could hear her with all that screeching, coming from bird and man alike. She turned her back and walked away as the geese and crows and ducks swarmed onto David, completely engulfing him.

A few yards away she paused and watched as he fell back into the water, the ducks ripping at him, the swans biting into flesh, the goose bobbing its head in triumph over a prized tidbit. She watched until the crows and starlings and grackles, seeing no more food, flew off to find roosts for the night. The ducks and geese waddled toward a rotting log in search of insects, while the swans floated serenely away, specks of crimson dabbing their white feathers.

Still chuckling about the phrase, Maggie turned into the darkness and headed home.

SOUNDS

Hammer, hammer, hammer.

Cheryl Goodwin pursed her lips, sighed and pulled the pillow over her head. Damned roofers.

Hammer, hammer.

Even through the thickness of feathers, she could still hear the whacking of the workmen's hammers on the slate roof next door.

She opened an eye. Read the clock. 7:07. In the morning, for God's sake, on her one day off this month—a Friday to make a long and very welcome weekend—and she had to be awakened by that damned whacking.

Someone started a buzzsaw. She winced.

She glanced over at her husband, Tommy, laying serenely on his back, one arm flung over his face. He was soundly asleep, would remain soundly asleep no matter what noise followed.

She envied him.

She sighed, punched up her pillow, closed her eyes. She would fall asleep again and she would sleep until nine, maybe even ten, and then—

A drill whined.

She sat up in bed.

"W-What?" her husband mumbled, only disturbed a little from her abrupt motion. Then he was asleep again, snoring mildly.

Snoring.

There'd be no more sleep for her today.

She shook her head, pushed the covers back and got out of bed. She went to the window in the hallway and stared out at the workmen. They went on their ways blithely, completely unaware of her baleful glare.

She knew the workmen had to get an early start or they'd be working too many hours in the 90-plus temperatures under a burning sun. But still. Couldn't they go about these improvements a little more silently?

She grinned at the thought.

She went into the bathroom, washed her face, and even over the running water she could hear the rapping of the hammers.

Try to ignore it, she told herself, not for the first time. She tried to blot out the alien sound, tried to concentrate on the rushing water, a much more serene sound. A gentle, soothing frequency, hypnotic almost, quiet and peaceful and—

Tap, tap, tap.

No good.

She stepped into the shower, turned on the water full blast, and only then under the stinging stream did the other noise fade away.

She finished, dressed, and swallowed an aspirin. It was going to be one of those days.

Downstairs she retrieved the rolled-up newspaper off the front porch steps, sat down at the dining room table to enjoy her first cup of hot cinnamon tea for the day. The dining room windows faced onto the house under renovation, and she could see the crew crawling like immense ants over the gray roof.

Before she could get more irritated, she got up and pulled the windows down. The noise dimmed a little, but didn't go away.

About fifteen minutes later Tommy came downstairs. "Mornin'," he said, as he bent over to kiss her. He smelled of some lemony aftershave, and she smiled.

"Sleep well?" she asked.

"As always," he said, going into the kitchen to fix his breakfast. "You?"

She shrugged.

"Woke up again, huh?"

"Yeah."

"Maybe you need some sort of sleeping pill, something from over the counter."

She sloshed her tea around in the mug. "Yeah, maybe, but I think I've tried just about every one out there. They work for the first night or two, you know, and then after that I keep waking up. In fact, I think they keep me awake."

"Well," Tommy said, sliding into the chair opposite her and dipping his spoon into his bowl of Cheerios, "maybe you should go to see a—"

"A therapist?" Cheryl asked, her voice a slightly sarcastic.

He looked at her. "Let me finish, okay? I was going to say a hypnotist."

"Oh. I hadn't thought of that."

"A guy at the office went to one—I could probably get the name, if you want—and he quit smoking. He used to smoke two—three packs a day."

She nodded thoughtfully. "Get the name, if it's no bother. I think that might be good. Sure is worth a try, I guess."

"Maybe you can take a nap today."

"Not with that going on," she pointed with her chin toward the windows.

"Isn't it kind of warm in here? Do you want the windows closed, Cheryl?"

"I wanted to cut down on the racket."

He gave her That Look—the expression she always hated, and always felt held more than a little condescension. "Hon, you've really got to do something about that. Face it, we live in a noisy world, and it's not going to get any quieter." He took his bowl out to the kitchen and ran water in it.

She made a face at his back, then looked down at her mug. She didn't know why she did that, except that she always suspected that he really didn't understand how horrible it was for her. How bad the level of noise could get.

"It would be much more quiet if we lived in the country," she

210 | KATHRYN PTACEK

said.

He stopped. "Hon, don't start on that again. I told you that with the cost of land, we just can't afford a place out there. At least right now. If one of us gets a raise, maybe we can sock the extra money away. Until then you'll just have to put up with a boisterous town. At least it's not the city."

She said nothing.

"See you later." He kissed her again, picked up his jacket and a few minutes later she heard him calling to the workmen and chatting for a few minutes, then the car started up. It popped and sputtered; the engine needed tuning.

Cheryl gritted her teeth.

With her tea mug in hand, she wandered into the living room and draped herself across the easy chair and turned on the TV. She didn't normally watch television in the daytime—after all, she was usually at work—but she was curious to see what was on at this hour. An earnest-looking host talking about incest, and some quiz show with lots of buzzers and flashing lights, a nature show about fishers going back into the wild, a couple of music stations, the weather channel, CNN, and others. She flipped through the stations one by one, then through them again as if expecting to find something else in their place, then finally turned the TV off. Too much noise.

From one of the houses across the street she heard the faint beat of rock music. Something by some heavy metal group.

Swell.

A car went by on the street, the windows rolled down, a Mozart concerto blasting out.

Not even the classics were sacred, she thought with a faint smile.

Enough of this. Cheryl stood, pursed her lips and looked around the room. So, what was she going to do with her day off? She supposed she could go to the mall and shop. But that meant a long drive, and hassling with the crowds and that maddening piped-in elevator music that followed her into every store. Couldn't people survive without having to listen to something every minute of the day?

No, the mall was definitely out. She did have to go grocery shopping, though.

The grocery was only a five-minute drive away; and once she'd claimed a cart, she started down the aisles.

She recognized some songs from the late '60s being piped in on the p. a. system; but now they'd been homogenized into bland elevator music. Again. Then the system crackled and a man's voice—perhaps it was the manager—came over the p.a. and announced that there was a special only today on lean ground beef. He kept droning on and on about all the different uses for ground beef. Finally, the ad ended, and the music—the Beatles' "I Want To Hold Your Hand", one of her favorites and slowed down considerably—came on in mid-tune.

That irritated her even more, but she wasn't sure which was more offensive—the lackluster renditions of the music or just the plain fact that there was music.

She didn't know why she hated noise so much; from her early childhood on she had been particularly noise sensitive, at least that's what her mother had called it. Cheryl had always disliked loud voices and sounds, and had always crawled into her parents' large walk-in closet when thunder boomed outside. She could hear the whine of air conditioning as she walked into department stores when no one else could. Sudden reports made her shiver. Once she had begun crying as a small airplane droned, circling over their house. Her father had said it was simply a stage that she would outgrow; only she hadn't.

It hadn't gotten better with age; it had grown worse, much worse.

Most of the time she had an uneasy truce with her sensitivity. Then there were the other times...days like today.

She headed down aisle one.

Somewhere, maybe a few rows over, a young child began crying.

Cheryl waited for the child to stop, but it didn't; it was building to an enthusiastic crescendo. It was a wonder its lungs didn't give out, she thought.

Her hands clenched on the cart handle. She braked before the paper products and tossed in a few boxes of Scotties, some packages of paper napkins on sale and half a dozen rolls of paper towels. Beyond that was bath soap, and she needed to pick up a few bars. Her hand paused just before she picked up the Zest.

The wailing grew louder. Obviously the child was going to be in her aisle before long. The high-pitched voice rose and fell in a pathetic undulation. The mother's voice was shrill and she was telling her child that the child really shouldn't cry.

Cheryl shook her head in disgust. The mother ought to just say no, and then bop the kid on the butt once or twice. That would stop the whining. God knows, it had happened enough to her when she was small. Of course, she hadn't been prone to pitching temper tantrums, either. That wasn't allowed in her family.

A gentle throbbing began in her temple; her headache was returning.

Cheryl pushed her cart toward the end of the aisle, trying to get away from the noise. But it followed her wherever she went.

She hurried through the produce section, lobbed lettuce and radishes and spinach and cucumbers into the basket. She would surprise Tommy with a really big salad. Normally they didn't eat quite that healthy, but tonight it would be a welcome change. All those wholesome vitamins, she thought drolly.

Somewhere else in the store another child began crying, picking up the refrain of the first.

Then a third started whimpering.

When she got to the check-out stand, Cheryl flung her items onto the belt as quickly as possible and watched the checker ring them up one by one.

"How can you stand to work in all this noise? These kids must drive you crazy."

The checker, a middle-aged woman with a big brown-black mole on her chin and a rather placid expression, shook her head. "Don't hear it after a while. It just sort of blends together pretty soon."

"You're lucky."

"Yeah, I guess so. That's twenty-three fifty. You should have been here when they were remodeling the store." The checker shook her head. "We had hammering and drilling from early in the morning to late at night, not to mention all the paint and glue smells. It was terrible."

Cheryl shuddered, paid, put her purchases in the car, then returned home. The workers were still next door; she had entertained some vague hope that they might have called it quits for the day.

Right.

After she put away the groceries, she took a couple of more aspirin, then wandered into the living room and sat down. She was going to read. Really she should do a little housework, but she knew she couldn't take the howling of the vacuum cleaner.

She opened her book, a thick historical mystery set during the American Civil War, and opened it to where she'd put her bookmark. She read for a while and only gradually became aware of another noise, a clanging and banging. She glanced out the window and saw the garbage men. Why, she wondered, when all the garbage cans were plastic now, did these guys have to make all this noise? The truck moved slowly down the street, the noise finally receding.

It was noisy at the office, too, where she worked as a staff writer. Her job was to translate computer talk into people talk, and the constant clatter of printers and phones and people talking, chairs squeaking, doors being slammed grated. Some days she wondered how any one—how she—could stand it. But no one complained about the level of noise, and she figured she was just being sensitive.

Too damned sensitive for her own good—wasn't that what her father always said?

At lunch she fixed a simple cheese sandwich and had a soda, and while she was sitting at the dining room table still reading, she heard a high-pitched whining. Like a buzzsaw, only she knew that sound very well. Even over the sound of hammering and the shouts of the workmen, she could hear that grating noise, though.

She stepped out onto the front porch; the sound grew louder.

Something bright flashed along the street. The whining came from it.

It turned out to be one of those remote control cars, and she watched as a man with his young son played with the car. Around and around it went, then up and down in front of her house. It was nice that he was with his son, she thought, but why couldn't they have found some silent toy, like a kite, to play with.

She found herself gritting her teeth, forced herself to relax, went back in and closed the front door and windows facing that direction.

Not good enough, but the best she could do.

She read until the kids came home from school, then her finger marking her place in the book, she looked out the window and watched as the junior high kids cut across her lawn. They were yelling to one another, and one of them held a large silver radio that blasted out some loud song with a fast beat. They cursed at each other and pushed each other around, and shouted, even though they were standing only a few feet away from each other.

Didn't kids speak in civil tones any more? In hushed tones? she wondered.

One of the kids broke away and clambered up the steps of the house next door.

Oh, no, she thought.

John was home, and she knew very well what would come next.

A few minutes later the kid stuck a trumpet out the window facing Cheryl's house and began playing scales. He knew somehow that she hated the sound of that damned instrument, so he was always faithful about practicing it every afternoon when he got home from school, and every evening before he went to bed. He even practiced on the weekend, which she thought was a bit excessive.

She tried to put the brassy sound of the trumpet out of her mind, but she couldn't.

It had always been hard to deal with, this noise sensitivity. She'd tried ear plugs years before, but they really hadn't helped. She tried ignoring the sounds, but couldn't concentrate fully.

Maybe the hypnotist Tommy had mentioned that morning would help, though; she hoped so. All these noises were driving her crazy.

It didn't help that Tommy snored so loudly sometimes at night that she woke up and was unable to go back to sleep until she came downstairs and camped out on the sofa. Even then, she'd be able to hear the snoring faintly, but at least it no longer kept her awake.

And he always kept the television volume much too high, she thought, just like her father had. Her father had been hard of hearing, though, and she could understand that although he refused to get a hearing aid. But Tommy was a young man, only in his mid-thirties, surely he wasn't that deaf. Maybe she would suggest that he have his hearing checked out.

She knew hers didn't need it.

At least, she thought, the boy and his father and the awful toy had gone off. Maybe the thing was broken; that would be good news.

Her mother had been the type to slam drawers and doors. If she was mad, slam went a dresser drawer. Or the door to the oven. Or the backdoor. With each jar, Cheryl had jumped. She was always glad that she came from a family of three rather than thirteen.

She went back to her book.

After a while, over the blasting of trumpet, she heard the ticking of the clock in the hallway. Tommy had bought that for their last anniversary. With each swing of the brass pendulum there was a resonant echo, like the striking of a padded hammer on wood. Almost a muffled sound. But not muffled enough.

She always kept the TV down low when she watched it alone;

in fact, Tommy would complain about the lowness whenever he entered the room, but she never had any problems hearing it.

The refrigerator went on. The appliance needed work, and for years it had made cooing noises, like a dove. Once, when they'd first moved in and the refrigerator which came with the place hummed on, she'd checked down in the basement because she could have sworn a bird had gotten caught down there. No bird, though; just the sound of the failing refrigerator, the sound that followed her throughout each room of the house. Sometimes at night as she lay in bed, trying to sleep, she could hear that persistent cooing.

Water dripped from the kitchen faucet. Drop by drop. She would have to remind Tommy again this weekend to get a new washer for the faucet. They were wasting too much water.

Her headache was back, and growing worse. It was centered over one eye and throbbed. She bet if she put her fingers on that spot she'd feel it pulsating. She got up and took some more aspirin, took a deep breath, and told herself to relax.

Somewhere, on the other side of the street, a phone rang and a man's voice, loud, answered it, and she listened to a conversation she didn't want to hear.

A car, gunning its engine, sped by.

Kids shrieked as they played in their front yards, running around and around.

Bluejays squawked and shrieked at each other as they perched in the mulberry tree outside her window.

A lawn mower growled two houses down.

Tommy really was pretty good about all of this, she told herself. She tried not to complain about the noise, because he really didn't understand. No one—not even her closest friends—did, because none of them could hear as well as she could. They all complained about varying hearing loss, and she always thought that they were the lucky ones, that she was the cursed one.

Someone with a weed wacker worked in the yard where the lawn mower still roared.

You're too sensitive, her father always grumbled, as if it were really something she could control.

The neighbor next door, father to the trumpet player, arrived home early and began working on the sports car he never drove. She could hear the racing of the engine, louder and louder, a grinding of gears, the beeping of the horn.

Another phone shrilled.

It was just that she never could seem to get away from the noise. It was always badgering her, assaulting her. She hated it.

A television blared.

Somewhere a woman giggled, a high-pitched irritating noise. Too sensitive.

A piano—someone playing "Heart and Soul" over and over—blended with the trumpet.

The pulsating pain returned.

Some teenager gunned the engine of his car, honked seven or eight times, then sped away.

A jet shrieked its way overhead.

An ambulance, or perhaps it was a police car, raced down the next block out, the wailing siren rising and falling, rising and falling.

Another lawn mower roared into life, while the kid and his father returned with the remote control car.

Too damned sensitive....

The refrigerator hummed on again, while in the basement the furnace rumbled on.

Her phone rang. And rang, and rang, and rang, and still she sat on the couch, and listened to all the noises of the house and her neighborhood.

* * * * * * *

Tommy parked the car in the driveway, waved to old Mr. Miller who was just finishing clipping his hedges two doors down. He went into the house.

"Cheryl, hi, I'm home."

He heard nothing but the ticking of the grandfather clock in the hallway. He listened for running water, thinking she might be taking a bath, but he didn't hear it. Maybe she was out back.

"Cheryl?" This time louder.

Still no answer.

He heard something in the kitchen then, and he realized she was out there, probably making dinner.

He stopped on the threshold of the kitchen. "Hi, hon, how are you?"

She stood at the counter with her back to him. She was cutting up vegetables for a salad.

"Hon?"

Was this a game, he thought with a sly smile? Then: was she mad at him for some reason and ignoring him?

He stepped closer.

On the counter, not far from the salad bowl, he saw an ice pick, and a smear of something red on the countertop.

"Honey, I got the name of the hypnotist; it's some guy who just—" he began, then stopped when Cheryl turned around and he saw the blood trickling from her ears.

SNOW

Jean drove away from the nursing home and didn't look back.

There was no reason to; her mother wouldn't be on the porch, waving in farewell like something out of a Norman Rockwell painting.

No, she would be hunched over in her wheelchair, in what was called the common room, and tears would be streaming down her cheeks.

Just as tears streamed down Jean's. She wiped at them, futilely, with her fingertips; rubbed the dampness across the leg of her jeans.

Something small and white whirled by the windshield. A snowflake, she presumed, because that was what the weather forecasters on television had been calling for over the past few days. Only nothing like they'd predicted had developed yet. But of course the snow had to wait to appear until today.

Today, when she needed bright sunshine and clear skies and the cheerfulness that went with them.

No; today she got glowering skies and gloominess; the trees that arched over the road seemed to bear down upon her and menace ever so slightly, and accordingly her spirits sank even lower. They were, after all, not very high to begin with. On this day, this day when she had taken her mother to the HarborHouse Nursing Facility, the day should have been brighter, to help her ease the pain for them both, if that were at all possible.

A flicker brought her attention to the road again as another snowflake danced across the windshield, accompanied by a second, then a third, then more than a dozen. One stuck to the glass, and she shook her head.

She had a long way to go yet. The drive to the facility took approximately two hours; going back to her house would take even longer now. She hoped, though, that she'd be there before the storm really started. She didn't like to drive in the snow, which was sort of ironic because she lived in the east. But she had never been able to handle the slipperiness, the fog-like blowing flakes, the freezing temperatures.

Now, however, the weather was a reverse sort of ally, forcing her to concentrate on the narrow two-lane road twisting before her, rather than think of her mother as she had seen her before she left. Etta had been glaring at her, that accusing look in the cataract-paled eyes, and her peeling lips had been pressed into a thin bloodless line, a disapproving line reflected in the hunch of her bony shoulders, the tilt of her gray head.

Her mother didn't want to go to HarborHouse; Jean had had no choice but to put her there.

After all, what could she do for the old lady now? In this past year Etta lost control of her bladder and her bowels; her blindness had increased; she didn't know Jean or anyone else half the time; didn't want to do anything yet complained that she was bored; had lost so much weight that with her sagging flesh and protruding bones she looked like some ancient refugee from a WWII concentration camp; had, indeed, become argumentative and querulous and demanding. Had become impossible for one untrained person to take care of.

There was no other choice, Jean repeated to herself over and over. No other choice.

More flickering, and she blinked and focused once more. The temperature must be dropping, she thought, because the snow had begun to stick to the grass alongside the road. It was fast becoming more white than green. She even hit a patch clinging to the road and automatically raised her foot from the accelerator, letting the car slow gradually. She didn't want to go too fast, didn't want to end up embedded in a tree.

The wind gusted, shaking bushes and tree branches, and pelting snow in a crazy-quilt pattern.

The tires thudded against the pavement, a rhythmic sound that soothed Jean, the sort of sound she used to fall asleep to when she was a child and her parents had gone driving in the country.

On the way to HarborHouse her mother had complained about the sounds. There was nothing wrong with Etta's hearing most of the time.

"This car is too noisy," Etta had said, as she gazed unseeing out the car window. "There must be something wrong with it."

"I just had it in for a tune-up, Mom," she said gently. "I think it's all right."

"Well, you're wrong. Something's the matter with the engine or something like that. I can hear it. We're going to get stuck. I just know it, I do."

"That's the tires thumping on the road," and she had wondered why she bothered to pursue this; the conversation wouldn't get her anywhere. Her mother would never concede that she was wrong. For that matter, neither would Jean.

Etta snorted, a disgusting sound. "Well, that's what you think, Sissy."

She hated it when her mother called her that; Sissy had been the childhood nickname for Peggy, Etta's sister whom Jean could not tolerate for a variety of reasons, all of them long-standing. For years now Etta had been mixing them up. Jean thought she got the short end of it.

Momentarily the car wobbled. White covered the blacktop, obscuring the dotted line, and she braked even further. There were too many twists and turns in these backwoods roads, and she knew she couldn't afford to take a corner too fast. God knows what would be coming around the turn then. Too many big trucks used these curving back roads rather than face the clogged interstate, but they never seemed to obey the lower speed limits. She sighed, finally switched on the windshield wipers. They blurred the glass momentarily, then swept it clean. Back and forth the blades went, their swooshing added to the drum of the tires.

Casually she glanced into the rearview mirror and for an instant saw cloudy-pale eyes glaring back. She blinked, and the eyes were gone, and she was staring into her own green ones.

She shook her head. She was letting her guilt affect her now. And she did feel guilt, even though she kept telling herself— just as her friends kept insisting—that she shouldn't feel this way. But it was easy to say, not so easy to follow. She knew she couldn't do any more for her mother; she knew Etta would be better off in a home that would provide around-the-clock attention; she knew that she was at the end of her rope mentally and physically and emotionally.

But.

There still remained that lingering "but." But maybe she was wrong; but maybe she was acting too hastily; but maybe things would work out somehow; but maybe she should give it a bit longer.

But maybe she wasn't wrong.

It had already been six years—more than six years—since her mother had come to live with Jean, and things had not improved. In fact, they had worsened. Back six years ago Jean had been engaged to marry, but when she brought her mother into the house, her fiancé had given her an ultimatum—if they married, Etta would have to go into a nursing home. She could not stand that idea, not then, and knew she had an obligation to take care of her mother, at least for a while.

She and Peter had broken up then. Occasionally they saw each other, in social situations, and he always smiled pleasantly. But he was married now to someone else, and each time she saw him with his wife, she felt a tightness in her chest—something else she blamed on Etta.

Of course, she didn't know if even now she would change what had happened, provided she could. She had a duty, after all; a family obligation that she had had to take on; she'd had no choice. If only, she thought and not for the first time, if only Peter had been a little more understanding. If only he had waited a while, then she might have come to the realization that her mother needed more help than she could give her. If only. But he had made her choose right then, had forced her back to the wall, and she'd had no alternative.

Her friends told her she was crazy to let Peter go, but she kept saying, Don't you understand? My mother has no one but me. One or two of her friends proved sympathetic, but the others kept saying what a shame it was she was throwing her life away for an old woman.

But it isn't just any old woman, she insisted, it's my mother.

Still, they shook their heads.

And that made her feel worse. Worse that she was in a way destroying her life, and yet she couldn't abandon the old ailing woman. Not yet.

Not until today.

She rubbed one eye, then glanced at the speedometer. The needle hovered just under twenty-five.

The snow had thickened, the wind roaring like a train through a tunnel as well, and she sighed. There were still forty miles to go, and it was going to take hours to get home. She would be driving in the dark, too. What great conditions—darkness and snowy roads. Swell. She wanted to be home, curled up on the couch, wrapped in a crocheted quilt, a cup of tea on the table in front of her, and able to sit and cry all she wanted to. But all of that would have to wait.

Momentarily the tires lost traction, and she spun the steering wheel to get herself out of the slide. The car righted itself after a heart-stopping moment, and she cautioned herself to be more careful.

The clouds seemed to be pressing down upon the treetops; they looked so low that she thought she might be able to stretch out an arm and touch them. They were dark, forbidding; and promised a lot more snow than they had released already. Maybe this would be the first blizzard of the season.

Curious, though, that she hadn't heard anything like this predicted on the news. Of course, that didn't mean anything, either. The forecasters didn't have much of a track record these days, not after a couple of missed hurricanes and non-appearing storms during the past two years.

The white outside the car was as chalky has Etta's eyes had become. Several years ago, she had been diagnosed as having cataracts in both eyes; the ophthalmologist and Jean had explained to the old woman what this meant, and how the cataracts could easily be corrected so that she could see again. But for some reason she wouldn't share with them Etta had refused the surgery. Distressed, Jean had gone over the procedure with her and said it wouldn't take long for her to recover. Again Etta refused.

And nothing would change her mind. So, little by little, she lost what vision remained to her. Now she could scarcely distinguish between light and dark. And yet this situation—one of her mother's own making, Jean thought—did not prevent her from making accusatory remarks about the problems of being blind.

As if it were all Jean's fault.

Of course, Jean's aunt had thought she should have forced Etta to have the operations, but Jean kept insisting that she couldn't forcefully take her mother to the doctor's office. It wasn't morally right.

Her aunt had called her a fool.

Maybe.

People, she noted ironically, were always very quick to offer advice about Etta, but she didn't notice any of them volunteering to watch her for an hour or two while she ran errands. Or taking Etta in for a weekend so that Jean could just be by herself. Again, she reflected, it was far easier to advise than to actually do something about it.

A shadow passed across her field of vision, and she peered out. The trees seemed to crowd closer to the road with each passing moment, and she thought it was by far too dark for this early hour; sunset was still an hour away, at least. She switched on her headlights, which sliced only a few feet ahead through the falling snow.

She sighed again, the tightness once more in her chest, as she remembered telling Etta that she would be going into a nursing home. The old woman had remained silent for a few minutes, then had turned her head away and said, muffled, "You don't love me any more."

Jean had expected this sort of thing, but it still hurt to hear those words from her mother's lips. "Of course, I love you, Mom. You know that I do. That's why I took you in six years ago."

"Then why are you abandoning me?"

"I'm not." She wished there could be more conviction in her voice.

"You are," the old woman accused. "You're going to take me to some hell hole."

"It's not a hell hole. It's a nice place, with some really great people. There'll be physical therapy, and people your own age that you can talk to, and during the holidays schoolchildren come in to sing Christmas carols and—"

"You've been there. You've already made up your mind. I don't have a choice in this." Her mother's tone had become more childish now.

"That's right, Mom," Jean said, forcing herself to reply calmly, "you have no choice in this. I can't take care of you any longer, and Aunt Peggy isn't willing to put her money where her mouth is and take you in, so I have no other options."

"You are a hateful daughter. You're no daughter of mine."

Ah, but she was. Why else would Jean have gone through all this hell for the past six years?

And even though Jean loved her mother—most of the time— it was not always pleasant.

There were the times when Etta didn't tell Jean in time that she had to go to the bathroom, the times when she had diarrhea and Jean had to bathe her completely from chest to knees, and when she was all nice and clean and in fresh clothing, she'd have it again, and they'd have to start over. There were the times when her catheter leaked, and soaked the bedding, so that Jean had to strip the hospital bed and take the urine-reeking sheets down to the basement and put them in the washing machine. Again. Just like she had the day before.

There were the times when somehow Etta had maneuvered her wheelchair around the downstairs while Jean worked or was out running errands. One time Etta had managed to turn up the thermostat, and when Jean came home from the grocery store heat blasted her when she opened the door. Her mother had set the temperature at eighty-five, a good eighteen degrees higher than Jean normally set it. Another time, Etta had manipulated her wheelchair around the room and had managed to pull out her catheter, which drooled urine on the good oriental carpet Jean had purchased only a few months previously, and then she had rammed the metal chair into the china cabinet, knocking down the old plates and dishes inside.

Of course, Jean had been glad her mother wasn't hurt, but the urine stains had never really come out, and she couldn't replace the china, which had been passed down from her Scottish great-grandmother and was the only thing they had from the old country. Not to mention that this had occurred on a weekend when the visiting nurse had gone home early from the office, and so Jean had had to diaper her mother until the following Monday morning when the nurse could come out.

Another time Etta tried to telephone Peggy, and had reached someone out in California, and had become frustrated and left the receiver off the hook. The line was still connected when Jean came home. Still another time Etta had turned on the stove somehow, put the tea kettle on and when Jean came downstairs, she found the water had boiled out. Luckily she had caught it before there was any sign of a fire. She shuddered to think what would have happened if she had been out that day.

Little things. They were all little things, really, but they soon became frustrating. Every week something happened.

Sometimes they occurred two and three times, and if Jean scolded her, Etta would pout and call her a damned bitch.

And that made Jean cry. Or at least initially it had, but after a while, after the next few times, she realized that her mother really didn't mean it—or did she?—and she shouldn't let it upset her. But it did, and so did the odd incidents, and the leaking catheters and the diarrhea, and the blindness and all of it.

Bothered her until she couldn't sleep at night. Bothered her while she tried to work. Bothered her until she realized she had to do something before she lost her mind.

Which meant the nursing home.

To be perfectly fair, there were good times, too. Good times. Jean knew there had been, but when she tried to remember them, she couldn't. Those pleasant memories were fading, too quickly replaced by the disagreeable ones. And she resented that as well.

The car lurched.

Jean blinked, bringing her mind back to the road in front of her. The wind whipped a branch on an immense tree by the road back and forth, and the limb clacked, and she thought of her mother's gnarled fingers, distorted by age and arthritis.

Snow muffled the sounds of the car's engine now, and she thought it was almost as if the car wasn't moving. But it was—she could see trees going past, then an open space where she could glimpse a field of snow. She should have come to the turnoff by now, or maybe she hadn't come as far as she'd thought. Or maybe while she was daydreaming she had missed it.

Great.

She checked the rearview mirror and saw nothing but whiteness behind her. There was whiteness ahead, too, and to the sides, and for a moment she felt as if she were being suffocated by a colorless blanket.

She shook her head, dispelling the feeling.

The process to get her mother into the nursing home had been fairly complicated; after all, Jean was dealing with a bureaucracy, and there had been any number of papers to examine and fill out and sign. Knowing how slow bureaucracies tended to be, she had thought she would have months before her mother would leave for the home; as it turned out, it had only taken weeks.

And then the day had come too soon, too unexpected for all her preparation. She had dressed her mother in her best dress and put shoes on Etta's feet, even though her mother no longer walked, and she had taken her down the ramp to the car in the driveway outside. She had managed to get Etta in without any problem, and they were ready to go. She had already packed her mother's suitcases the day before and put them in the trunk ahead of time. She figured there would be the minimum of fuss that way.

And then the two women had driven in relative silence to HarborHouse, and when Jean had seen Etta settled in after a few hours, and had finally decided she should leave, Etta had whispered, "Don't leave me."

"Mom," Jean began, then stopped. She didn't know what to say, because she was going to have to leave, and that was all there was to it.

"Don't."

Jean closed her eyes against the tears that burned there.

"I'll be back," she said, as she walked away. She refused to look back.

"Don't leave me."

She swallowed a lump, then hurried out to her car and away from the nursing home.

And now, as she drove through the snow, all she could think of was her mother's last words, and the tone in which she'd whispered them.

"Don't leave me, don't leave me, don't leave me," the words thrummed in Jean's mind which each rotation of the car's tires.

She blinked away tears, slowed the car again as her vision blurred. She had to be careful. It would be dark soon, and she wasn't too steady driving right now. She didn't want something to happen.

The windshield wipers whispered, "Don't leave me, don't leave me. Don't."

The snow had thickened in the past few minutes, until it was like a curtain that hung across the road. The car crept forward, hesitant on the slippery blacktop. Again it slid, and she concentrated on getting back into the right lane.

She could only see a few feet ahead now, and she wondered why she hadn't seen any traffic on the road since leaving HarborHouse. Perhaps most motorists had heard the forecast and decided to simply stay home. Which she should have done.

Except that she couldn't put off any longer what had to be done.

"I had no choice," she said aloud, and the sound of her voice seemed strange.

The wipers still worked, but now they made no noise, not even a whisper. She couldn't even hear the tires on the road any longer. There wasn't even the sound of the wind rustling through the trees.

She would be glad to get home. Home, which would seem too big with just her in it now, and so empty. She would be alone for the first time in six years. Free to do whatever she wanted without disturbing her mother who always complained about Jean's "racket"—her whistling, her off-key singing, the music she enjoyed listening to. It didn't matter what it was, Etta complained about it; everything was always too loud.

No, she couldn't think about that. Had to look at the road and watch the snow and worry about ice—

At that moment a clearing appeared on her right, and automatically she glanced toward it and saw an ice-covered pond. And something else, and as the car swept past, she reacted with a small motion that translated into a jerk of her arms, and the car swerved. She fought for control as the car spun around and around. Finally, it plowed into a snow bank off to one side of the road, and slammed to a stop, snapping her forward. Luckily she wore her seatbelt, and so wasn't too badly shaken up. She suspected that she would have more than a few bruises tomorrow morning, but at least none of her bones were broken.

For a moment she sat there, trembling, her eyes tearing from nervous reaction. She put her head down the steering wheel and wept a little. After a few minutes she felt better, and she wiped at her face with a wadded up tissue she found in a coat pocket.

She took a deep breath. She had to do something now. She tried to back up the car, but the tires spun hopelessly, digging into the snow even deeper. She swore, and hit the dashboard with the palm of her hand, and cursed more at the pain. She closed her eyes and leaned back and told herself to count to ten. When she reached twenty-five, she tried to move the car, putting it into first, then quickly into reverse, then back to first, then reverse again, hoping the rocking motion would loosen the snow's grasp of the car.

But it didn't.

Finally, she turned off the headlights and the ignition. She didn't want to wear down the battery, not if she were going to have to spend the night here.

She wondered about walking back to the nursing home. It couldn't be that far. She glanced at the dashboard. She must have come seven or eight, maybe ten, miles. No, surely it must be more than that by now. She could walk that, not easily, on any given day, except a snowy and cold one. Today that would seem like a hundred miles or more.

She huddled inside her oversized coat and stared ahead at the gloom and tried to figure out what she should do. She couldn't just sit here. She was a few yards off the road now, and she feared that if anyone came by, they would miss her. She ought to get out and signal someone. Just in case.

But it was so cold out there, and the snow was falling even more heavily than before. She breathed deeply, watched as her breath frosted.

She had no choice.

She had to get out.

Besides she should go back to that pond. Had to find what she'd thought she'd seen. A light from a house across the pond maybe. Some sign of civilization. Help of some sort.

She got out, and thrust her car keys into her pocket. She didn't bother to lock the car. Who would think to stop and steal anything during a snowstorm?

Snow blew into her face, and she shook her head, as if that would get rid of it. Then she pulled up the hood of her coat and started traipsing back to the spot where she'd lost control of the car. She reached the place—it wasn't hard to find—after a few minutes and glanced toward the pond again. There *was* a light there. A house? She hoped so.

Jean clambered down the small slope to one side of the road's shoulder, slipping and sliding a little. Finally she reached level ground again. It was difficult to walk rapidly, because the snow was deep already, and it sucked at her feet, slowing her down.

She kept her head tucked onto her chest; she didn't like the snow blowing into her eyes. Ever so often she glanced up to be sure the light was still ahead. Once, she thought she ought to give up and return to the car, but she had come this far and there was no sense in giving up. Not yet at any rate.

She tried to whistle, but the sound died in her throat. The wind brushed across her face with a chilly caress, and she thrust her hands deeper into her pockets.

There was no panic, despite the storm, the cold, the longing to be home—she never thought she would not get out of this situation. After all, things—good and bad—had always worked out in the end for her. Always, during her life. This time it would be no different.

The light seemed closer now, although it was hard to judge distance in the snowstorm. She kept plodding onward, and when a quarter of an hour had elapsed, she stopped and stared at the light which came from a building not so far away.

It couldn't be, she told herself; she had left that behind hours before.

But it was.

HarborHouse.

And there, just a few yards in front of the porch, a dark

seated figure, snow collecting on it, icicles forming on the metal, waited.

Jean approached, reluctant, yet compelled to see who it was.

"Don't, don't," the wind breathed while ice crackled around her.

Jean reached for the nearly fleshless claw held out to her.

"Don't leave me," her mother whispered.

Jean took the cold and trembling hand, and she bent over as the snow gathered at her feet.

"Don't," the wind soughed. Overhead the branches clacked like bare bones. "Don't."

"I won't leave, Mom," she promised. "Not this time."

The wind sighed.

The light on the porch winked out.

THE VISIT

The first day I noticed the angel it was snowing.

Snow and angels went together, I thought as I looked out the window into the backyard. But in October?

It was two-thirds of the way through the month, and the weather had been peculiar all year long for this part of the southwest, so why not expect heavy snow in October? At least it wasn't July. Now *that* would have been ridiculous.

I stood watching the angel, who was busy darting through the drifting flakes, looking as if he—or was it a she, or possibly an it? Had some ecumenical council somewhere determined the sex of angels? And just how was that done anyway?—wanted to pick up his robes and roll and roll and roll.

The ground wasn't quite white yet, so the angel would probably get more dirt than snow on his flowing robes.

Angels with dirty faces, I thought, the old movie title floating into my mind.

After a while the snow stopped—there was hardly more than half an inch coating the ground, and the angel stopped his dancing or whatever it was, and turned to gaze at me through the window.

Involuntarily I stepped backward. Then I realized what I was doing, and gave a little laugh. The angel could have seen me at any time. Why did it bother me now? I'd been standing in front of the picture window for an hour.

Framed.

Outlined.

Vulnerable.

I shifted uncomfortably. There was no reason to be afraid of an angel, after all.

* * * * * * *

The second day I saw the angel, the wind was blowing, propelling the clouds through the turquoise sky as if they were mere pieces of fluff. The day was warmer than the previous one, and there was the smell—the tease—of rain in the air. I watched the angel dance in the wind—rainbow raiment twisting this way and that with the air currents, long coppery hair spinning outward from his head.

I thought of all the phrases that involved angels: your guardian angel watches over you, my mother always insisted; be an angel, my maiden aunt said to coax me to do something I didn't want to do; how many angels can dance on the head of a pin ran the old religious debate. Angel of the morning...a song; Teen Angel...another one. An angel on Broadway meant someone who supplied the money for the production of a play or musical. Angel dust...used to be good stuff, now it was a drug. You lay down in the snow and moved your arms and legs vigorously and "made" an angel.

Angels to the left, angels to the right, angels, stand up, sit down, fight, fight, fight.

I smiled briefly, then wondered if my thoughts verged on the heretical. I didn't think Father Sánchez would approve much, but then Father Sánchez hadn't approved of much of what I'd done, starting with when I left the church at the age of eighteen. He hadn't approved of Andrew or our marriage or what came after. He had approved of Patrick, though, and that had been good. But then Patrick—

No, I told myself. I didn't want to think of little Patrick or Andrew. That way lay madness. Or at least more pain, pain that I couldn't control, pain that racked my mind and soul. And hadn't I, through sheer force of will, driven that pain from my heart, hadn't I built walls around myself so that I could retreat to this neutral spot and think of nothing, feel nothing?

Hadn't I?

I watched a few minutes longer, then slowly backed away, never turning my back on the creature that danced in the wind.

I didn't know why the angel made me uneasy, but he did. Maybe even a little fearful.

Angels were good, weren't they? They were *godly* creatures, after all.

I remembered that when I was a little girl, long before I went to school, I had contracted chicken pox so severely that I had almost died. My mother told me later that I had insisted that I saw someone—something—in the corner, an angel, perhaps, "come to take me away." She always dismissed it a mere fever dream. But what if it were true? I wished I'd asked my mother about it when I was older, but I left home for college, and then later my parents had died in a car crash, and so much had been left unsaid, unfinished between them and me.

Come to think of it, they probably wouldn't have approved of Andrew either.

I breathed deeply and thought I felt a pain in my chest. Nothing physical, I assured myself; just some little shard left over from the breaking of my heart.

Outside, the angel whirled and twirled, and my attention returned to him.

Angels....

Angel food cake...angelfish...angel hair pasta...Los Angeles, the city of angels...there were so many phrases, so many times that angels touched our lives, I thought. If you had an angel on your shoulder, you were lucky.

* * * * * * *

The third day I saw the angel it was raining.

Water gushed from the leaden sky, drenching the poor creature. His—her—its hair lay in strings across its thin face. The robe once so beautiful sagged around the creature's asexual body, and even the feathers of its magnificent wings drooped.

It stared at the house...at *me*...as if the rain and its miserable condition were all my fault.

I ached for it. It looked so lonely. Like me. Should I invite it in for a cup of tea and a chance to dry off? What would happen if I went to the back door and called to it? Did I want to know?

Yes.

No.

Yes.

I walked into the kitchen and stood there, my fingers resting lightly on the knob, and thought about what lay beyond.

Something...unknown.

Something...marvelous.

Something...angelic.

Something wonderful to touch my life...finally.

I'd better do something before I chickened out.

I whisked the door open and stared out into the pattering rain, but the angel was gone.

* * * * * * *

He didn't show up the next day, nor the next. A week later he was still missing.

Or whatever you wanted to call it. And I felt the loss far more than I wanted to admit. I had been alone for years now, since Patrick, since Andrew, and I had grown accustomed to it, and it didn't bother me.

Or so I had thought.

But now it got to the point where I would get up at different times of the night to check my moonlit yard to see if the angel was there.

But he wasn't.

I was relieved, and yet...there was a hint of disappointment.

The mornings were gray.

Imagine, though, I told myself as I checked in my car's rearview mirror to see that my lipstick hadn't transferred to my teeth, if I'd mentioned the angel to anyone at work. Imagine if some of them had come home with me to see the angel. Imagine when the angel didn't show up.

The guys in white suits would come for me with butterfly nets, I told myself, and laughed nervously, the sound too loud in the car's confined space.

When I got to work I hiked my way to the building from the lower lot. I always parked down there to force myself to walk those extra yards. I waved offhandedly to a cluster of fellow workers who greeted me, and I smiled politely, although I didn't really hear what any of them said. I had worked in this office, shuffling bureaucratic papers in this state government office, away from the public and all of the people there and their pitiful stories, for nearly a decade now, and I didn't think I knew anyone here better than I had the first time I walked through the door.

My walls kept them out.

My walls kept me in.

Once in my cubicle, I reached for the morning paper and scanned the headlines of the front section.

I was searching, as I had been since first I'd seen the exquisite angel that snowy morning, for some mention in the local newspaper.

Nothing.

Not even a paragraph buried in the back section, right before classified.

Or possibly they weren't admitting it. Or else they *had* and the men with the butterfly nets had already come for them.

Still it would have been comforting to see some reference, no matter how small, of another sighting...somewhere, anywhere. Some little blurb to reassure me that I really wasn't losing it.

How nice to see something like "Penny Warren of Pennsauken today reported seeing an angel. Ms. Warren invited the angelic visitor in for decaf and doughnuts, whereupon the angel bestowed her with many wondrous gifts and then left, declaring that Ms. Warren's homemade doughnuts were the best he'd ever tasted."

Then I could call up Penny Warren back in Pennsauken and we could chat about our mutual strange experience, and there would be some comfort in knowing...knowing that I wasn't alone.

But angels wouldn't come in and chow down on glazed and raspberry filled doughnuts.

Would they?

And what kind of wondrous gifts would an angel give someone? Long life? Wealth? Health? For God's sakes, I told myself, *angels* aren't *genies.*

Or maybe angels brought the gift of removal of memories? I wouldn't mind that. Memories brought pain, and pain brought awareness, and—

No. The walls slid down silently, and I forced myself to smile, alone in my cubicle. My practiced smile, my friendly yet impersonal smile, my smile that said nothing is affecting me, I'm quite all right, thank you.

But it really didn't matter, did it? No one else had seen the angel, an angel...any angel. Only I had. Or perhaps others had seen them but said nothing. They didn't want the butterfly nets coming after them.

An angelic visitation.

I was far from being a saint or a virgin, so I wondered that an angel would call on me. He hadn't spoken to me, though, so was it a *real* visitation? I wished that I still went to church, that I could talk to Father Sánchez or someone about this. Was I blessed by this event? How should one feel when one was blessed? I didn't feel any different. Or did I. I patted my hair, aware for the first time that I did this too often.

But, I thought and took strength in that thought, I might not be alone. Perhaps the angelic visitations numbered in the dozens...the hundreds...the thousands.

Literally an angelic invasion. Hundreds and hundreds of celestial beings sprinkled through this country and others. Maybe it signified the coming of better times, the coming of the end of the world. Maybe it meant nothing.

Maybe it meant ultimately that we weren't alone, that someone waited.

Maybe it didn't mean that at all.

I sighed, and shoved the paper aside and got to work. I had too much to do today without dreaming about angels and such nonsense. I focused on the numbers and not the pitiful excuses, and told myself for the millionth time that I really enjoyed my work.

Only once more that day, and that was right before lunch-time, did I think of the angel and that was to tell myself that I would be better prepared next time—next time I'd have my camera at hand. I'd take a photograph of the angel, and then I'd have the film developed, and there, that would prove that I was seeing an angel.

Prove to whom? I asked myself.

Prove to myself, but by now I was wondering if I had really seen it.

* * * * * * *

But I *had* seen the angel, because the very next day it was back in my yard.

It just stood there in the yard, not doing anything. It wasn't dancing. Just standing. The wind didn't blow; there was no snow or rain. It was a perfect October day with the sky overhead a rich turquoise.

The angel was staring at my house, staring at *me*, I decided, and I wanted to be somewhere else.

I was nervous and wanted to stay away from the window, but I couldn't. All I could think of was the angel. I had to go to work, but couldn't. I couldn't bring myself to go out the door. Even though the angel was in the backyard, he might come around to the front yard. He might block the driveway. I might hit him with my car. What happened if you accidentally killed an angel? I frowned. Wasn't there a story a long time ago about something like that? I couldn't remember, but I figured it couldn't have had a pleasant ending. They rarely did.

I could still remember the sound the car made that day...that gentle *thump*...and then I slammed on the brakes and I was out on the driveway in an instant, and there was the little broken body of Patrick who had been playing under the car. I would have known that, too, if Andrew and I hadn't been fighting as usual, if I hadn't stormed out of the house, hadn't thrown the car in reverse without checking...checking as I always did.

Except that day.

I couldn't face the car today.

Too many memories, and my wall seemed to be crumbling in spots.

So I called in sick, and spent most of the day flitting from window to window, looking out. The angel was there all day, too, just standing and looking.

Gooseflesh erupted on my skin, and I rubbed my upper arms.

I tried to read some of the books that had been piling up by my couch, but couldn't concentrate. I tried to watch some soaps on the television, but all I saw was the angel standing there.

Finally, I stood and told myself this was nonsense, and that I had to face this thing once and for all. I didn't have any home-made doughnuts, but I had a box of ginger snaps. Maybe he'd like a couple of those.

I went to the back door and opened it. If I expected a gust of wind or something equally dramatic at that moment, then I was disappointed.

The angel continued to look at me.

I smiled.

The angel smiled back.

I breathed a sigh of relief. This wasn't so bad after all.

"I would like to invite you inside," I called, using my friend-liest tone, and I smiled my bureaucratic smile because I no longer knew how to smile otherwise. "There's so much to speak of."

"So much," the angel echoed.

He glided toward the house, toward me, and it wasn't until he was on the patio and only a few feet away, that I saw his eyes weren't the heavenly cerulean blue I had envisioned, but rather a flat *dead* black; and his skin wasn't porcelain white, but rather the pasty color of something diseased.

It took a few seconds before I recognized Patrick.

I think I said God help me, but by then it was too late.

THE CHILDREN'S HOUR

The first phone call came, as she'd always dreaded it would, in the middle of the night.

The sharp peal pierced dreams and sleep, and by the second ring, she was reaching over for the handset.

"Hello?" she asked without a hint of sleep-slur.

"Darcy, is that you?"

"Yes." She sat up, bedclothes falling away from her chest, and reached to flick on the bedside lamp. Her hand hesitated. Some things were best delivered in the dark.

"This is Irene Baldwin, your mom's neighbor?"

"Oh, my God," Darcy said. Something fluttered in her throat, and she pressed a hand against her chest. Breathe, breathe, breathe. "Oh, my God," she repeated. "What happened? What hospital is she in?" She was up and out of bed as one gruesome scenario after another played in her head—her mother tripping on the top step of the basement stairs; her mother getting out of bed in the middle of the night and, disoriented, falling; her mother keeling over with a heart attack...a stroke...a who-knew-what...

She'd need at least two days change of clothing, probably, and she'd have to have Mr. Romero check in on the cats. She tried to remember if she had a meeting tomorrow at work, but she couldn't—

"Gracious no, honey, she's not in the hospital."

Abruptly Darcy sat down. "She's not?"

"No, I'm sorry to make you think that."

Now, Darcy could hear another voice in the background...she frowned in the darkness, as if that would make her hear more clearly. Was that her mother? "Mom?"

"Yes, she's fine, dear. That's her, in the living room, giving me whatfor for calling you." Mrs. Baldwin chuckled. "I'm sorry to disturb you, but I thought you should know. I went to bed at eight like always, and then I got up in the middle of the night—you know, these old lady bladders aren't strong like they used to be—and I saw her lights still on. I thought that was mighty strange because your mom doesn't stay up all that late, and here it was past midnight and all. So I put my wrapper on and come over and found her."

"Found her?" Darcy repeated.

"Yep, the poor thing was on the floor. Just sitting there like she'd wanted to be there. Still in her clothes. Just grinning at me."

Darcy rather suspected her mother had not been grinning like Mrs. Baldwin said. She could well imagine what her mother had said upon her neighbor's arrival. "So she's okay?"

"Well, yes. Nothin's broken, and she's not hurtin'. But I thought I should call you. I hope you don't mind."

"Not at all, Mrs. B. You did the right thing." She hesitated. "Could you hand the phone to Mom?"

"Certainly, dear."

Darcy heard some muffled sounds, an exclamation from her mother, a mollifying tone from Mrs. B, and then her mother growled, "Don't come."

"I'm coming."

"No. I said, don't come."

"I'm coming."

"No. I don't need you here."

"I'm coming, Mother."

"No. I don't want you here."

"I'm coming!" Darcy screamed into the receiver, slammed the phone down, and burst into tears.

* * * * * * *

She was on the road in less than an hour, her clothing and whatnots tossed hastily into an overnight bag.

Before she left town, she gassed up the car, bought a six-pack of canned soda, chips, and chocolate cookies. She knew what she needed in the time of a crisis.

Now, she wiped her greasy fingers against the leg of her jeans, and glanced at the car's clock. 4:15. She'd been on the road less than half an hour. Two and a half to go.

Why had she moved so far away? she asked herself, not for the first time.

Because her mother drove her nuts, she answered for the umpteenth time.

She pictured her mother sitting on the floor, looking serene as Mrs. B poked her head into the house to see if she was okay. Had her mom slid off the couch? Or had she just decided to settle on the carpet for the night? There was no use speculating. No use.

But of course, she couldn't help thinking about it. The whole scene played over and over in her mind, and she sighed, then cranked up an oldies station on the radio to keep herself awake.

4:47.

She'd called her sister, who lived only sixty miles away, but Becka hadn't been there, Philippe her live-in boy toy said. She's off on a business trip, and he'd sounded miffed. So, she'd tried Becka's cell phone number. Nothing. She figured Becka didn't want to be bothered with reality while she attended the buyers' conference. Darcy had asked her not to ever turn the phone off—just in case there was emergency, but Becka had laughed and said, "It's always an emergency with you, Dar."

"Yes," she muttered aloud, "it's always an emergency with me, because I'm the only one who responds to these things." She realized she had a death grip on the steering wheel, and forced herself to relax. Their older brother was worse than useless when it came to anything dealing with Mom, who thought the sun and moon rose with Jimmy, and so the serious matters of their elderly mother's life had fallen to the two sisters. Or rather the one sister. The baby of the family, and where's the fun in that?

The Stones wailed about not getting satisfaction, and she pressed another button, paused when she heard one of those all-night talk shows.

The miles and minutes flew by as she listened to one crackpot caller after another relaying, in excruciating detail, firsthand accounts of hovering mother ships, Bigfoot, alien abductions, take your pick from column A and column B of governmental conspiracies, leprechauns and fairies.

Now, that was a new one. Usually these kooks kept to their UFO sightings. But leprechauns? Fairies?

"That's it," she said aloud. "I'm a changeling. That has to be it." Mom and Becka and Jimmy were all dark-haired and dark-eyed, but she had blonde hair and blue eyes, and some-where when she was a baby, a fairy sneaked in and took the little dark-haired infant away and slipped Darcy in while no one was looking. It was the only explanation. It just had to be. She couldn't be any more different, in about every possible way, from her older siblings. Talk about taking one from column A and one from column B...

She giggled, realized she'd just swerved off the road onto the shoulder, and hauled the car back onto the highway before she hit the guard railing.

Telling herself to stop thinking nonsense, she cranked down the window to let the cool air wash over her.

Finally, just after seven, she pulled into the driveway. The porch light was on. She opened the screen door, found the inner door open.

"Mom?" she called. She stepped into the small foyer.

"I told you not to bother to come," her mother's querulous voice said.

"Hi to you, too."

Darcy walked into the living room, and there sat Helen

Woods, the Queen of the May, back against the sofa, her news-papers scattered around her, cat on her lap, a glass of some clear liquid—water, Darcy hoped—at hand. As usual, the television blared. Mrs. B was gone, even though Darcy had begged her to stay; no doubt her mother had driven the well-intentioned neighbor away.

Darcy wanted nothing more than to rush over, wrap her arms around the frail form, and ask if she was okay, but years of being pushed away kept her where she was.

"You okay?"

Her mother's black eyes glared in the morning light. "Yes. I told you I was. I don't know why you drove down here. You've got better things to do, I'm sure, with that big fancy job of yours."

Yes, the big fancy job that I'm not at today, and thank God I have a sympathetic boss.

"You're my mother. I had to come. I *wanted* to come."

"Oh, I'm so sure."

Always sarcastic. Darcy sighed. There was no sense arguing; she'd never won an argument, wasn't likely to at this point. Her mother could always trump her, always had, always would. Maybe that's why Jimmy was the favorite. He never argued, just smiled and caved.

"I told that meddling fool not to call you. Probably spied on me. Probably wanted me to fall."

"Did you fall?"

"Of course, not," her mother said, as if she thought Darcy had lost her marbles.

Alice through the looking glass. That's what she felt like. She'd tumbled through to some bizarre world where things weren't quite right.

"Well, let's get you up off the floor."

"I don't need help."

"Okay." She waited. "Well?" she asked when her mother didn't twitch a muscle.

"I'm thinking about standing up."

"Yeah, and I'm thinking about kicking your butt," Darcy said as she leaned down to help her mother stand.

"Darcy! Is that any way to speak to your mother!"

"Strangely enough, yes."

With little effort, she got the elderly woman to her feet and checked for bruises; she found no broken bones, no scrapes, so that was good.

"When did you last eat?" she asked as she lead her mother to the kitchen table.

"I had dinner last night. No, wait, lunch? I'm not hungry. Don't make anything. You'll just waste it," she said sharply as Darcy opened the fridge. Some eggs—expiration date not past, she noted with surprise—cheese, and half a loaf of bread. And thou beside me in the wilderness, she thought, nearly giggling aloud. Once again she realized how surreal things became once she returned home. Had it been like that when she was a kid? she wondered.

"Don't go to any trouble," Helen said as her daughter cracked a handful of eggs into a frying pan.

"Yeah, right."

Her mother kept denying she was hungry, but when Darcy set the scrambled eggs and toast down on the table, Helen fell upon her food as if she hadn't eaten in days. Which was probably what happened, Darcy figured as she nibbled her unbuttered toast.

The cat meowed, and Darcy tossed a clump of eggs to it. The animal looked healthy, which was good, but she could smell the acrid tang of cat pee, which meant that her mother had probably not bothered cleaning the litter box in days.

"You just sit there and rest, Mom," she said as she stood up.

"Don't do all that stuff. I have a girl that comes in to clean."

"The girl", who was nearly sixty, hadn't been to the house in decades. The old woman kept up a steady barrage of criticism and complaint while Darcy washed and dried the dishes. She cleaned the litter box—shuddered when she saw its condition—then quickly scrubbed the bathroom.

"I don't want you doing that. You always use the wrong kind

of soap."

"I'm using the cleanser I found in here, Mom."

"Well, it's the wrong one."

It's always the wrong one. Or I always do it the wrong way, or not well enough or...whatever.

Shortly afterward, she noticed the paper bags in the hallway; they'd been tucked into the shadows when she first arrived. She started unloading the groceries that been sitting out in the hall God knows how long. She found a carton of orange juice, opened it up and winced at the smell, and poured the contents down the kitchen drain.

"That's a waste of a perfectly good juice."

"Mom, it's rancid. Or whatever juice does when it goes bad. When did you last have groceries delivered?"

Helen thought about it. "Last Wednesday."

"Oh God." Darcy fetched a bucket and mop and cleaning cloths and sponges and proceeded to clean the downstairs, her mother managing to find fault with everything she did.

Darcy just ignored it all. She didn't want to rise to any of the baiting. That would just give the old bag secret satisfaction. Old bag. God, the things I think about my mother. It hadn't always been like that; but recently all her mother did was criticize, nag, and pick pick pick at her. Jimmy and Becka were the same way; nothing Darcy did was good enough for any of them. She wondered what it was she'd done that made them dislike her so much.

"—just like those children who come in here."

Darcy glanced up from the bucket she was filling, her attention caught. "What?"

"She talks," Helen said, rolling her eyes. "I said, you're as bad as those children who come here...never listening to what I say, never speaking."

Darcy frowned. "What kids?"

"Children, Darcy. Kids are baby goats."

"Yeah, yeah. What about these kids?"

"They come in the house."

"Your house?"

"Yes."

Darcy waited for more. "Children from the neighborhood?" she prompted.

"Yes, they march right in here as if they owned the place."

"And?"

"I don't like it. It's not respectful."

"What do they do?"

"They just sit there—" she indicated the living room with a thrust of her chin— "and watch the TV."

Children from the neighborhood entering this house? They'd be more likely to skip into a nest of vipers or the den of a dragon.

"They never speak, even when I talk to them."

They never speak, Darcy thought as a cold shudder inched down her back, because they don't exist. And not for the first time, she realized they—she, and Becka and Jimmy—had to do something. Mom was losing it. For the most part, she could take care of herself—if eating only marshmallows and graham crackers was taking care of yourself—but...but there were things now that showed Mom wasn't able to "do" for herself.

Darcy left her talking about how cute the children were with their long blond hair and bright eyes, and went to call her sister. Something had to be done. Today. Her mother couldn't stay alone any longer.

"She still not back," Phillipe said peevishly, as if it were somehow all Darcy's fault.

"Well, please tell her it's supremely important that she get back to me. It's not an emergency—yet."

"If you insist."

"I do." She hung up and hoped her sister was screwing some new boytoy at the conference; that would show ol' Phil a thing or two. She tried Becka's cell phone again. Still nothing. Sighing, she called Jimmy next.

"I can't come today."

"Why not?"

"I have a tournament game this afternoon. Mixed doubles at

the club."

"Jimmy, I wouldn't be asking you, if I didn't think it was important—hell, it's fucking crucial!"

"Darcy, don't be a pottymouth," he said mildly.

Oh God, she thought; they've let the inmates all out. Pottymouth? That from a grown man.

"I think that Mom needs to go with one of us, or into a home or a hospital or...something."

"Really? She was fine when I was there last."

"Which was?"

"This weekend. I took her out for a bite to eat, and we came back to the house and watched an old Robert Mitchum movie on TV, and then I tucked her into bed and went home."

"And she didn't say anything strange?"

"Strange? Like what?"

"Like something about neighborhood kids coming into her house."

He laughed. "Are you kidding?"

"No. That's what she's saying."

"C'mon."

"Really."

"Oh, you sound so serious, Dar. I'll try to get by later on."

"Thanks," she said as she hung up. "For nothing."

Back in the kitchen she discovered her mother had lined up medication bottles, like plastic soldiers, on the table. Darcy quickly counted fourteen of them. Surely her mother wasn't on all of that. She checked labels. Expired prescription. Expired. Expired.

"Jimmy's coming over later."

Helen darted a look at her. "Why did you bother him? He's got important things to do."

"He's playing a fu—stupid—game this afternoon. He can damn well miss it and come visit."

"Jimmy visits me all the time. Unlike some people I could name."

That would be me, Darcy thought with a grimace. She swept

the bottles into a plastic bag. "I need to call your doctor," she said as her mother protested. "I don't think you should be taking all this crap."

"And now you want to kill me!"

You have no idea, she thought grimly as she stalked into the next room.

* * * * * *

Two hours later she had the medicine mess taken care of, with half the bottles tossed out. The doctor hadn't sounded very concerned. Then again, it wasn't his mother, just another Medicare case to him, and what did he care, when he got paid by Medicare no matter what he did.

She realized that Helen's confusion could be from the medicine. Or small strokes. Or Alzheimer's. Or dehydration or lack of food. Or...or...or...Who knew? She set an appointment for the next day—Jimmy could take her, she thought with sadistic glee—then called the grocery to see what food her mother had ordered. She cleaned the rest of the house while she waited for her brother to show up. She had to keep busy; had to keep herself from thinking too much about those imaginary kids.

Eventually, she bundled her mother up, and they went off to a diner for lunch. Helen complained the entire time that Darcy's selection of restaurants wasn't good—not like Jimmy's—but when she asked her mother where she and her brother had last eaten, the old woman fell silent.

Home again, Darcy set about straightening up the living room, tying up months-old newspapers for the recycling center, tossing out used paper plates and plastic cups she found tucked here and there. She dusted. She vacuumed. Then she sat with her mother and waited for Jimmy to show up.

More hours dragged by.

"When do the kids come here?" she asked.

"Any time they want. Sometimes I'm in bed, and I hear them."

"What do you do then?"

Helen's eyes widened slightly. "I get up, and I tiptoe to the door, and I peer in. And they're just sitting there staring at the TV! It's hypnotized them, you know. They sit there and stare and stare, and they won't talk to me a bit!"

Nuts. Her mother was fucking nuts, and she put her head in her hands and squeezed back the tears.

* * * * * * *

Jimmy didn't show up that night, nor did he call. Darcy stayed overnight, and finally somewhere around noon the next day, he strolled in. Darcy watched her mother's face light up and felt her teeth grinding together. She wished that her mother looked like that when she came into the room. Oh, stop whining, she told herself, but tears still dampened her eyelashes.

Jimmy gave no explanation of why he hadn't come the day before, nor did Darcy ask. She had heard all his excuses before, and frankly she was tired of them.

"Hey, it's my best girl," he said, gathering their mother's hands in his and dropping a kiss on her forehead. "How you doing?"

"I could be better," she said, shooting a dark glance at Darcy.

Jimmy chuckled. "I bet."

Helen grinned slyly.

Sharing a little inside joke at her expense, Darcy thought, and realized she had to get out of there now.

"I'm going home," she announced.

"I told you not to come down here," Helen said, the corners of her mouth turning down.

"Yeah, whatever." She looked at her brother. "I'll call you later, Jimmy."

"Sure, Dar. Hey, Mom, there's a retrospective of old Rock Hudson and Doris Day movies on in a bit. Wanna watch?" He was up and across the room to the TV.

Darcy stood there. Already dismissed. Already forgotten.

She watched her brother laughing with her mother, plumping up the pillows on the sofa, and realized she wished they'd both just drop dead.

She turned around and left.

She got home in the afternoon and laid down on her bed and tried to capture some of the sleep she'd missed last night as she dozed in her mother's musty guest room, but she couldn't. All she could think of was her mother's happy expression when her brother walked in. Okay. I'm jealous. I admit it. But she's that way with Becka, too. Hell, her mother was that way if the meter reader came by. Her mother always had a smile and a good word to say to anyone. Except Darcy.

It's not fair, it's not fair, it's not fair, she thought as she buried her face in her pillow.

But then who ever said life with parents was fair?

She sighed, closed her eyes, and told herself not to think. She had just drifted off to a welcome sleep when the phone rang. She stiffened. Oh, my God, what now? But it was Becka on the other end.

"What happened?" her sister asked without preamble.

Darcy explained.

"Is that it? I thought it was an emergency."

"It is. Well, almost is. We have to do *something*, Becka. The time has come. Mom can't take care of herself any more."

"I was there last weekend, and she seemed fine to me."

Jimmy was there last weekend, too, Darcy recalled. Were they having a secret party—without her? "Of course, she seemed okay. She playacts or something in front of you guys."

"Well, how is it that you're the only one who sees this stuff, huh? How come her doctor doesn't say anything?"

"Her doctor is a quack and doesn't care as long as he gets his Medicare co-payment. And as to why I see these things, and you and Jimmy don't...well, maybe it's because I don't have my head up my ass like you do."

Silence. Then Becka chuckled. "Oh, come on, Dar. Lighten up."

"Fine. Ha ha. See. I'm lightening up."

"God, you had better find a man soon. You need a good screw."

"Thanks for the advice. Talk to you later." She hung up, lay back down and with a heavy sigh, told herself to lighten up. Maybe her sister was right. God knew, she did need a good screw. But her sister seemed to do enough for both of them, though.

Meow, she thought, and smiled for the first time in two days.

* * * * * * *

The second call came three weeks later while she was at work. She was in a department meeting with her boss droning on and on, and her mind wandered, so she didn't realize at first that he'd stopped and that Carol from the front office was standing at the door. Everyone was looking at her.

"What?" But she knew even before Carol said anything.

"A call for you—an emergency."

She was up and out of her chair in one fluid motion, nodding to Michael who looked sympathetic, then half-walking, half-running down to her office to take the call.

"She's on the floor again," Mrs. B said, more concern in her voice this time.

"I'm on my way," Darcy said and rushed back to the conference room, spoke a minute with Michael, then off she went, not bothering to go home and pack.

I should have had Mrs. B call Jimmy and Becka, she thought. Maybe if they heard it from her lips, they'd believe. I should have asked her to call an ambulance, then told her I'd meet her at the hospital.

When Darcy rushed into the house, Mrs. B was still there, patiently listening to Helen talking about the children coming into her house.

The neighbor looked up. "I'm sorry," she said plaintively.

"Thank you, Mrs. B. I appreciate all you've done."

"I have to get home. I left Frank alone."

"Thanks again." She knew that Mr. B had health problems of his own.

"Well, Mom, what the hell are you doing on the floor?" This time her mother wasn't sitting. She was lying there on the carpet, the cat curled up at her side.

"Don't be sarcastic, dear. It doesn't suit you."

"Oh, I know that all too well." She crouched by her mother. "Did you fall?"

"No. Yes. Well, I mean, a hand made me stumble. It reached out and grabbed my leg. I was startled, you know!"

"A hand?" Darcy looked around. She didn't see any errant hands flopping around and thought for a split second of that old Michael Caine movie. She muffled a giggle.

"It's not a laughing matter," Helen said sternly.

"I'm sure it's not. Let me give you a hand," and she nearly laughed aloud. She took her mother's hands, and Helen cried out in pain, and Darcy grabbed the phone and called 911.

The ambulance reached the house in mere minutes, and Darcy watched the EMTs load Helen into the emergency vehicle. Would her mother would tell them about the hand?

She called Becka and left a message with Phillipe that their mother was headed for the hospital and *yes*, this *was* an emergency, so he should get off his butt and go get Becka. Curtly she told her sister what had happened, told her to call Jimmy, then hung up, and headed for the hospital.

She sat in the waiting room, while the doctor on call saw her mother. Where were the fairies now? she asked herself. She could do with a magic wand or fairy dust or something just about now. She wanted Mom young and okay again; she didn't want to have to face the decision about putting her in a home, selling the house, getting rid of all that stuff. She wanted it okay again.

Helen was simply bruised. No broken bones.

"Well, thanks for running up my medical bills," her mother said. "All those x-rays are expensive!"

"Medicare pays for them, Mom," Darcy said wearily.

"Don't be so sure, Miss Smarty."

"I checked. They do."

"Hmmm."

Sometimes her mother had no answer for things, and for that Darcy was grateful.

"You know, those children were back today—" Helen began, but at that moment Jimmy and Becka strolled in, some six hours after Darcy'd called them. "Here's your brother and sister," her mother said, the glee in her voice unmasked.

"Oh, good, let the party begin."

"What?"

"Nothing."

"Mom, we came as fast as we could," Jimmy said.

By snail, no doubt, Darcy thought.

"What's wrong?" Becka asked.

"Nothing. Darcy was overreacting again. She always had an overactive imagination, you know."

Becka and Jimmy stared at her. As if she'd made up the whole notion of her mother falling and having bruises.

"You dragged us down here for nothing?"

"She was in pain. I called 911. I didn't know if she'd broken something. It happens. Bones snap in old people."

"You'd like that, wouldn't you?" her mother asked, casting a sly sidelong look at her.

Darcy didn't dignify it with an answer. "Let's go."

"I'll ride with Jimmy."

"Fine. Meet you back at the house."

She got back there before they did and started cleaning up. Maybe she should see about a cleaning service for her mother. An hour went by, and the three weren't back. She kept cleaning. Another hour crept by. Finally, half an hour later they walked in the door.

"Jimmy and Becka took me to dinner, which is more than you ever do," Helen said. "Family, you know, stays together."

"Yeah, right. I'm the one that starves you, huh?"

"You said it. I didn't."

She tried to talk to her brother and sister, but they were concerned about her mother and found things to do rather than talk to her. By midnight they had gone home; it was just Darcy left.

"I'll stay the night."

"If you want."

"Would it kill you to say you'd like me to stay, that you'd like me to be around."

"You'd like that."

Darcy tucked Helen into the bed, and thought for a moment about staying downstairs on the couch, but shook her head. She had to sleep in a real bed tonight; she was bone tired. She went upstairs, stripped off her clothes and hung them carefully on a hanger, then found an old nightgown of hers and slipped that on. Sleep eluded her for a long time. She thought about all that her mother had said, all that she claimed she had seen. Didn't anyone but Darcy think there was something seriously wrong here? She kept going over her options, one by one, and felt exhaustion—mental and physical—seep into her. She had to rest, had to stop thinking about this. Had to...

It seemed that she'd hardly fallen asleep, when she sat up abruptly, awakened by a sound. What sound, though?

Her mother.

Heart pounding, she leaped out of bed and fairly flew down the stairs to the old den now converted into a bedroom. "Mom." The bed hadn't been slept in. Not knowing what to expect, she stepped to the door of the living room.

She saw something dark on the carpet.

She took a few steps into the room.

Her mother. Lying face up on the floor.

"Darcy." The old woman's voice was weak. Light from the streetlamp crept in through the venetian blinds, and Darcy thought she saw a bit of blood trickling from the old woman's mouth.

Darcy stared at her. "Do you need help up?" She waited for

the usual sarcastic comment, but none came this time.

"Darcy. Call."

Darcy blinked. "Call the paramedics again, Mom? Call Becka and interrupt her while she's screwing her brains? Call Jimmy and make him miss his beauty sleep? Call Mrs. B? If I turn on the living light, she'll come over here."

"Children. They grabbed me. K-knocked me down."

"What? The children were here again? Not speaking, huh? Well, Mom, I've got news for you. There are no children in the neighborhood any more. Everyone here is some old geezer or geezerette, and their childbearing days have been over for decades. These so-called children exist only in your head. Your sad, demented head."

"Chil—"

"Yeah, right. The children, the children, the children. There are *no* children."

She plopped down onto the couch, only a few feet away from her mother, and grabbed the remote control. She clicked the TV on, watched as the screen turned grey.

Her mother gasped, then started coughing. Darcy flicked a glance toward her, saw her chest rise and fall slowly.

The grey-white light of the television seemed almost hypnotic, and she changed channel after channel with the sound down. She never liked it loud like her mom did.

She kept her eyes on the screen and nothing else, so she felt rather than saw them slip onto the couch on both sides of her. When she finally looked, she saw why her mother thought they were children. Slight of frame, they weren't very tall, and they had long light-colored hair and intense blue eyes. They didn't say anything, but they didn't have to. And she knew they'd heard her plea, that they wanted to help her. They believed her.

"You know, Mom," Darcy said aloud, "you're right—family does stay together."

Third's time a charm.

Darcy sat back and waited with the fairies, their eyes glittering in the dim light, for her mother to die.

SOLITAIRE

It all started as a sore throat. Nothing much, really. I'd had sore throats off and on all through my life; this was just one more in a long line of petty annoyances. Hardly worth the bother, hardly worth going to the doctor, right?

Wrong.

The sore throat worsened, and by the time I realized I was truly ill and went to the doctor and he ran test after test, it was too late.

Can you imagine that in this day and age, that *something* is too late? We have all these advances in science, preventive this and that, with thousands of drugs for just about every illness—real or imagined—and yet...yet, sometimes medicine doesn't cure it all.

I had the choice of a lengthy course of poisonous chemicals being pumped into my body to prolong my life a few months, or I could go the route of more natural remedies that would manage the pain, but do nothing to give me extra days.

I opted for quality. Mike thought that was the best approach, too. All through the ordeal Mike, my husband of eleven years, was there with me, holding my hand, stroking my forehead, letting me lean against his shoulder to cry.

At night he held me and whispered to me of his love, and we talked about the places we had visited, the people we had met, and more often than not I fell asleep so easily, secure in the comforting circle of his arms. I tried not to think about the children we would never have now; after all, I had him. Thank

God, for that.

How devastating it was, then, for me to discover Mike was cheating on me.

I learned of his infidelity a month into my dying. In bed, I hoped I could nap, but sleep eluded me. I hadn't taken the pills that Mike normally gave me at lunch—I had found them in the pocket of my sweater as I trudged upstairs and figured I would take then in an hour or so when I got up.

So, I kept my eyes shut and pretended I was sleeping and hoped that somehow I would drift off, and that's when I heard the first sound...like a woman's voice. I heard it again, then shrugged mentally. No doubt Mike had a radio or the television on, even though it was the middle of the day. Then I heard his voice—I couldn't make out the words, just the tone. And the woman responded.

My eyes popped open, and I pushed up to a sitting position. I waited. Again his voice, and her response. I eased off the bed so it wouldn't squeak, then stepped softly to the door. I opened it just a crack.

The woman laughed...more a giggle than a laugh, I guess, and I ground my teeth. "Oh, Mike, don't do that." Her tone was husky, almost throaty.

"I thought you liked it," he said, chuckling.

Somehow I knew they weren't talking about food.

"Oh, oh, yes, I do. Oh, yes, yes. Oh, honey." She trilled, then gave full voice to her passion.

Mike grunted. I imagined each thrust he made into her, his skin slick with sweat, his face so intent on his passion.

Their voices blended, wordless, as they surrendered to their lust, and then I heard more murmuring, and her squeal and sustained gasp as he came with a muffled bellow.

The room seemed to blur for a moment, or perhaps it was my tears.

Mike had told me right after I'd been diagnosed that he wanted to make love to me, but only when I wanted to. I had just been happy these past weeks that he held me and murmured words of love. The physical aspect had been too tiring, even though we'd tried a couple of times.

I could understand that he was frustrated—I was, too. I wanted him to make love to me, but it was too exhausting, too hard. I wasn't long for the world; at least he could have kept it zipped up while I was still here.

I wiped the tears off my cheeks, felt the anger growing.

Quietly I shuffled down the short hall to the head of the stairs. I knew the placement of each creaking board in the floor and managed to avoid them all.

I reached the first step, went down slowly until I was halfway down the stairs. And there on the couch in the living room—my good imported Italian leather sofa—was my husband, his hairy butt in the air, as he sprawled across—

Good God! It was Fiona, my sister. She lay under him, a blissful expression on her sallow features. Feeling faint, I grabbed the banister for support.

I must have made a noise—how could I not have?—and Fiona's eyes flew open, and we stared at one another. She tried to look triumphant, but she must have seen something in my face, in my eyes, that scared her, because suddenly she pushed at him, and Mike thought she wanted to nuzzle him, so he started kissing her neck.

"Get up, get up, get up!" she demanded.

"I'm up, sweetie, for you."

"She's here!" Fiona shrieked at him.

He raised his head, and his jaw dropped. Seeing me wasn't something he'd anticipated. What, I wondered, had been in those sleeping tablets to put me out so thoroughly? And just how long had this *tête-à-tête* been going on?

I took another step down.

The room got a little shimmery at that point, and I must have let go of the banister because the next thing I knew I tumbled down the stairs, all the while Fiona screamed and Mike shouted.

Then blackness.

Then a bright light, and then blackness again.

And when I woke I was sitting in the living room in one of the wingback chairs I'd just had recovered last spring. The couch was bare of human occupants; in fact, there was no sign of Mike and Fiona.

I guess I must have passed out, and they propped me up in the chair. That seemed a trifle odd, even cold for them.

The doorknob rattled and the door swung open. Mike was in his best suit—the one I insisted he buy when he went on that last trip to Boston; had she been at the hotel waiting for him?—and Fiona was decked out in a black designer dress and a trim hat, complete with veil. Fast dressers, I thought; last time I'd seen them they'd been buck naked.

I grinned—inappropriate, I know, but I couldn't help it. "So, why the long faces?"

They ignored me. Fiona went to my husband, and he wrapped his arms around her. She started weeping as he held her close.

"Hello!" I called.

"I didn't want it to be like that," Fiona whispered.

"I know, sweetie, I know," he said in a soothing voice. "I didn't, either. I mean, God...you know...."

She nodded.

"Hello?" I said again.

"Want a drink?" Mike asked.

"Sure."

He brought back a bottle of wine and two glasses and poured for them.

"I'd like a glass, too," I said. The doctors hadn't said I couldn't drink. And besides, what was it going to do...kill me? I laughed.

Again they ignored me.

They started talking in low tones about some dreary funeral they'd attended. Fiona alternately wept and sipped her wine. And just when I thought I couldn't take it any longer—all this sad talk about who was there and who wasn't —she stood up, letting her wine glass drop onto the carpet. And try getting *that* stain out, I thought sourly.

"I feel horny."

Mike grinned wolfishly. "Me, too, babe."

And right then and there, in front of me, they stripped and started screwing on my couch again.

That was it! I stood up, and I went over and grabbed Mike's butt and pulled him off her and the couch.

He gaped at Fiona. "Why'd you kick me off?"

"What are you talking about?" she said.

"You pushed me."

"I pushed you," I said irritably. I studied my sister's naked body. Really, any bigger up top and she was going to have to have a boob tuck. But then men always did seem to go for the big breasts. I wonder if Mike knew those breasts weren't that way because of nature but rather the surgical work of one Dr. Gannon.

I remembered when Fiona was just a flat-chested, wide-eyed child, who followed me around, mimicking every action. It had so annoyed me.

But I had shown her how to use tampons and what to look for in a boy, and how to fix her hair and dress nicely. I guess I had taught her a thing or two.

Mike came back to her, and I gave him a good kick. My foot connected solidly with his derriere, and he landed on Fiona. "Get off me, you ox!"

"Ox!"

"Ow, you're hurting me!"

"You think that was hurting? I'm gonna hurt you now." He grabbed her and hauled her across his lap and began smacking her butt really hard, one stinging blow after another. She cussed and sobbed as he spanked her, her butt turning cherry red, then all at once she got turned on, and so did he, and they ended up doing it twice. Twice!

Utterly disgusted, I walked away, and as I headed up the stairs, I glanced at the mirror over the mantle and paled. My God, I looked like I had seen a ghost.

But I had.

Me.

* * * * * * *

I stared up at the bedroom ceiling. I was dead. How did this happen? I wasn't supposed to die for months and months. Well, months, at least.

The fall down the stairs...when I lost my balance, I must have done something serious, like break my neck. Or maybe I just hurt myself really badly, and they left me there to die by inches. I could imagine them dressing after their illicit foray on the couch, then going out to dinner, and at 7:05 Mike glancing at his imported watch—the one I gave him on our tenth anniversary—and saying, "Well, she should have kicked the bucket by now."

And they'd have a leisurely drive back to the house—*my* house—and tiptoe in to see if I was still breathing.

What if I was? Did they help me shuffle off this mortal coil by smothering me? Probably not. Any medical examiner could find traces, indicating death by that method. No, I had died of natural causes. A freak accident.

Damn it. Isn't that ironic? Dying woman dies through ridiculous tumble down the stairs.

Damn.

So, what the hell was I going to do about it?

I was in the guest room, and I could hear the energetic squeaking of the bed springs as they screwed again in *my* bedroom across the hall. My God, they were worse than crazed rabbits! I tried to remember when Mike and I had ever done it more than once in a day. I couldn't recall such an occasion, not even when we were first dating and then married. He was a one-time type of guy. Until now, I guess.

That pissed me off. Had he been saving himself? Wasn't I good enough of a lover? Why did *she* get all the best?

"It's not fair," I said to myself. "It's not. I get a husband who barely does his husbandly duty, and I get cancer, and I die in some dumb accident, and she reaps all the glory. It's. Not. Fair."

I got up and marched into our bedroom—excuse me, *his*

bedroom—and watched them going at it. He must be taking something, I thought; he wasn't this vigorous even at the beginning of our marriage. I grabbed the sheet, which was partially under him, and gave it a good jerk. His body popped up in the air a few inches, then flopped down.

He screamed wordlessly because he'd landed on a certain intimate body part.

I smiled and returned to the spare bedroom. My work that night was done.

For the next few days I haunted them. As it were. I did little things to irk them, things to make them wonder if they were losing their minds. Yelling, they accused the other of taking the toothpaste tube or burning the toast or turning off the alarm clock. It amused me greatly to see them sniping at one another.

I guess Fiona had moved in at some point, which I thought was rather tacky, given I'd just been laid to rest. But I suppose they thought they could just throw caution to the wind or whatever now that I was dead and buried and not around to put a crimp in their sleazy affair.

During the day while they worked, I wandered around the house, not really doing much of anything. Being a ghost was lonely business, I discovered all too quickly.

One day I tried to follow them to work, but I couldn't. I got no farther than the bottom of the driveway. I watched them drive off in their separate cars. I looked up and down the block, and four houses down I saw Mr. Mancini, which was odd, because Mr. Mancini, 100 pounds overweight and with high blood pressure, had died two years ago from the one-two punch of a stroke and heart attack while mowing his lawn in ninety-five-degree weather. And there he was, roaming around his yard, a lost soul without his lawn mower. Occasionally he stooped to pluck a dandelion out of the Kentucky bluegrass.

I waved. He waved.

So, I wasn't the only ghost.

I called to him, but the wind whipped away my words. Besides, Mr. Mancini had been hard of hearing...no doubt because of all that lawn mowing. I mean, there's something wrong with a man who cuts the grass every two days....

Apparently I couldn't leave my property, and he couldn't leave his. Maybe that was just the way it was. Or maybe there was a way of leaving, but I just didn't know how yet.

Inside once more, I wandered from room to room. I picked up a photo in a silver frame and stared at the happy couple there. Mike had a full set of wavy hair then and was twenty pounds lighter, and I looked so much younger...and alive. We'd been at Hoover Dam on our first road trip. This was the Western State circuit—we'd taken a month and driven through Utah, Nevada, and Arizona. It had been wonderful, and at the time I had thought we would have other such vacations. Somehow, though, they never worked out.

The following morning I watched Mike and Fiona leave for work, and once again I faced another day of doing nothing. I sighed. Being a ghost was dull. Maybe I should get some chains and drag them around for a while. I grinned at the prospect.

On Monday I was out on the driveway early, long before they left for work. Carefully I set a number of heavy-duty tacks and nails on the driveway. I put them all over for maximum effect. This ought to be fun, I told myself.

Mike backed his car out and hit the first nail, then the second, just as Fiona backed her car out. Well, it was quite amusing to see them grappling with the steering wheels as all four tires on each vehicle went flat. Fiona blamed him, for some reason, while he just shrugged and picked up the cell phone and called the car service.

I drifted back inside, though, after a few minutes; I was bored already of my pranks, but I didn't know what else to do. I could read, I suppose. There were a lot of books I'd intended to pick up, but had just not found the time. Now I had lots and lots of time. The first book I selected was a leather-bound volume of Shakespeare's sonnets.

I touched the maroon cover, remembering when Mike had given the book to me during our courtship. He had memorized a full dozen sonnets, and each night he presented me with a small present—a single rose, a silver locket, an embroidered handkerchief—all while he whispered the sonnet. On the final night he gave me the book and asked me to marry him. Who could resist?

I put the book down and went upstairs to the spare room and laid down with my eyes shut.

Damn.

Several days later I poured the entire shaker of salt into the soup bubbling on the stove. Their faces were quite something when they took that first spoonful at dinnertime.

They seemed to fight often, too, something Mike and I never did. We were rarely cross with each other. Sure, we had our disagreements, but we never screamed at each other, not the way they did. Had he been building up a decade and more of resentment? Was that why, in the end, he had turned to her? What did she offer him that I hadn't?

Well, for one thing, she wasn't wedded to her job. Mike and I had wanted children, but I had kept putting it off. My job, I'd claim; it's not a good time to get pregnant. It was never a good time. Eleven years later it hadn't been a good time, and then I got sick and...well...now there was time enough, but....

I kept up my petty harassments. I moved books, shifted knickknacks, all things calculated to drive them nuts. Nothing too harmful. Not yet, I told myself.

One day Fiona nervously told Mike that she thought the house was haunted; he laughed. She cried and said she wanted a psychic to check out the house. Finally, after a drink or two and a few kisses from her, he relented, and the following week they brought in a psychic, a slender reed of a man with a silver goatee, who surveyed the living room and announced the presence of a ghost.

He peered everywhere except at me. He said he would rid the house of its unwelcome guest.

Unwelcome! And me, who had selected the imported carpet and the brushed silk drapes to match. Me...who had gone through sample book after sample book to find the right wallpaper for every single room, not to mention the upstairs hallway. Me, who had lovingly laid the expensive Spanish tile on the kitchen counters and grouted it carefully. Me...unwelcome.

Go ahead! I thought. Get rid of me. I dare you!

He brought in a crew of what were supposed to be ghost-busters, I guess. They waved various impressive-looking instruments around, and I watched over their shoulders as the gauges registered a Presence, and after much mumbo jumbo, Mr. Goatee announced that the ghost was gone. Fiona cried and hugged him, while he patted her shoulder in a fatherly fashion. Mike shook his hand and slipped him a check, and while they were congratulating him and having a celebratory drink, I went outside and released the handbrake on their van—it rolled back-ward down the driveway, just as a police cruiser drove by.

I waited until all that was cleaned up and Mr. Goatee and his overpriced and highly ineffectual friends had left, then I pulled a few books out of the bookcase, and Fiona fled upstairs. Mike just stared, then got up and followed her.

The next day she insisted that they had to sell the house and go elsewhere. Mike said no.

She moved out. Mike drank more and more after that, and sometimes as he sat on the couch and knocked back one beer after another, I'd sit in the wingback chair and talk.

"And remember that time, Mike, when my mother needed help, and you were right there for me? A lot of husbands would have just stood around and been utterly helpless. But you didn't. You helped out."

He belched, and eventually passed out.

It was true, though. He'd always been good to my mother, a woman who'd had a devastating illness when she was nearly fifty. He had been gentle and kind and always helpful.

I didn't want to think about that. I didn't want to think about all the good things we'd done together, about the great times we had. I wanted to think about the bad times, the bad things. Except there weren't any. And all I could think about were the many little gifts he'd surprised me with, the things he'd done around the house to help me out, even though he worked just as long as I did at the office. In short, all the things I had taken for granted when I'd been alive.

But still it didn't add up. Why had he gone to my sister when I was dying? I just didn't understand it.

After Fiona left, Mike had a succession of girlfriends, who moved in, then moved out, usually after no more than two weeks. Each one got more floozie-like as time went on. I really had no idea he had such bad taste—I mean, all that bleached blonde hair and overdone eye makeup. Tsk, tsk. I messed with them, too. I took their cosmetics, hid their pills, ripped favorite outfits, and after a while, they ended up screaming at Mike, packing, and storming out of the house.

That just make Mike drink more.

Once, I waited on the bottom step of the stairs and when he walked down in the morning, I grabbed his foot, and he tripped and fell. He didn't go far—just the one step down and all, but he managed to twist his ankle. I was hoping he'd break it, but no such luck. I wanted to hurt him, as badly as he'd hurt me. Somehow he managed to get out to his car; hours later he returned on crutches and with the ankle tightly wrapped. He was very careful after that, and I decided I really couldn't mess with him now, no matter how much anger I still had toward him.

Then for a year or two it was just Mike and me. Sitting around the living room every night. He drank, I talked. Sometimes he spoke aloud. Sometimes it seemed like he was talking with me. He wasn't, though. He just talked about the times we had, and how he missed me.

Too late, I thought. Too damned late.

During the day while I was by myself, I moved figurines and knickknacks around, tossed sofa pillows on the floor, rearranged books. At night after work, Mike—without really looking at what he was doing—would just pick up the pillows, ignore the books out of sequence, and set the figurines back in their original positions.

"I know it's you, honey," he said, staring around the room, as if searching for me. "I know you drove Fiona off, and the others as well. But you're not going to drive me away. This is my house, too."

In answer I flung a book at him; it clipped his cheek, drawing blood. He took a swig, wiped the blood away, and closed his eyes. He did not speak to me again.

Finally one morning he woke up from an all-night binge and managed to stagger to his feet and take a shower. Then he swept up all the bottles and cans, and went to work.

He came home and made himself a meal, and while he was eating his tuna and noodle casserole, the doorbell rang. He went to the door, and Fiona was there. She wanted to be with him again. He pulled her to him, and they stood, arms wrapped around each other, for a long time.

I wanted to do something to scare her off, but I didn't think she'd flee this time. I just went upstairs to the spare bedroom and closed my eyes. But I didn't sleep; I just sort of seemed to not exist then, and I can't begin to tell you how much I appreciated that.

Shortly after that they married. Mike no longer drank, and their lovemaking was less wild, more loving, even tender. Within months Fiona's waistline began expanding. Mike and Fiona had a party at the house and all our friends attended, and there they announced they were pregnant. Everyone patted them on the back, hugged them, kissed Fiona, and I had to go upstairs. I wanted to cry. That could have been me with Mike. That could have been our baby.

Only it wasn't.

I had put it off. And put it off and off and off and off.

Am I the ghost? I wondered. Truly the ghost? Or is Mike and all my memories of us together? Maybe those are the true ghosts.

I didn't like that idea. I spent more and more time upstairs in the spare bedroom. I knew every inch of the ceiling there, every cobweb, every crack in the plaster.

I had to listen to them readying the nursery. They'd selected the empty room next to our bedroom—excuse me, *their* bedroom. Fiona chose the sunny yellow paint and the wallpaper and ruffled curtains, while Mike did all the work himself. Funny, he hadn't been that handy when we were married.

The nursery was pretty, too, with Noah's ark on the wallpaper, and stuffed animals lining shelf after shelf. Brand new top-of-the-line crib and changing station and a rocking chair that had been my mother's. They had a fancy baby monitor positioned on a table, while a cute mobile with stars and moons dangled over the crib.

I spent a lot of time in the nursery, and seemed like it was only days later when Fiona called to Mike, and he ran upstairs, grabbed the overnight bag they kept by the bedroom door, helped her downstairs, and off they went. I stood at the nursery window and watched the car turn the corner. Mr. Mancini, out on his lawn, waved when he saw me. I started to raise my hand, then dropped it.

I sat in the rocker to wait. I waited a long time then, because they didn't return for two days, and with them came the baby.

I watched as Fiona tenderly put the infant in the crib, watched as later on she nursed Mike's little daughter. He stayed with them for hours, washed the baby, diapered and cooed at her. They stood, hand in hand, and watched their child.

And I hated them for it. They had each other, they had the baby. I had nothing, nothing except another spirit who couldn't even hear what I had to say.

It wasn't fair.

That night the proud but exhausted parents went to bed, and I stood by the crib and stared down at the beautiful little baby. She had lots of dark hair, like Mike when he was a child, and her eyes were large and round—like Fiona's had been when she was born. I guess you could say that she looked more like her mother than her father. I gazed in awe at the tiny fingers as I stroked her diminutive fist.

And for the first time since I died, I wept. Tears flowed down my cheeks as I watched her and listened to her soft snoring, and I thought about how unfair all of it was.

I was doomed to an eternity of solitude. It. Wasn't. Fair.

I stroked the baby's hair again and trailed my fingers down her chubby cheek, down to her onesie. I straightened a pink bow there and realized for the first time she was part of my family. We had a *bond*, and I smiled through my tears.

I didn't have to be alone. Not at all.

I put my hand over her mouth and pinched her delicate little nostrils together. It didn't take long; she was so tiny, had so little air in her to begin with.

I went back to the spare room and lay down and listened as Fiona rushed in when she didn't hear anything on the baby monitor, and listened as she screamed and screamed and listened to Mike howl in despair.

I listened all night...while I waited for my baby to come to me.

EACH NIGHT, EACH YEAR

My father is dead.

He died two years ago.

But every night he visits.

He comes to me, each night of each year.

I am in my childhood bedroom, tired and asleep after a long day at my place of work and an all too-long evening alone. At first I don't hear anything. But gradually I become aware of a sound.

It is in the hallway—a faint scuffling, a wisping of a breath-like sound.

And despite knowing what it is, despite what I have witnessed each evening for the past two years, I still get up and go stand in the doorway of the bedroom that has been mine in this house since I was two years old. Each night, each year.

While the house is dark and there is only a faint nightlight in the bathroom across from me, I can see. I can see what is in the hallway.

It is my father, and he is crawling.

He is on his hands and his knees, creeping across the stained shag carpet, and his lower jaw, covered with grizzle, is quivering as if he is speaking, but I do not hear any words. Occasionally his nails, grown longer than most men wear them, snag on the loops of the carpet.

He is crawling as he has done before and before and before.

As he did the first time I found him. He had been sleeping on the couch in the living room, having gone there from his bedroom where he said he couldn't get to sleep. And he claimed he couldn't stand up from the low-slung sofa when he wanted to return to his bedroom for the rest of the night. So he crawled. He did not call to me, even though I was in the next room. I would have come to help him stand; I did not sleep heavily in those days when I was tending him.

I would have come to help.

But he didn't call.

And so I found him.

I bit my lip and knelt down and slowly, carefully helped him to his feet. Hanging onto me, he shuffled into his room. I eased him down onto the hospital bed that he hated so much. I took off his bedroom slippers, worn down at the heel, and put them under his bed.

I asked him if he wanted water; he said no; and I remembered all the evenings when I was a child that he brought me one last glass of water.

In the dryness of the night air, a sweetly rotting smell suddenly pervades the room. It is the smell of his cancer, which invaded his bowels, and has eaten its way through his body to his liver, and which somehow in three years had not managed to kill him.

Somehow he hangs on.

I ask him if he wants anything. Of course, he says no. He does not want to bother me, he says. I tell him it's no bother, dad, because I'm up already. He says no, go back to sleep, honey. I'm fine, just fine. We do not look at each other.

I go back to my room and lay down on the narrow bed. My feet hang over the end just slightly. With my hands clasped behind my neck, I stare up at the ceiling in the darkness.

And after a while, as I knew it would, a light goes on in his bathroom. The light spreads outward, through his room and down the hallway so that small objects in the bedroom suddenly stand out sharply in the semi-darkness, and I listen. I hear the sound of running water. He is up again, washing out his colostomy bag as he does so often during the day. He has never let me help him with that procedure, never let me see what he does even though I have told him I wanted to help. I have only seen that horrible opening with its metallic rim in his stomach just once. That terrible obscene unnatural opening.

My father is proud.

I wait until the light is gone, and I hear him shuffle back to bed. He groans, and I close my eyes. I hate to hear that from him.

I wait in the darkness, waiting for him to call me, and finally I hear him snore, and know that at last he falls asleep.

I wait for sleep to claim me, but it doesn't. I am awake when dawn comes with the coolness of a breeze and the sound of stirring birds.

And when I can put it off no longer, I rise and wash my face and my hair and take a bath. This is the bathroom where he had the hemorrhage that indicated for the first time that something was wrong, very wrong. When I came home from the hospital afterward, I found dried blood across the seat of the toilet and run down onto its base, splashed into the tub and beyond, and flecked onto the wall behind the commode. I scoured these stained surfaces, wiping away every trace of the blood. But I still see it, see it even though it's no longer there.

I apply my makeup and dress in good slacks and a tailored blouse with long sleeves which I will roll up later in the day, and while my hair is still drying, I glance into his room.

Of course, I got rid of the hospital bed after he died. Three days after his death I went through all his things and gave most of them away—his few coats and pants and shirts and the three pairs of new pajamas I had bought him at Penney's but which he'd never worn—to a Catholic mission for homeless men located downtown. Two men in patched flannel shirts and baggy pants and oversize shoes came to get the boxes of clothes I had packed. They did not speak to me; I watched them as they hefted the boxes into the back of a silver pickup. The other pieces of furniture, a bookcase and badly painted chest of drawers and an old music cabinet he had salvaged from the city dump when I was a child, I gave to neighbors.

My father's room is bare of furniture, but not of memories.

I remember when I was seven or eight, and he would lie down in the afternoons for a nap when he was home from work or on the weekends after he'd mowed the front and back lawns. I would come in and lay on the other half of the double bed, and we would talk for a few minutes, and then I would get drowsy, and fall asleep. And when I awoke, he was gone.

Under the window overlooking the backyard, he had placed an old kitchen table. It was yellow-topped, with rounded chrome legs, and very ugly. He stored his art supplies there, kept his drawing board with the water-color paper taped to it. He had a German beer stein filled with camel hair brushes in various lengths and fullnesses, and in plastic boxes he had brought home from work he had rubber erasers, and broken pieces of charcoal in several shades, and leftover paperclips and brittle rubber bands and a couple of pretty rocks he had picked up one day when we were picnicking in the Manzano Mountains.

In his closet was an old ice cream bucket, the kind made of heavy tan cardboard. He always used it as a hamper, even though the laundry hamper was just outside his door. But he would put his underwear and socks—always black or dark blue—into it. Mostly he dropped them on the side of the bucket or on the floor around it, and I remember my mother complaining that she couldn't understand how he could miss it so often, and then not bother to pick up the fallen sock. She thought it was very unfair of him. I used to smile, thinking it was such a small matter.

At the other window, facing the neighbors' backyard, is a honeysuckle bush, long overgrown. In the summer, when my father cranked his window open wide, you could smell the fragrant flowers and watch the bees darting among the delicate yellow and white blooms. One day while he stood there, a BB tore through the upper pane of glass, missing his head by only a few inches. Our neighbors' son was testing his new air rifle. My father marched over to their house and took the BB gun away because he said the boy—just a year older than I—was not responsible enough to use it. He put the gun into the trunk of our car, and when I asked him for it, he refused. I never saw it after that. The boy saved his money from his allowance and paid for the new window. We never talked of the incident after that.

I leave the bedroom, and glance once at the other silent, other empty bedroom next to it. It is my mother's. Or rather, it was. She died six years ago. A stroke came upon her late one night—I had seen her only a few hours before—and then she was gone, a vein in her head bursting without any warning. It was only a few months later that my father was diagnosed as having cancer. It cannot be a coincidence, I think.

I eat my breakfast of toast and unsweetened tea in the dingy kitchen, at the table where he used to eat his breakfast, and I remember making him oatmeal. He never wanted anything else, just oatmeal. Oatmeal was filled with fiber, and he had read that that was good for you, was supposed to prevent cancer. Only it was too late; he had bowel cancer by then. But still he ate the oatmeal every day.

I cooked it for him, and set the bowl in front of him, and watched him as he picked up the spoon, watched as the spoon made its quavering way to his mouth. I would look away, afraid I would cry.

I used to cry a lot around him, and he cried with me. Tears can be cleansing upon occasion, but these were not. They only made us feel worse. But somehow we couldn't help it.

I grab my purse and my jacket, and car keys and head out the front door.

I test the door. It is locked, as I knew it would be. I test it again. A habit taken from my mother, I guess, who always checked things two and three times.

I drive to work, a long commute, even on the freeway. I am employed at the University of Albuquerque across the river from the city. It's a good job, not too difficult but with some challenge, with mostly pleasant people, and I am well-paid.

And while I work, I do not remember.

* * * * * * *

You don't look so good today, Diana says right before we get ready for lunch. She sits at the next desk in this large office, and we talk often during the day while working. She is probably my closest friend, my only friend. Aren't you sleeping? she asks.

I shrug. Not really. I tell her that I've been having problems at night.

She puts down her pen and looks at me sharply. What sort of problems?

I fidget with the handful of paperclips on my desktop, unbending and bending them into grotesque shapes. Problems, I say.

Insomnia?

Sort of, I mutter. I cannot meet her eyes. I take a deep breath, then look up abruptly. I have a ghost in my house, I say lightly, thinking she will smile. It's my father.

She exhales sharply, as if she has been holding her breath. Her expression has not changed. At least she has not laughed at me.

I wait for her to speak, but she doesn't say a word. Had she heard me? I ask her.

I heard. A ghost? Of your dad, you say?

I nod.

A ghost.

Yes. Every night since his funeral I see him crawling up the floor of the hallway, just the way he did that one time right before he died. It's awful.

Even in the daytime, the image remains too bright, too persistent in my mind, and I close my eyes briefly, as if that would clear the picture.

It's been over two years since your dad's death, Diana says, as if I do not know how long it's been. I don't think it's a ghost, Becky. Not really.

Why not? Why isn't it a ghost?

I think you're just dreaming. I mean, how do you know you're not? Why do you think you're awake?

Well, I see it so clearly—

Which means it can't be a dream? Of course not! Come on, it's just memories. For some reason—and I'm not sure why—you still feel guilty about your dad's death and what happened just before it. So your mind, which still hasn't let go of all that, is conjuring up these weird images. They're *dreams*, Becky. That's all. It's part of the natural grieving process. Yours has taken two years; some people take a much shorter time, while others never get through. It's an individual thing. You can't rush it, you can't stop it. But you can work it out—mostly through talking. You haven't done that, you know. Not really.

I know, I say. I feel guilty again.

Come on. It's not the end of the world. You're having some bad dreams, but that's all. Your memories become your dreams, and that's why you think you have a 'ghost.' She laughs. You don't believe that, now do you?

I smile. You're right, Diana, you're completely right, of course. And for the rest of that day I feel remarkably better.

But then at five I most head home once again, head back to that silent house.

* * * * * * *

It is nighttime again, and for once I am in bed by ten. It is early July and too warm, with no breeze to cool me off, and I have only a light sheet across my body. I hope I can sleep through the night without awakening, but I know I won't be able to. I haven't been able to since I tended my father those last months. Not in two years have I slept completely through the night. I awaken each night, time after time, waiting to hear those sounds, waiting to hear him call my name.

And sometimes he would do that, so faint that at first I didn't hear him. When it happened more and more, I awoke at the slightest sound.

But I would get up and go into his room. What did he want?

I would ask, and sometimes my voice would be sharper than I wanted.

He wanted to know what time it was. I would look at his clock with its luminous dial on the bookshelf behind his head, and I would tell him. One-seventeen; three-thirty- three; four-oh-five; five-fifteen. Whatever time it was then.

Sometimes he wanted a drink of water, and I would hold his head up with one hand, as I guided his icy hand to the flexible straw in the glass and to his lips. Sometimes it ran out of his mouth, and I would wipe his face softly, as if he were a baby.

Sometimes he wanted nothing, but I think he wanted just to see me, just to make sure that I was really there in the other room, that he hadn't died yet.

Sometimes I would get up and go into his room, even though he hadn't called me, and I would watch him as he slept. Would watch his thin chest rise and fall so rapidly. Surely he couldn't be asleep, not a natural sleep. But he was.

Sometimes, as I watched, his breath would catch and hold for an impossibly long time, and I would wonder if this were it, if this were the moment of death, but then he would exhale, and I knew it wasn't time.

Each night, each day I wondered how much longer it could be.

I prayed for his death. I didn't want him to live any longer, not when it was like that. Not when he wasn't the father I had known all my life, the tall and athletic man who was never sick, who never felt pain.

He had accidents. Sometimes he couldn't make it to the bathroom in time.

Once he peed on himself in the kitchen as he stood at the sink, and I yelled at him when I saw the yellow puddling at his feet. I dabbed at his thin legs and the floor with paper towels, and I was crying for him, and for myself, but mostly I think it was because he was reduced to this, such a feeble old man, so unable to fend for himself.

It is nighttime, and I cry, my pillow uncomfortable, my

cheeks damp, and I ache inside.

* * * * * * *

I am watching the television, looking at it with the sound turned off, trying to read the lips of the actors and actresses, trying to guess what's going on. I think what I make up is much more interesting than what is really going on, and sometimes I laugh aloud, the sound odd in an otherwise silent house.

I am staying up late. I am trying to prove to myself that this is only a dream as Diana claims it is, not a ghost.

I yawn and stretch and realize that I'm getting tired, and here it's only after nine. But I can't go to bed. Not yet.

I decide to step outside; perhaps the cool evening air will wake me up. I go out to the backyard and look up into the sky.

The air over Albuquerque has grown thicker with smog these past years, but you can still see the stars, can still watch them.

My father used to sit out here on the patio for hours every summer evening. He'd sit on a webbed chair with a can of beer in his hand and stare up at the sky. Looking for flying saucers, he would say with a knowing grin, and I would giggle.

The memory feels good, and there is no ache inside. Simply a warmth.

Memories, I tell myself, can be good, as well as bad. I grin.

As I watch, I see something shimmer in the sky...a shooting star, or perhaps only the lights of a distant airplane. I prefer the former.

The temperature is dropping. Even though it's summer, the nights can be cool, and I shiver. I go back inside, and decide it's time for bed.

I take a quick bath, and see no blood in my mind's eye, and I brush my teeth, and pull on my short nightgown, and go back to my bedroom. As I brush my hair, I hear a sound outside my room.

I frown, lay the brush across my knees. Wait and wait and wait.

And once more I see my father.

I am not sleeping. I am awake. Too much awake.

Diana was wrong.

* * * * * *

My father is a ghost, and he comes to me each night, each year. I do not think he means to, but I don't think he has any choice.

I bring him here.

It is my guilt that calls him.

Even though I did all I could, I didn't do enough. There had to be something more that I could have done for him. Something. I don't know what. But there had to be something else.

I look back, and I'm not happy with what I see. I yelled too much. I crabbed at him. I didn't mean to, but I did. Sometimes it was just too much for me, day after day like this, and I would raise my voice. He would always look at me with his yellow-brown eyes, look at me and say nothing, and I would feel terrible, and I would apologize at once. But no words could take back the tone I had used. To my father.

I forget the times when he asked me to tie his shoelaces, and he would sit on the organ bench because it was high and thus easy for him to sit on, and I would kneel in front of him and gently tie the laces, tie them for the seventh or eighth or ninth time that day. I forget the times when I helped him into the bathroom and he would send me away. too proud to let me see. I forget the times when I read to him from the newspaper, or talked about what I had done at work that day. I forget.

I remember only the yelling, the anger, the resentment that my life was dying with him.

During the day for a few hours I had aides come in to take care of him. They were expensive, but there was no choice if I was to continue working and bringing in money to support the two of us. Luckily, Hospice provided an aide for a few hours a week, and that was good; that was some respite.

But every evening when I came straight home from the office he was already in bed, his thin chenille bedspread pulled up to his chin, two winter-thick blankets spread across the bed. Even if it was July and August and in the '80s or '90s, he was freezing. Always cold, because the disease sucked the warmth from his blood. In the day, he wore a Haines tee-shirt under a heavy flannel shirt, thick woolen trousers and a bathrobe over that. And he turned the heat up when he thought I wasn't looking.

I turned the thermostat down when I thought he wasn't looking.

On the weekends my father and I were on our own. No aides came then. It was just the two of us, or an occasional neighbor or friend who dropped by to chat and to see how things were or to bring some food for us, and which I nearly always ended up eating because he wanted nothing but oatmeal because nothing else tasted good to him any longer. Things were the same, the neighbor would see after a few minutes; my father was still dying inch by inch, breath by breath.

Often on those long weekends we would sit in the den, the small room off of the kitchen, and he would be in his green plaid chair that he had salvaged from my grandmother's house, his hands clasped along its padded arms, and I would sit on a wooden kitchen chair that I had brought into the room. Every morning when he rose, he always built a fire in the Franklin stove that he had installed some years ago. He had built the fire wall of brick behind it, the floor of brick under it, and the half-wall of brick between that room and the kitchen. My father had never been trained as a mason.

We would sit in that hot room, thick with smoke from the Franklin because he didn't want the windows opened, and there would be silence.

Sometimes the television was on, but the volume was down low because he was going deaf, and it didn't matter to him any longer what was being shown on the old black-and- white. Yet he would look at the flickering images so that he wouldn't have to look at me.

Sometimes he would say he wanted to tell me some things, and I would ask what things. Just things, he would say, almost slyly. I would wait for a few minutes, and when he didn't continue, I would ask him again, though sharply this time, what he meant.

He would turn his head, and he would look at me with those yellow-brown eyes, the eyes of a wolf, and he would say, things.

Things he disapproved of in me, things he thought I should have done with my life, things we had disagreed about so many times in the past. Just things.

He never told me. I asked him now and then, but he just said later.

I kept telling him there would be no later, that he was dying, and he would say no, he wasn't. He wasn't dying at all.

I would start to cry then. I would put my head down and grab the Kleenex I kept in my pocket, and the hot tears would come, and my shoulders would shake even though I didn't make a sound.

He would want to stand up then, but couldn't, and so I would go to him and take his bony hands and help him to his feet, and watch as he shuffled from the room.

I would watch that sad form, and my eyes would fill with tears again. This was the man who had built the wall of bricks without instruction.

* * * * * * *

I have a ghost, and I want to exorcize it. But I do not know how.

The ghost of my father lives with me, inside my mind and out.

Each night my father comes to visit me, to remind me what I did not do, to remind me of all that he did not say to me.

I did what was best. At the time. I thought. I did what I could do. I regret the yelling, the harsh tones, the bitterness, but I can't take them back. You can't change what has happened in the past, can you? What is done is done, no matter the regrets.

And yet...why not?

Why can't I take them back, now after two years? Two years that I've given to mourning, to a life inhabited only by myself and the ghost of my father. Why not?

If I do, will his ghost go away? Will he leave me alone, my father, so that I can sleep through the darkness, be rested for at least one night?

I am scared. I want to take back all those ugly things that I did to him when he was dying, and yet if he goes, what will I have? He is my only nightly visitor.

He is dead, I tell myself.

He is a ghost, and I am rapidly becoming one myself.

I swallow, lick my lips.

I take them back, I say aloud in the darkness. I take them back, all those angry tears and furious words, and childish impatience when he took too long to feed himself or to pick up a pencil or to finish his sentence. I take them back.

I take them.

Back.

* * * * * * *

It is nighttime. I am in my bedroom.

I grow aware of a scuffling, a breath-like sound. As I lay in the dark, I hear the sound grow louder.

And knowing, I still get up.

It is dark as I stand in the doorway of the room, but I can see clearly. I can see what is in the hallway.

It is me, and I am crawling up the length of the hallway.

ABOUT THE AUTHOR

KATHRYN PTACEK has been a writer and freelance editor for a number of decades, and has published many novels, articles, short stories, columns, and reviews in various genres. She's the editor of the *Gila Queen's Guide to Markets*, as well as the monthly *Newsletter* for the Horror Writers Association. Originally from New Mexico, she lives in Newton, New Jersey, and is the proud, but broke, owner of a 129-year-old Queen Anne Victorian house, which she shares with five cats and the ghost of her late husband, writer Charles L. Grant. She likes to garden, read, putter with beads, and collect gila monster stuff.

www.ingramcontent.com/pod-product-compliance
Lightning Source LLC
Chambersburg PA
CBHW050355260626
47156CB00003B/732